ALCHEMIST

THE ALCHEMIST ACADEMY SERIES: BOOK ONE

ACADEMY

MATT RYAN

For information on new releases or if you want to chat with me, you can find me at:

www.facebook.com/authormattryan
or www.authormattryan.com

Cover: Regina Wamba
www.maeidesign.com
Editor: Victoria Schmitz | Crimson Tide Editorial
Formatting: Inkstain Interior Book Designing
www.inkstainformatting.com

ALCHEMIST ACADEMY

BOOK ONE

CH.1

"If you weren't so fat, we could go up this hill faster."

I sighed. My life felt like a never-ending sigh. *Fat?* They didn't feed me enough for me to be fat. I took slow breaths, fighting down my anger. I didn't want to get too angry; strange things happened when I did.

"Can't you go any faster?" my little stepbrother spouted from his sidecar.

I gritted my teeth and shoved the pedal down harder, propelling the bike up the last hill on Orange Street. The gears ground with each rotation. It would have been easier if his damned sidecar weren't dragging me down.

Spencer adjusted the backpack on his lap. A satisfied, smug smile spread across his face when I began to breathe hard from the effort. I wanted to detach the sidecar and send it sailing back down the hill. But I didn't.

Near the top, I slowed down, longing for the reprieve of the backside of the hill.

"We're going to be late again," he said.

"When have we ever been late to school?"

Spencer fumbled with the question and shifted the backpack on his lap again. "We could go faster if you didn't weigh us down so much. You're just a fatty, Allie." He laughed to himself. "Fatty Allie."

I took a deep breath through my nose and frowned. I tried to be Teflon, but his words weren't sliding off my shoulders as they should--maybe none of them did. He and his mother found sport in besting each other with spiteful comments aimed in my direction, adding a pebble to the ever-increasing pile on my shoulders.

I saw him looking at me. I steeled my face, not wanting to give him the reaction he wanted to see.

"I bet your mom was fat just like you. Your full name on the birth certificate reads 'Fatty Allie'."

My eyes went wide at the mention of my mom. That wasn't a pebble, but a boulder, and it broke down the fragile barriers already shoddily constructed. He smiled as he saw me fuming. Letting him get to me sent me to another level of anger.

We crested the top of the climb. My legs burned and my hands squeezed the worn-out grips as I looked down the hill.

Spencer laughed and kept repeating, "Fatty Allie." I glanced down at his little face. He felt so proud of the new nickname that he didn't even seem to realize all of my teeth were showing.

The hill tilted down and the bike gathered speed. Normally, I would coast down this particular hill, giving my legs a rest. But I didn't want to hear Spencer's voice today, or his stupid laughter. I pedaled harder.

The bike started listing from side to side as our speed became dangerous, the sidecar bouncing and clattering noisily. The warm summer air blew my hair back and dried the sweat from my skin. I glared at the bottom of the hill, wondering how fast the bike could go.

"Slow down." There was a hint of fear in his voice.

Good.

I didn't plan on slowing down; I wanted to give the little punk a ride he wouldn't forget. I gripped the handlebars hard and felt rage filling me. The handlebars shook, sending the whole bike into violent vibrations, but I paid no attention and kept pedaling … feeding my anger into each step.

Spencer gripped the front bar with a terrified look. I heard the bolts that connected his sidecar to my bike rattling loose.

"Allie."

Interesting. He said my name without some kind of insult attached to it.

"Please, slow down. I won't call you Fatty Allie anymore."

The "please" shocked me enough that I stopped pedaling and took deep breaths, releasing some of my anger. The bike slowed down as the hill leveled onto a flat street. But it was too late. The sidecar rattled harder and sent my handlebars into violent vibrations. I leaned forward, gripping them tighter, trying to stabilize them.

The sidecar detached from the bike and swerved toward the curb. Spencer screamed as it hit the cement curb and bounced over it, and he and the sidecar sailed into a hedge in someone's front yard.

I slammed on my brakes and tossed the bike to the street as I jumped off, then rushed to the site of the accident and pulled the sidecar out of the hedge. Spencer's pale face glared at me, but he appeared to be okay.

"You could have killed me!"

"I'm sorry. I didn't know the thing would fly off." But that wasn't entirely true. I knew if I focused my hate on something, it tended to break.

Spencer shook his head in disbelief. He unstrapped his seatbelt and climbed from the sidecar. "I'm walking the rest of the way." He swung his backpack over his shoulder, narrowly missing my head, and huffed off toward school.

I watched him, trying to catch my breath. Did he even know how to get to school? Eh, it was only a block away and I was sure he'd be fine without me.

I shouldn't have gotten angry like that; it wasn't his fault, it was his mom's—my stepmom. She'd taught him that I wasn't much more than a nuisance in their lives, a terrible side effect of her marrying my dad.

The bike was lying in the street. I pulled it over to the sidecar and propped the two against each other. After searching, I found one nut and spun it back on the bolt, connecting the bike and the sidecar. Hand tight, but it should hold.

By the time I got to pedaling, I heard the faint sound of the school bell.

Making quick time without a passenger, I finally got to school. A few other late arrivals were darting into the building. I followed them, but kept to a walking pace up the stairs and into the school. I enjoyed the silent halls, devoid of the hustle and bustle of just minutes before. The smell of early-morning anxiety was still hanging in the halls as I approached my homeroom class.

I opened the door and glanced at the wall clock. I was three minutes late, but the teacher was cool. Mr. Briggs was younger than most of the other teachers, and still felt as if he could fit in with the teenage crowd. His frozen smile greeted me as I entered the classroom. I didn't expect a chastising, but something, some words, and his silence weighed on me. He stared at me as I walked past his desk.

"Sorry," I said, and the words seemed to snap him out of his trance.

"Allie, let's not make this a habit." He pointed to my seat.

My seat was all the way in the back of the room. It had the advantage of having no one at my back, but the distinct drawback of moments like this one. When I arrived late, I had to do the walk-by.

On the way to my seat, I received the standard looks of

disgust from the Dolls. At least that's what I called them. They were a group of girls who always acted as if I was vomiting on their desks when I walked by. I tried to ignore them, but they did grate on my nerves, as much as I hated to admit it.

"Nice shirt," I heard Bridget whisper and snicker. The other two rolled their eyes and leaned away from me. Oh, Bridget, the lovely ringleader. Everything she said gave them reasons to snort, and their favorite target seemed to be me.

Even with the awful people, I loved school. It was away from home, from Spencer and my stepmom. I sat down and slid my backpack under the chair.

"We have a guest today. Her name is Ms. Duval." Mr. Briggs stood and gestured to a woman behind him. His tone seemed different. More monotone than his usual tired, cool-guy cadence. "She's asked us to be part of an experiment."

Some of the kids in the class groaned.

I hadn't noticed Ms. Duval. She was standing in the corner of the room, dressed in a white lab coat with a sleek black skirt underneath. She pinned her blonde hair back and stood next to a large cart full of glass vials and jars, like a mad scientist's chemistry set.

"Thank you, Mr. Briggs." She pulled the cart closer to the teacher's desk. Some of the glass clattered during the movement.

Ms. Duval surveyed the class and for a brief moment, her gaze held mine before moving on. She looked younger than Mr. Briggs. Her pretty face didn't match her stern expression as she crunched up the space between her eyes. I bet *she* wouldn't have let me slip in late.

"I'm here to conduct some simple experiments. If you can all line up over here." She gestured to the side of the room lined with windows. "Now," she snapped when no one moved.

I shot out of my chair and thought of my stepmom's orders. I moved with the rest of the class and lined up.

"I'm going to have you come forward, one at a time, and mix together a couple of items to see what reactions we'll get." Her voice took on a sweeter tone and she gave a smile us that displayed too many teeth and didn't reach her eyes.

I positioned myself near the middle of the line. I didn't want to be first, but I didn't want to be last, either. I was a bit curious as to what experiment this woman wanted us to do. I stood to the side of the line, trying to get a look at what she was having the other kids do.

A finger tapped me on my shoulder and I looked back.

"Those shoes match your shirt," Bridget said, looking down.

I searched her eyes for sincerity and came up short. "Thanks." I turned around.

"You going to march into war with those?" she continued to comment to my back.

I ignored the criticism and snuck a glance down at my shoes. Black army boots with a one-inch heel. They looked awesome to me, but they were nothing a Doll would wear. My jeans covered most of them anyway. I didn't even need to look at Bridget's shoes. I was sure she had on her designer ballet flats. It was Monday, so probably the pink ones with red flowers. And now I wanted to look. I resisted the urge and watched the front of the line.

Tommy walked up first. I heard a few words about mixing and in a few seconds, he'd poured a couple of vials into the bowl and mixed it with a wooden spoon. The contents of the glass bowl looked like blue Kool-Aid. After a pause, she motioned for him to move on. Tommy shrugged and walked back to his desk.

My mouth crunched to one corner as I tried to figure out the experiment. On the rare occasion we had a guest, it normally involved a lengthy lecture, or some dude trying to get the school to sell candy bars. This woman had just laid it out in a few seconds and had formed a line for us to dump some crap into a bowl. If only all guest speakers were so efficient with their time.

Tabitha stepped up and did the same thing as Tommy. Ms. Duval motioned her away and she walked back to her seat. No explanations, no words. I liked her already.

My mind raced at what could possibly be behind this activity. There must be some sort of big reveal after everyone had done their experiments. Like, she would tell us how susceptible we were to rapists and kidnappers because we had just obeyed without question some stranger wearing an official-looking jacket.

The rest of the students in front of her mixed, poured, and stirred the blue Kool-Aid. And each time, Ms. Duval hurried them away. I tugged on my shirt as the person in front of me mixed the stuff in a bowl and was sent off.

I was next.

When I stepped forward, Ms. Duval gave me a thin smile and handed me a tube of clear liquid. She slid a glass bowl toward me.

"Just mix the two chemicals together and stir. But try to put some emotion into it. Think about the thing that makes you angry." She clinched her fist and growled as she said that.

I frowned at her and looked at the vial holding what looked like water. The bowl held a small pile of white flakes, like someone had shaved a bar of soap into it.

She wanted me to be angry? I had an ample supply of that.

I thought of going home after school and the crap I'd be dealing with when Spencer ratted me out about the sidecar. He'd probably accuse me of trying to kill him. A chant of "Fatty Allie" played in my head. I didn't need another thing to think about.

I poured the vial of liquid onto the soap flakes. The liquid bubbled and steamed. I stared at the steam and shoved the wooden spoon around in the mist. Something solid hit the spoon and I stopped stirring. Ms. Duval leaned close to the bowl and blew. The steam dissipated and a white stone about the size of a golf ball rolled around at the bottom of the bowl. Ms. Duval picked up the bowl and swirled the stone around in it. It sounded solid as it clanked against the glass.

"Interesting," Ms. Duval said.

I fidgeted under her gaze. "Is that supposed to happen?"

"Yes." She plucked the ball from the bowl with a piece of cloth and dropped it into a bag. "What's your last name, Allie?"

"How did you know my name?"

"I overheard Mr. Briggs calling you that. Last name?"

"It's Norton. Why?"

Her eyes had widened a tad when I said my last name. "Just for my research."

I glanced at Mr. Briggs sitting at his desk, wondering what kind of guest experiment this was, but he just sat there, smiling and looking forward.

Ms. Duval pointed to my desk. "You can go back to your seat now, Allie." She waved off Bridget, the next person in line. "That's all the time I have for experiments today. Perhaps another day we can finish up."

No grand reveal? I frowned and watched the rest of the class take their seats.

"Thank you for participating. You have helped me more than you know."

She pushed her cart toward the door. Her eyes met mine again and I looked away. They felt like they were looking deep within me. I stared at my desk and waited for the sound of clanking glass to stop before looking at the door again. I felt kind of ripped off, being left in the dark after so much buildup. I sighed and looked around to see if my fellow classmates were showing any signs of wonder.

After Ms. Duval had pushed the cart out the door, she walked back and stood next to Mr. Briggs. She brushed her gloved hand against the back of his neck, holding it there for a second before rushing out the door.

Mr. Briggs got up from behind his desk, looking around the room as the door closed behind Ms. Duval.

Tommy raised his hand.

"Yes, Tommy?"

"No offense, Mr. Briggs, but what the hell was that about?" Tommy asked.

Mr. Briggs shook his head. "Language, Tommy. Come on. What are you talking about? Now, if you can all get your American History books out, let's continue with the Civil War on page eighty."

Many in the class groaned and the room filled with the sounds of shuffling backpacks and books landing on wooden desks. I saw in their faces that they were already forgetting about the strange woman with a chemistry set and the stone rolling around in the glass bowl.

What had I made?

I wanted to ask Tommy's question again, but the class appeared to have moved on and Mr. Briggs had begun to speak about General Lee. I pulled my history book out and shook off the strange encounter with Ms. Duval.

I wasn't going to complain too much. I loved reading. I read history, fiction, fictional history, whatever I could get my hands on. Even at lunch I had a secret place away from the quad and the Dolls ... away from everyone. It was located between the shop and art classes, where a tucked-away tree stood. I could spend most of my lunch reading under that tree. It was usually the highlight of my day.

The history book felt heavy in my hands and while I wanted to read, I couldn't stop thinking about Spencer and what my stepmom was going to do when she found out her precious boy had gotten scared by our tiny sidecar accident. Ugh, it was his birthday as well.

CH.2

"Get started on wrapping the rest of his gifts and then get out back to finish his decorations." Janet flung her purse over her shoulder and held it tight. "His special cake is finally ready and I have to go to town and pick it up. You'd better not mess up a thing on his birthday, Allie. You have thirty minutes, and I expect everything to look perfect for him by the time I get back." Her eyes narrowed and she sneered, waiting for a response.

"Yes, Janet," I said.

Spencer had told her all about his brush with death. Tears had fallen as Janet soaked up his exaggerated tale. When he was finished, she took away all my books for a month and grounded me. She knew I liked books, but she also knew I loved to get out of the house and go to my place in the woods. Being grounded meant many more hours of enduring crappy comments and menial chores. Being stuck in a place I didn't want to be and wasn't wanted in was so much worse with no escape. The house would be my prison for the next month.

Janet pulled the back door open and looked at me. I never knew what my dad saw in her bone-thin body and pointy nose. She glared at me through her narrow glasses. It was going to be a long time before she forgot about me almost hurting her little man.

"And don't think you're getting a single piece of cake." Janet chuckled. "From the looks of it, I'll be doing you a favor." She left through the back door, looking happy about her remark about my weight.

Another fat comment. I knew I wasn't fat, but the words stung because she wanted them to. Anyone compared to Janet would be morbidly obese.

Every year I thought my dad would leave these people. We had no real ties to them. Spencer was his stepson. Who knew what guy had spawned that thing. With my dad gone for so long, Janet and Spencer had begun to feel like my family. It'd been ten years since the last time I'd seen my mom, and with each passing year, the memories of her faded, no matter how much I tried to grasp them. They continued to fall between my fingers.

My heart pounded as I thought about my dad dancing with my mom in our old kitchen. I had grabbed at their legs and joined in. I couldn't remember why we'd been dancing, but they had seemed so happy that night. That was the last night I had seen my mom.

I walked to the kitchen table, and the presents sitting there brought me back to the present. I had gifts to wrap.

The first gift was a new video game of some sort; I didn't really pay attention. Then, the trading cards Spencer loved to collect. I stuffed some paper over them and plopped them on the pile. Next I pulled out an iPad. The white box gleamed and the Apple logo shone as I ran a finger over it. I had asked for this gift, laughing, knowing I would never get it, or any present for that matter. To give it to Spencer felt like another punishment. I would've read books and used it for learning, while he'd just download games and muck it up with Cheetos residue.

I opened the box and slid out the iPad. It shook in my hands as I thought about Spencer throwing it around carelessly. Janet knew he wouldn't care about this gift as much as I would. She knew I wanted it, but she was giving it to him, and even worse, making me wrap it for him. I could hear her stupid laugh in my head and I felt rage building inside me.

The screen cracked.

I gasped and looked down at it, bringing it close to my face in disbelief. It couldn't have been me. I hadn't pressed hard, not hard enough for cracks to spread over the whole screen. I stared at it and wiped the fingerprints off the screen like I was cleaning up a crime scene. I knew I had broken it and I knew it was my anger again. I must have some uncontrollable muscle spasms when I got mad, I figured. This time I hadn't even gotten that mad. It must be getting worse.

I glanced around the kitchen and stuffed the iPad back in the box, making sure to seal it back in place. With any luck, Janet would blame the broken glass on shipping.

With the gifts wrapped, I went to the back yard.

A couple of white folding tables had been placed on the grass. A few bags lay on them, full of Spencer's decorations. The backyard wasn't very big, but it had a white privacy fence around the perimeter, plenty of space to hang the decorations.

I rummaged through the bags and was pulling out the tablecloths as I heard my neighbor start up a lawnmower. I sighed and realized I'd be dealing with that noise the whole time. The air started filling with dust and bits of grass as that unseen person pushed the mower through the grass. I saw the top of his head move past the fence, brown hair bobbing over the white pickets. Mrs. Crabtree had probably gotten herself another landscape boy.

I turned back to the decorations, a *Star Wars* theme this year. I shrugged and draped the cloth over the table. I pretended I was setting up another kid's party. Maybe the nice girl down the street, who was about Spencer's age. She'd appreciate these decorations.

Lawn Boy was doing another pass near the fence when the lawnmower sputtered and died. He glanced at me before he disappeared behind the fence but in that split second I caught his eyes and part of his face and wondered what the rest of him looked like. Oh, well, let him figure out that mower and I could get these decorations up.

Next, the streamers. The vinyl fence seemed as good a place as any other. I pulled out pieces of tape and stuck them on my lip. I unwound the streamer and yanked a strip off my lip.

"Ouch!" It had ripped some skin off my lip and I tasted blood in my mouth. "Son of a—"

"You okay?"

I fell backward and landed on my ass.

"Oh my God, you're bleeding." Brown Hair leaped over the fence and landed on the grass next to me.

He was gorgeous, and I stammered for words. I touched my lip and looked at the blood on my finger.

He reached down, took my hand and pulled me to my feet.

"Who are you?" I asked.

"I'm Mark, your neighbor."

"No, you're not. Mrs. Crabtree lives there."

"Not anymore. My mom just bought the house."

"I didn't know she was selling it."

"My mom has a way of convincing people." He laughed, and his bright smile made my stomach warm. He looked down at our hands, still entwined. I let go of his and he smiled again. "You have a first aid kit in the house?" Mark looked behind me.

I sucked on my bottom lip and felt the damage with my tongue. It didn't feel too bad, and the salty, metallic flavor was already dissipating. Could you bandage a lip? Besides, I didn't know this guy. I wasn't about to go inviting him into my house.

"I'm fine."

"You sure? Let me take a look."

His hand touched the side of my face and I jerked back. I didn't like being touched, even if it was some hot guy with his hands on me. "Sorry," I said. "I just need to get these decorations up."

"Well, let me help you. Decorations can be dangerous, you know?"

I stared at him, trying to use my best psycho detector. He was about my age. His clothes were stylish. Clean shoes. Most importantly, his eyes had some sorrow in them ... even if he tried to mask it with his perfect smile. I couldn't tell if he was being honest with me, but he didn't seem dangerous.

He chuckled. "I only came over here because I heard a yelp."

"I didn't yelp." My hands went to my hips.

"Call it what you like. It sounded like a yelp to me. Like a puppy calling for its mom."

"My mom's dead."

Well, that happened. I couldn't spend one minute in a normal conversation before ruining it. He'd probably leap back over the fence.

His expression blanked out for a second and then he looked hurt. "I'm so sorry. I didn't mean anything by it. I lost my dad a long time ago."

A fellow half-orphan. I wondered if he'd gotten the fairy tale evil step-parent to boot.

The subject needed to be changed away from my mom. "I don't think you're a psycho." The words tumbled out of my mouth and I felt even dumber.

He ran his hand through his hair and smiled. "You never

know. I could change on you at any moment."

"Just so you know, I know kung fu."

"Ooh. I'd better be on my best behavior, then."

I grinned and felt something deep in my gut. I wanted to keep the banter going, but I took out my phone and looked at the time. Crap, I had ten minutes to get all the decorations up. The chatting would have to wait.

"Get those streamers up on the fence," I commanded.

"Yes, ma'am." He saluted.

I rolled my eyes. "I'm Allie, by the way."

"Pleasure." He bowed, then went about putting up the streamers.

I busied myself with setting up the tables and organizing Spencer's presents. And every chance I got, I watched Mark. His fit body showed through his thin t-shirt and I wondered what he might look like with that shirt off.

The thought of it shocked me. Not the image I conjured up, but my actually thinking it and conjuring it. I had to stop watching him.

We finished with a few minutes to spare. I'd have to go to my hideout soon. I didn't want to be anywhere near the celebration of Spencer's birth. "Thanks, Mark."

"No problem. It's kind of fun setting up a kid's party."

"Not if you knew the kid."

"I don't have a sibling, but I'd be happy to help out with their birthday."

I didn't want to explain my crappy situation. I'd probably

already given him enough reasons to be wary of me with the whole "my mom's dead" thing. I didn't need to pile my home problems on top of it.

"He's my stepbrother," I said with disdain. I hoped it didn't come off as too bitchy, but I couldn't help it.

He nodded. "My mom never remarried."

"Well, thanks for your help. But I'd better get going...."

"How does a guy go about getting an invite to a party like this? With all these decorations we put up, I bet it's going to be a smash."

He wasn't making it easy. I might as well scare him off. It wasn't like he'd be interested in me anyway. "I'm not invited to the party, so I can't really invite you. I have to stay away until it's over."

He raised an eyebrow, probably waiting for me to say I was joking. *God, I wish I was*, I thought. His expression changed to a question as he realized I wasn't.

"If they aren't expecting you to be here, then they won't know you're missing."

"Missing?" I did know some kung fu, and stepped sideways in a defensive stance.

He laughed. "You aren't the trusting type, are you? I meant we should ditch this party together. It's my first day in Summerford. Maybe you can show me around?" He raised his hands. "I promise, I'm not some psycho. I just find you interesting. I think it'd be cool to get to know you better, seeing as we're neighbors now."

My face flushed. I turned away.

"Mark?" a woman's voice called. I knew that voice and turned back around.

"Over here, Mom."

A familiar stern face peered over the fence. "Oh, you found a friend already?"

"Mom, this is Allie."

Her eyes narrowed and I wondered if she recognized me from school.

"Hi, Ms. Duval," I said. "We met at school today."

Mark's eyes went wide. He stared at his mom. After a few seconds, I wondered if I should say something more.

Her gaze passed over him and landed on me. "Oh, yes," she said, and smiled. "Allie, nice to see you again."

"I can't believe you." Mark stepped closer to his mom.

"It's time to get back home. I will not have foot-tall grass growing around a house I own, and you've got a lot of unpacking to do."

"Just a minute. And I only have one bag, Mom."

"Mark, *now*."

He took a deep breath and turned to me. "Sorry, Allie. We'll have to postpone that date." Then he leaned in close and whispered, "I'll meet you at the side of your house in thirty minutes." Winking, he darted to the fence.

Date? Meet him in thirty minutes, and he was hiding it from his mom? I hated being part of anybody's lies, but I felt trapped.

"Alright … nice meeting you," I offered lamely.

He climbed over the fence and hopped down to his side.

I stared at the fence, breathing through my mouth and thinking of the things he'd said and done. I was probably reading too much into it, but I almost thought he'd been flirting with me. Actually, I was sure of it.

The front door of the house opened.

Janet was home.

I ran through the kitchen and opened the door to the basement, eased the door closed behind me, and tiptoed down the stairs. Light was shining in through the small basement window, illuminating the pile of laundry next to the mattress on the floor. Just like I'd left it last time, and the musty smell still remained. *How pleasant.*

I reached behind the paint can on a shelf and pulled out my tattered copy of *A Tale of Two Cities*, then rushed back up the stairs and inched the door open. I watched as Janet walked into the kitchen. Quietly, I crossed the family room to the side door. I knew she hadn't noticed me because she hadn't screamed, nor was I given some mundane, last-second chore to do before her horrible friends arrived.

The side yard had grass on the ground, and was only a few feet wide. I liked it there. A fence enclosed the whole thing and I found it to be a quiet place I could escape to and read.

The loud air conditioner kicked on next to me. So much for being quiet. I sighed and moved away from it. If I got lost in the book enough, I wouldn't hear it.

Who runs the air conditioner when it's only seventy-five

degrees?

Fifty pages in, I set the book down and looked at the top of the fence. It had to have been thirty minutes by now. The party guests had arrived and a cackle of laughter flooded out from Janet and her friends. The little one should be opening his presents soon, and the thought of them finding the broken iPad sent my heart racing.

There was a tap on the fence and my new best friend jumped over, landing next to me. Warm air blew past me and carried with it the distinct smell of Mark. Like soap with a hint of something else I couldn't place.

"I came to rescue you."

A lump formed in my throat and I croaked out, "I don't need a rescue."

Mark glanced back at the gate blocking the party from me. "I just spotted your little brother opening presents."

"Stepbrother."

"Fine, let's get out of here. I promise to get you back before either of our moms notice."

"Stepmom."

He reached out and offered both hands. I placed mine in his and he pulled me all the way up to my feet. Wiping off my butt, I glanced down the narrow fence line toward the sounds of the party. I heard the *oohs* and *aahs* from the crowd as Spencer opened another present.

"Come on," Mark said. His soft hand enveloped mine. I normally didn't like it when someone touched me, but this... this was okay.

I followed him to the front gate and he let go of my hand to open it. *He's just being neighborly,* I reminded myself. *Then why is he looking at me like that?* Each time he did it, my stomach fluttered and I sucked in a quick breath.

We walked past all the parked cars and down the street lined with houses. Each house was the same design, but each owner seemed to take pride in their lawn and the small landscaping differences.

"Where to?" he asked.

I shrugged. "I don't know."

"Oh, come on. There has to be somewhere you go, somewhere unique."

My eyes lit up. "There is, but you have to promise to not tell anyone else about it. It's sort of my little space away from it all." I gave him a stern look and waited for his nod.

"I can keep a secret."

CH.3

My hands grasped at each two-by-four nailed into the tree. At the top of the makeshift ladder, the hatch door flopped open with a little push and I climbed through into the room. I took quick inventory of anything that might be embarrassing. I grabbed my worn copy of *Fifty Shades of Grey* and tossed it out the window just as Mark's head popped through the hatch door.

"Aren't you a bit old to have a tree house?" Mark asked, looking around.

"You can be seventeen and still enjoy stuff, you know."

He hoisted himself into the room and hit his head on the ceiling. "Ouch." He rubbed his head.

I saw judgment spreading across his face as he scanned the room. It had a single chair by the window and a pile of books stacked next to it.

"It's awesome. Did you build this?"

"Nah, I was just walking in the woods one day when I found it."

"So, naturally, you claimed it?"

"I guess. I've never brought anyone out here before."

"Until now? Well, I'm honored to be your first guest." Mark bowed and then walked to the window. "You can see the rooftops from here. Isn't that red one yours?"

"Yeah, I think so."

"Oh my god, you've read *To Kill a Mockingbird*?" He picked up my tattered copy.

"Yeah, like five times."

"Atticus Finch is a hero of mine."

"Most of the boys around here wouldn't know Finch from Potter."

"I'm not most boys." He set the book down and stared out the window. He had a wonder to his look, like he absorbed everything with an infectious positivity. Even the dark clouds around me felt brighter with him around.

"No, you're not. Where did you come from?"

"We ... well, we...." he stammered, then tried again. "We came from Baker, California. Home of the world's largest thermometer. What about you?"

"I've lived here most of my life."

"You like Summerford?"

"God, no. The people here are awful. The school is terrible."

I didn't know why I was trying to make it sound so bad. Was I trying to be cool?

"It can't be all bad. A pretty girl like you... In a town like this."

His calling me "pretty" set off a mixture of alarms. Bridget had mastered the use of sarcasm to such a high degree that it felt natural to question any compliment sent my way. I touched my straight black hair and looked at my pale skin.

"I...." I didn't know what to say, and glanced at the hatch.

"You don't take compliments well, do you? What would one of the boys in this town say? How about, 'You look as fine as a polished John Deere'?"

I chuckled. "They might say, 'You look as fancy as a pig in a parade.'"

He laughed. "I have no idea what that means."

"I don't either." I smiled. I couldn't help but smile when he did.

He took a step closer to me. "I know we just sort of met, but I feel like I know you. Is that crazy?" he asked.

His soft eyes melted my insides. I felt the same comfortable way. It seemed stupid, but I did. Like an idiot, I wanted to tell him all about my family and my problems at school. Of course, I bit my tongue.

Mark turned from the window and rubbed his stomach. He took in a quick breath and opened his mouth but then closed it.

"You okay?" I asked.

"I'm fine." He took his hand off his stomach. "I'm sure it's nothing, but I just have to ask you something about my mom. She visited you today at school, right?"

"Yeah, for some strange chemistry experiment. She had

each of us mix up something."

He moved closer. "What did she have you do?"

"We poured something that looked like water onto a pile of flaky stuff in a bowl."

He rubbed his chin. "And then what happened?"

"Why does it matter?" I crossed my arms.

"It's the difference between our relationship being simple or complicated. Did it just melt into a liquid?"

"No, it misted and turned into a white stone."

Mark winced and rubbed his eyes. "There's something you need to know, Allie." He sounded as if he was about to dish out a lecture.

I set down the book *Wool* on the shelf and waited to hear what I needed to know.

He opened his mouth and raised a pointed finger....

"Mark," a woman's voice called from below.

He closed his eyes for a second and moved close to me, then put a hand on my shoulder and his perfect face moved near mine. My thoughts went wild in preparation for a kiss, but his lips landed close to my ear.

"Don't trust my mom," he whispered. "And don't make another thing for her."

"Mark, get down here now. I know you're up there."

He turned from me. "Coming, Mother." He stood and watched my face.

My mouth hung open. Flirting was one thing, but this was just weird. Don't trust his mom?

Mark opened the hatch and climbed down the ladder. Through the opening, I peered past him to Ms. Duval standing below. She had her arms crossed, but when she saw me looking she smiled and waved.

"Hello, Allie. I hope Mark was being appropriate."

"He was a perfect gentleman," I called back to her.

Mark shook his head as he took the last steps off the ladder. When he reached her, Ms. Duval whispered into his ear. Then she said, "Allie, I like to get to know all of Mark's friends. Could you please join us for some tea?"

Mark took a step behind his mother and shook his head, mouthing the word *no*.

His words hung around in my head. *Don't trust my mom.* "I think I'd better be getting back to my house."

"Very well, but I won't take no for an answer next time. After all, we're neighbors and I think we're going to be seeing a lot of each other."

Mark waved to me. "To be continued. Remember what I said."

Ms. Duval put a hand on his shoulder and nudged him away.

CH.4

Janet was pissed.

School had been canceled today because of some electrical fire. I knew she relished the time she had by herself, and with my dad gone for most of the year, she had plenty of it. I wasn't even sure where he was, maybe the Middle East?

"You're going to have to watch Spencer," Janet said.

"Mom, I'm ten now. I can watch myself."

She patted his head. "The big one-oh."

"I can watch him," I said.

"I wasn't asking," she spewed. "I'll be gone for a few hours and when I get back, I expect your chores to be done."

I stopped my eyes from rolling. Janet hated that. "Yup."

"Only Spencer is allowed into the fridge or the pantry."

He smiled. It gave him some power over me, being the one who knew the combinations on the locks.

She knelt close to his face. "If anything happens, sweetie, call me on my cellphone." She frowned at me before she left.

With Janet gone, Spencer went into the kitchen and worked the combination lock on the refrigerator. He hovered over the lock so I couldn't see it. I left the kitchen and went to the backyard, anything to get away from his snotty face. I stared at my first chore of the day: cleaning the mess left over from the party.

I clutched a vinyl *Star Wars* tablecloth and pulled it free from the tape holding it down. At least they didn't want to save it all; I could destroy it as I tore it all down. Spencer would never have the same themed party two years in a row.

The pile of trash grew as I grabbed, yanked and tore down their celebration remnants. Even his wrapping paper lay on the grass, next to the careless people's red cups.

"That's a serious mess."

I jumped back from the voice and clutched my chest. "Jeesh, you scared me."

"Did I?" Ms. Duval said over the fence. "How about that tea?"

Mark's voice pounded in my head. *Don't trust her.* "I've really got to clean this stuff up."

"I told you I wouldn't take no for an answer the second time." Her stern face left no room for arguments.

I put my hands on my hips and glared at the paper wrappings and plates scattered around the yard. How much trouble could there be in tea? Maybe Mark would be there. "Let me get Spencer set up."

How to keep a ten-year-old busy? First I set up his video games on the big family room TV, then I gave him an invitation to come to the backyard and help clean up if he wanted. With Spencer definitely not coming to the backyard, I left the house.

Ms. Duval was still standing behind the fence, her head peeking over. I walked toward her, and when the fence opened, she was standing on the other side.

I stopped. "I didn't know we had a gate back here."

"I can't have you climbing over fences, now, can I?"

I tentatively stepped through the opening and entered her backyard. It was about the same size as mine, but the grass was overgrown except for the strip leading to the broken-down mower. Ms. Duval shut the gate and I jumped at the noise.

"Please, let's go to the dining room."

I followed her into the house and took a seat at the table. The house looked mostly empty, save for a few open boxes scattered around. She brought out a pitcher of iced tea and poured me a glass.

"Thank you." I took the glass. "Is Mark here?"

"He'll be home soon."

I sipped the tea. Cool and refreshing. I drank more and looked around the room. A few boxes were unpacked, and a full hutch stood next to door way to the dining room. Beakers and vials lined its shelves. I took another sip and studied the different objects, many I remembered from the cart she had brought to school.

"You like it." Ms. Duval stood and walked over to it.

"Another one of your chemistry sets?"

"I'm not a chemist."

"Oh, I thought Mr. Briggs said you were."

"He did. I just didn't correct him. It's impolite to correct people in their houses."

I nodded and kept studying the displayed items. "What are you, then?"

"I'm an alchemist."

"Like, you're trying to create gold?"

She laughed—a pleasant laugh that I was shocked to hear.

"Some do, but not me. I'm more interested in the achievable goals. Like what you did in school yesterday."

"What do you mean? I just mixed two ingredients together. I didn't even choose what they were."

"Then why didn't the experiment work for any of the other students?"

"They must have done different things than I did."

"Why don't you tell me about the iPad you broke yesterday?"

I stood up from my chair. "How do you know about that?"

"I spent a bit of time at the party yesterday with your stepmom. She blamed it on your inability to wrap a gift properly. She's a wretched woman, isn't she?"

Maybe Ms. Duval wasn't so bad. I sat back down. I was sure Janet had gone on and on about what a fool of a stepchild she had, who couldn't even wrap a gift without creating a disaster.

She continued, "But that's not how it broke, is it?"

"I don't know. I just held it and it broke."

"Were you feeling anything the moment it broke?"

I looked at my hands and then back at the door. I couldn't look her in the eyes, but I felt her stare. "I was mad," I blurted out.

"This isn't the first time your anger has caused things to happen, is it?"

I thought about the sidecar falling off. "No."

"What if I told you only one in a hundred million people can do what you did yesterday?"

"I'd say you're crazy." *There goes my mouth again.* I hoped I hadn't offended her.

She smiled coolly. "You have a gift, and I suspect, a very strong one. If you like, I can show you something." She opened the door to the hutch and pulled out a couple of vials and a mixing bowl with a spoon. She placed them on the table in front of me. The bowl looked like a large metal salad bowl with a long wooden spoon sticking out of it.

"Certain people, *special* people, can infuse their emotions into matter. It appears you have that gift."

I raised an eyebrow and checked the tea in my glass. Maybe she'd laced it with something. I couldn't have heard her right.

"Okay, I can see you're skeptical." Ms. Duval raised an eyebrow and I squirmed in my seat. She pushed the bowl closer to me. "Just mix these two ingredients while you think of something that makes you angry, and I think you'll see exactly what you're capable of when you put your mind to it."

"Just pour them in this bowl and mix?"

"Yes, but you must focus your anger into them for it to work properly. Is there a strong memory you can summon to make yourself angry?"

"I think I can find one." *Or a hundred.*

Curiosity moved my hands to the vials. Blue liquid in one and clear in the other. I shifted in my seat and lifted the vials above the glass bowl. I took a deep breath and thought of Janet and Spencer last month on my birthday. They'd thought it funny that no one knew it was my birthday until a letter came from my dad. Keeping the letter from me, they'd laughed while I chased Spencer around the kitchen, trying to get it from his hands. I screamed when he tore it into pieces.

I poured the liquids into the bowl and stirred the spoon around, creating a maelstrom. It bubbled and swirled. White mist filled the bowl. Ms. Duval leaned over and blew. I coughed at the fumes and waved them away from my face.

She raised the bowl in her hands. Her eyes went wide as a round blue stone about the size of an egg rolled around, then she adjusted her expression back to a sweet smile and placed the bowl on the table.

I looked at the blue stone, settling at the bottom of the bowl, and reached my hand in.

"Don't touch it!"

I nearly fell off my chair. Ms. Duval grabbed the bowl.

"You have to be more careful. These things are ... delicate." She pulled a cloth from the hutch and used it to pick up the blue stone. She dropped it into a penny purse, then snapped it shut.

"What is it?" I asked.

"I noticed you've taken a liking to my son."

I choked on some of the tea I'd just sipped. "Yes, well, we only just met."

"I can tell he likes you." She smiled and sat down across the table.

He liked me? I'd picked up on his little flirtations, but hearing another person say the words made me feel all warm inside. I smiled and took another sip of tea.

"Why, I haven't seen him look this healthy in weeks. I should thank you."

"What do you mean? Is there something wrong with him?"

"Oh, I thought he might have told you. Please don't let him know I said anything. He'd be mortified, I'm sure."

I frowned at Ms. Duval and looked to the door, hoping Mark would arrive and I could look at him, inspect him. "I didn't notice anything wrong. He looks ridiculously fit, actually."

"He feels if he keeps himself strong and fit, his body will be better at fighting the disease. We've kept it bay for so many years, but it's a losing battle." Ms. Duval wiped her eyes.

"I'm so sorry. I had no idea. What do the doctors say?"

"They said to make him as comfortable as I can and give him as normal of a life as possible. I just thought you should know before you get too involved."

She made it sound like he was dying. I leaned forward and set my glass down. My hand started shaking. "There has to be something we can do. What's it called? I can Google it. I bet there are alternatives."

Ms. Duval leaned forward and set her glass on a coaster. She whispered, "There *are* things that can be done, but—"

"What's going on?" Mark interrupted.

I jolted upright in my chair and wondered how much he'd heard. He breezed into the room wearing a thin black shirt and jeans. I scanned his body, searching for something to show me what the problem was. His eyes narrowed and he looked from me to his mom.

"Honey, you're home early," Ms. Duval said. She shot me a look with a slight nod of her head.

"Hey, Mark. Your mom invited me over for tea." I grabbed my glass and took a sip, but I kept my eyes on him. He looked as healthy as anyone I'd ever seen. Could this be what Mark had been talking about with his mom? Was she lying as a tactic to keep me away from Mark?

He looked at me for a second with hints of anger dancing at the corners of his eyes and mouth. Guilt swept over me. He had told me not to trust her and here we were, having tea.

He glared at his mom. "I told you to leave her alone."

"We were just having a friendly chat."

"I think I'd better get going," I said.

Mark took the glass bowl off the table. He gazed at me and sighed. "What did you do?"

"I just mixed a couple of vials together."

He took a deep breath and scowled at his mom. She held his gaze with contempt and I felt years of tension built up between them. They locked eyes and I held my breath, waiting to see who'd look away first. Mark gave in and gripped the edges of the bowl with his white-knuckled hands.

"I'm going to go," I said.

"Come on, Allie. I'll walk you home." He set the bowl on the table and gave it a spin before giving his mom one more sharp look.

Before the bowl stopped spinning, I was out of there. In the backyard, Mark stopped next to the fence and put a hand on top of it.

"I thought I told you not to trust my mom," he whispered.

"She wouldn't take no for an answer. It was just tea until she busted out a chemistry set."

"Alchemy."

"Whatever." I fumbled around with my hands. I wanted to ask him about his illness and why he hadn't told me. Was it even real?

"I'm sorry." He touched my arm. "But there's something you need to know about my mom, and I think about yourself. She can change things … create stuff from other stuff." He took a deep breath. "What did she have you do in there?"

"I created a blue stone."

"Did it have white swirls around it?"

"Yeah, I think so."

He ran his hand through his hair, messing it up, but he still looked hot. "You made something she couldn't, something most people can't."

I shook my head and frowned. "What are you trying to say? Is your mom some kind of witch?"

"No," he whispered. "She's got the *touch*, just like you, but she barely has it. She wasn't good enough at the academy and they booted her." He glanced back at his house. "She's more than pissed about it."

"Okay." I dragged out the O. "Well, I've got to get going. Hope you and your mom have had fun messing with me."

Mark stepped closer. "I'm not messing with you, but I don't want you to come over here anymore. It isn't safe. She'll use you again."

What I heard was, *"I don't want to be with you."*

"Fine." I stood in front of the fence and searched for the gate opening.

He grabbed the top of the fence and pulled it open. Bowing, he swayed his arm toward the door, granting me entrance to my own yard. I started to walk through the gate.

"This doesn't mean I don't want to see you again," he said.

I stopped and turned back to him, smiling. "I'd like to see you as well."

"Listen, I'm sorry for losing it back there, but if you knew what my mom does to people like you…."

"Use my magical powers to make stuff. I get it."

He laughed. "It wouldn't be so funny if you knew how close you are to the truth. I tell you what, I'll see if I can prove it to you tomorrow at school," he said.

"You're going to Summerford High?"

"Yeah. Did you think I was some kind of dropout?"

"No, I just … I don't know what I thought." The words clogged in my throat and terrible thoughts raced through my mind. With his looks, he'd be swallowed up in a second by the Dolls, but if he was with me… Excitement spread through me. With Mark at my school, things were going to be interesting.

"I'll see you tomorrow," was all I got out.

CH.5

Janet drove us to school the next day, while the bike and sidecar were being repaired. She said she'd expect me to do extra chores until every cent was paid back. I didn't argue the demand. What would be the point? Besides, I was searching for a particular face among the throng of students moving around in front of the school.

I didn't see him out front as I left the car.

When I entered the school, hubbub filled the main hall: the clatter of lockers and shifting feet. I tried to walk tall, looking over the heads of the underclassmen walking around. Mark was tall enough to stand out in the crowd, but I didn't see him anywhere. After a while, I felt foolish for looking and walked to class.

"Hello, Allie," Mr. Briggs greeted me from behind his desk.

"Hey," I said.

It was a few minutes before class was supposed to start and only a few kids were in the room. As I scanned their faces, some glanced up at me, but not one made an attempt at a human greeting. Tommy leaned back in his chair and gave me a nod with a look that belonged in a selfie. His tight sports shirt clung to him as he flicked back his blond highlighted hair.

Mr. Briggs asked, "Allie, what did you do on fire day?"

"Oh, nothing much." *I just made some blue stone in a glass bowl for some weird alchemist witch.*

I darted to my desk at the back of the room.

As each person walked into the room, I perked up with anticipation, only to be let down when they weren't Mark. Then the Dolls strolled in, led by Bridget. She was wearing short shorts and a tight T-shirt with the words *Grand Tetons* stretched across her chest. I pulled my eyes away from the glaring attention grab and watched her shoes step toward me: white slingbacks with a pink bow near the toes. Who wears heels with short shorts? But dammit if she didn't pull them off.

She raised an eyebrow and glanced at me before she swung around into the seat two in front of me.

The bell rang. I looked at the clock and settled into my chair. Mark wasn't in my class.

"Everybody chill down and let's just rap for a minute," Mr. Briggs said. "I want to talk about the fire yesterday. It appears to be an act of vandalism, and if you hear anything or know anything, let me or any other teacher know."

It was probably a kid who *really* didn't want to go to school.

I laughed to myself at his request. Like anyone would come forward and rat out another person for getting everyone out of school for the day. Even though I was pissed about having to spend much of the day around Spencer, I wouldn't say a thing. Let the teachers figure it out.

The classroom door opened and Mark strolled in. I leaned forward and took him in as he handed Mr. Briggs a piece of paper. I had hoped he would wear something plain, something awful, but he hadn't obeyed my wishes and was wearing black slacks with black shoes and several perfectly layered shirts. He'd even styled his hair to frame his face. He looked even hotter than before, and it didn't take long for the rest of the class to take notice.

The Dolls exchanged open-mouthed glances, and my heart sank. There was absolutely no way they wouldn't snag him.

Mark looked at the class and did a double take when he saw me. Our eyes met, but Bridget must have thought he was looking at her, because she gave him a small wave. She tilted her legs into the aisle, making sure he saw her tanned, silky legs.

Mr. Briggs stood up from his desk. "Class, we have a new student, Mark Duval."

The class greeted him with a mixture of grunts and hellos. Mark waved to the class as a whole and smiled. I wanted to grab his warm, beautiful smile and keep it for myself. I didn't want the rest of the class to share in it.

"You can share a desk and a book until we get you one of your own." Mr. Briggs handed him a folding chair and gestured toward the class.

"Okay, thanks." Mark looked at me and nodded.

Again, Bridget missed the difference of inches in his stare. Maybe she never even thought it was possible for someone like Mark to look past her, but she shuffled her books and slid her chair over to make room. The other Dolls slumped in their chairs as they expected Mark to sit next to Bridget.

But he didn't. He never even looked as he passed her. His smile was all for me.

"Hey, Allie," Mark said.

I felt the heat from Bridget's stare and I did a quick glance to confirm. She scowled at me and then at Mark's back. Swinging around, hair whipping, she sat rigid and upright, her hands clasped on the desk. She scooted her butt sideways and centered her chair with the desk.

"Hey, Mark." I moved over to make room.

"Pretty cool we're in the same class."

"Yeah, small world."

After a few hours, I started getting used to being elbow-to-elbow with him. I could tell he was a serious student. He didn't fake his interest in Mr. Briggs' lecture; it was genuine.

I watched him from time to time and he'd catch me and smile before returning to the lecture. He and I shared the history book and he read it intently, like I would a Jane Austen novel, his eyes ping-ponging back and forth as he devoured each page.

"You done with this page?" he asked.

"Yes." I wasn't, but I didn't care. I'd already read most of the book at my leisure.

He turned the page. I skimmed through it and then purposefully leaned in closer to him, fake-reading the right side of the page.

The lunch bell rang.

Mark looked up, disappointed. "I guess we'd better get some food." He stood up. "Come on. You can show me around."

I nodded and followed Mark out the classroom door. The loud hall didn't give me a chance to tell him where we were going, so I pointed and he followed. I led him to the end of the hall and to the back door.

He put his hands on my shoulders and leaned close to me as we shuffled through the crowded doorway. "I like your outfit."

I'd wondered if he'd notice my low-cut white tank and black jacket, basically the only thing I owned that even resembled fashion. I'd even tried on my makeup this morning. "Thanks. You look nice as well." I turned so he couldn't see me and closed my eyes. I swore I'd find something witty to say to him at some point.

Past the door and down the stairs, the crowd of kids split up. The open eating area was called the "quad." I surveyed the area, looking for the place everyone else bought lunch. Typically, I brought my lunch and scurried off to my tree, but Mark wasn't carrying anything with him. He was a buyer.

"I think it's over there," I said.

"That's the gym," he laughed. "Maybe *I* should be taking *you* to the food court." He took my hand and pulled me into the motion of the crowd.

I resisted for a second before allowing his contact and direction. Glancing around, I wondered if anyone else was watching us holding hands. Mark seemed to think nothing of it and I tried to match his confidence, strolling next to him, keeping my hand intertwined with his. A few eyes turned my way and I lowered my head, moving closer to him.

He let go of my hand, wrapped his arm over my shoulder and pulled me snug against his side. "Lift your head up, Allie." He laughed when I lowered my head more. "You're so cute."

He led me to the chimichanga line. I'd seen a few other kids carrying around this treat on plates, but I never wanted to wait in line for one. I was curious, though. The thought of a deep fried burrito was intriguing.

In a matter of seconds, Mark had started up a conversation with someone standing next to us. He released me and shook hands with the guy.

"Me? Santa Fe, New Mexico."

I raised an eyebrow at Mark's declaration. What happened to Baker, California and the world's largest thermometer? I looked up as Mark conversed with Tommy, of all people. Tommy glanced at me a few times, but seemed more interested in talking with Mark.

A breeze kicked up a scent—bubblegum and slut. Bright colors hit the corner of my eye, forcing my attention to the approaching Dolls. I positioned myself on the other side of Mark as they approached.

Bridget took point in their triangle of skank. She strutted with one long leg in front of the other. It was a waste of time, however, because Mark never looked up to appreciate the display. He kept talking about some sport or other and Tommy was eating it up, laughing and joking along.

"Hey." Bridget announced her arrival.

Mark turned and looked at her. "Hello."

"So, you're the new guy, and we wanted to welcome you to Summerford High." She talked in a long, drawn-out sigh.

"Thanks. It's been a friendly town." Mark glanced at me and smiled.

I strategically kept him between me and Bridget.

Bridget leaned to her left and tilted her head, making eye contact with me. "Is that Allie back there? You know, Mark," she flirted, shifting her attention to him, "you could hang with us over at the gym bleachers." She pushed her Tetons forward, but Mark showed no interest in her mountain chain.

"Thanks, but I'm going to hang with Allie."

No one ever brushed Bridget off, and I watched her face crunch up with confusion and anger.

"Excuse me?"

"I'm in line with Allie. I don't want to hang with you at the bleachers."

A few people in the chimichanga line oohed. Bridget's head jerked around at the people in line who were mocking her. She stopped moving, raised an eyebrow, and then a stupid I-know-a-secret grin covered her face. She wagged a finger and laughed.

"Oh, I get it. You're one of *those* guys." She jutted her pinky nail back and forth.

"What's that supposed to mean?"

"Oh, come on." She pointed at me. "Is she your hag? Or is she some makeover project you plan on submitting to Bravo?"

The Dolls laughed and cuddled together. The line froze in silence.

I looked at Mark's face. He didn't seem to care at all about the comments, offering only a smirk of amusement. But I wasn't as calm and accepting of someone trashing one of my friends.

I rushed for Bridget with my fists clenched. Mark put a hand on me and held me back. Bridget noticed my aggression and laughed again.

"Let her go. Bring it on, bitch," she said.

"Don't let them get to you," Mark whispered in my ear. "It's what her type wants. You're better than they are."

"Yeah, keep holding your hag back, twink," Bridget taunted.

Mark sighed and kept his hand on me. I wanted to punch her stupid face. He faced her and stuffed his hand in his pocket for a second. I thought he was holding something in his hand, but then it was gone.

The chimichanga line had all but stopped as each person turned to watch the spectacle unfold.

"Bridget, I know you don't mean what you say. People aren't born like this." He pointed at her. "They're made. So, what's your story? What made you this way? Was it some guy?"

Bridget's eyes went wide and she looked at her friends. "You don't know me."

"A college guy, I think. He probably said all the right things one night, and then you made the terrible mistake of thinking you'd found true love. Didn't you?"

"Shut up!"

"You didn't realize how much alcohol he was bringing you. You trusted him. You worried he could never like a person like you, but he did for a little bit, didn't he?"

"How..." she stammered. "You don't know shit," she said, but I saw the tears building in her eyes.

What was Mark doing, and how?

"And then he did things to you, didn't he? Terrible things."

She wiped her nose and looked at the people surrounding her, judging her. Tears streamed down her face. I put a hand on Mark, but he pulled away and stepped closer to Bridget.

"Only it wasn't just him. Everyone got a turn, didn't they?"

Bridget's face became red with anger. She pointed her finger and opened her mouth, but Mark cut her off.

"I want you to know it wasn't your fault. You're a beautiful person, Bridget, just not on the inside. You've let this guy ruin you. He made you this way. You're letting him win. You need to forgive him, not for him but for you. Screw the asshole who made you this way. Kick him in the balls a million times in your head if you have to, but stop being a bitch to the people around you. If you can act like a human being, I'll be here for you — *we'll* be here for you." Mark grabbed my shoulder and held me.

Bridget was sobbing. I hadn't noticed how quiet everything had gotten. The Dolls pulled at her and tried to console her, but she yanked away from their arms and pointed her finger at Mark.

"You don't know shit, and you'll regret this." She pointed at me. "You both will." She brushed off her friends and stomped away.

The anger left me. I watched Bridget disappear into the crowd of kids surrounding us and I felt like chasing her. At one time, a long time ago, we'd been friends. I never knew what had happened to her. Now I felt sorry for her, and wondered if Mark had been right. Had some guy literally screwed her over? How did Mark know?

I looked at him quizzically as he stared at the space Bridget had occupied.

"I shouldn't have done that," he said, and shook his head. "It wasn't the right thing to do, and I created an enemy for you."

"We weren't exactly besties to begin with."

"Yeah, but it wasn't right. I need to make it right."

Maybe he'd pushed it a bit far, but it was over and in the past. No take-backs.

"Line's moving," someone said from behind us.

Mark ignored whoever it was and grasped both my hands in his. He locked eyes with me with an intensity that felt like he was grabbing my soul. I held my breath and waited for whatever he needed to tell me.

"You made something for my mother yesterday, something

extremely rare and very valuable." He pulled the small penny purse from his pocket. "I took it from her. You remember this?"

"Yes." I gawked at the small bag.

"This can turn back the clock a couple of minutes. If both of us use it, maybe only a minute or so. I'm not sure."

I shook my head and scowled at him. I didn't like being played with like a child. "That's not possible and you know it."

"Hey, can you speed *up* the clock and move the line forward?" the guy behind us asked impatiently.

Mark ignored the comment. "I told you I'd prove it to you today. If you won't believe me, then you'll have to see for yourself."

He took my hand and held it palm up next to his. He turned the bag over above our hands and the stone rolled out, stopping where our hands intersected. The stone began to flatten and he took my hand and clasped it over his. I felt the spherical rock begin to melt into my skin.

A loud noise sounded, like wind blasting, but I didn't feel anything. I closed my eyes and felt the ground under my feet fall away. Grasping at the air, I yelped, and Mark held me tight. Another second and my feet landed on solid ground. The howling noise disappeared.

"Hey," Bridget said.

I opened my eyes and she was standing there, staring at Mark. The puffiness around her eyes was gone; her face was back to its normal spray-on-tan color.

"Hello, Bridget," Mark said.

I looked from him to her and wanted to shake him. What had he done? Had he actually turned back the clock?

"So, you're the new guy, and we wanted to welcome you to Summerford High."

The déjà vu made me nauseated. This couldn't be possible.

"Thanks for the offer, Bridget. Might I say you look great today?"

I stared at him as he flirted with her.

She smiled and pushed her shoulders back. "Thanks. You look good too. So, we'll be at the bleachers in the gym if you want to hang."

"Thanks. We'd love to visit with you guys." He wrapped his arm around me and kissed the side of my head.

Bridget raised an eyebrow and looked me up and down. "You're with *her*?"

"Yeah." He squeezed me. My dumbfounded look did little to confirm the notion.

"Whatever." Bridget turned and walked toward the gym. She glanced back over her shoulder and stared at me, looking as if she was trying to figure me out.

"Hey, can you move the line forward?" the guy behind us asked.

I was the one to ignore the tremendously hungry guy this time. I grabbed Mark's hand and yanked him out of the chimichanga line. I glanced at each person nearby and kept pulling him along.

"No fried burritos, I guess," Mark said, staggering along

with my pull, obviously finding the whole thing amusing.

I had no room for amusement and wanted answers. Somewhere private, though. I hurried along past the gym and the shop classroom, all the way to my tree. Standing under my tree, I turned and crossed my arms, facing Mark.

He had a whimsical smile spread across his face.

I opened my mouth, wanting to curse him about how what he'd done wasn't possible, but I had witnessed it with my own eyes. We'd gone back in time, if only for a couple of minutes, and not another soul seemed to notice.

He stood with his arms crossed, waiting for me to speak. I took in a deep breath and tried to find a question that wouldn't make me sound like a crazy person. "Show me something else."

He laughed. "You're the alchemist, not me."

"Prove it." I wanted to find something to mix. I wanted verification. It couldn't be real.

"My mom keeps the stuff in her hutch."

"Fine. After school we're going to see your mom. I want some answers."

His expression changed from whimsical to serious. "No, my mom will use you to make stuff. You don't know what you're getting into with her."

"You don't get to do this. You don't get to just drop this in my lap and act like it's something normal. It isn't." It hit me right then and there: I didn't even know this guy. "Wait, are you normal?" Maybe he was something or someone entirely different, hidden behind the veil of a cute face and a hard body.

"I'm as normal as you are."

"I won't take no for an answer. If I can do these things you claim, I need to know for myself. I have to see it, or I'll go completely insane … if I'm not already." I put my hand on my forehead and felt a headache building. I hated not understanding things around me. I kept people away for the most part and kept those around me close. Even Janet and Spencer, as awful as they were, were comfortably dependable. If this ability was part of me, I had to understand it and bring it into a comfortable realm.

"How about this: we meet at the treehouse right after school, okay?" he offered.

"Only if you bring something I can make. Some alchemy thingy. You got it?"

Mark stepped closer to me. I licked my lips a little as he moved his face near mine.

"I made so many mistakes today." He put his hand on my shoulders. "I never should have used that stone on Bridget," he said, then let go of me and looked behind him as he laughed. "Do you have any idea what's going to happen when my mom finds that stone missing? She's going to kill me."

"Just bring something."

"Fine, but we're going to start off small. Alchemy is a dangerous path, and I don't think you even realize it yet. People will do terrible things in order to acquire these stones." He again looked behind him, toward our houses.

CH.6

I paced at the foot of the tree with my arms crossed, staring at the path leading to it. Ever since Mark's time-jumping act, it was all I could think about. Did every stone do something different? Was there a book on what different combinations of ingredients made? I wondered what the first thing I had made for Ms. Duval did. My mind refused to slow down and it scrambled with a million questions at once.

The bushes rustled and Mark appeared with a bag in one hand. It had better be what I'd told him to bring, I thought. He regarded me with a smile and lifted the bag, as if he was presenting a fresh kill. "Signed, sealed and delivered," he said.

I shook my head and wondered if Mark had a list of lame sayings in his back pocket, or if he saved them all for me. The corners of my mouth tugged up at his dorky smile. It was hard not to smile around him. He had an adorable way about him … endearing, with a mixture of mystery. I mean, why the hell was he so interested in me?

The bag swayed in his hand like he might be trying to hypnotize me. I knew he saw my interest because I was making no effort to hide it. I had to know how this all worked and if it indeed was real.

"Come on," I said. "Let's go up to the tree fort."

I scanned the nearby forest. I wasn't sure why; I just felt as if we were doing something nefarious. Like going to hide and smoke a pack of cigarettes, or sneak a beer from the fridge.

The two-by-four ladder creaked under my feet. I flung the hatch open and climbed into the small room. Mark was climbing much more slowly, mostly because he was holding the bag in one hand and climbing with the other. I paced around the opening until he climbed into the room.

He closed the hatch and took what seemed like an hour to open the bag and place the bowl and two vials on the shelf in the corner of the room. "So, you just —"

"I know what to do," I interrupted, brushing up against him in an attempt to move him aside.

He held firm and smiled at me. "You are one anxious person, aren't you?"

I crossed my arms and tapped my foot. "I'm sorry, but I need to prove, or hopefully disprove, this crap. I can't handle the uncertainty for much longer."

He shook his head and raised a brow. "Well, you'd better get used to not knowing anything. This stuff is just the surface of the alchemist world. Once you start dabbling, it's only a matter of time until they find you."

"Who's *they*?"

"The Academy, most likely."

"The place your mom was kicked out of?"

"Yeah. Though she wasn't kicked out exactly. She just didn't graduate. Something about not showing enough promise. Some alchemists are weaker than others." He paused to streak back his hair with his hand.

"So some are stronger than others?"

He nodded. "My mom has talked a lot about the Academy, and she trained me for much of my life, hoping I would have the touch like her."

"But you don't?"

"Would she be bugging you if I did?"

"I suppose not." I stared at the three items on the shelf and then back at Mark. He pushed on his stomach with his fingertips while smiling at me.

"Are you okay?" I asked.

"Yeah, why?" He moved his hand away from his stomach.

I knew he didn't want me to know, so I let it go. I would find the right moment to talk with him about it. Besides, I had a shelf of ingredients waiting for me to mix.

"Can we get to it?" I succeeded in keeping a calm tone, but my mind wanted to yell the words out and grab the items to mix together.

"This is the simple mix of two liquids. The blue one is ammonia, and the second is water from the tap."

"I'm mixing two liquids together. Really? Your mom had some flaky stuff in the mix before. How is this going to turn into anything?"

"You'll never know until you do it."

"Fine."

He moved aside and I sidestepped to stand in front of the table. I took the first glass vial and poured it in.

"Oh, I almost forgot." He handed me a thin wooden spoon. "Your mixing stick, my lady."

"Thanks."

I poured the blue liquid in and watched it mix with the clear water. I stuck the spoon in and stirred. The anticipation of something happening put me at arm's length from the bowl. The water didn't froth or steam up like the other ones … it just looked like a bowl of water. I pulled the spoon out and tapped it on the edge of the bowl before placing it on the table. The liquid swirled under the momentum I had built and then slowed down to still water.

"Did I do something wrong?" I stared at the liquid.

He eased up next to me, gazing into the bowl. "What you did wrong is a lack of emotion. You have to channel a bit of yourself into the mix, otherwise you'll be just another rube."

"What's a rube?"

"Someone who can't channel their emotion into the mix."

"Channel my emotion," I parroted. The two times Ms. Duval had had me mix, she'd told me to feel my anger. It wasn't hard for me to summon.

I stood next to the bowl again, and in a second, I had the rage I wanted. Spinning the spoon around, I felt the essence of the water ... and a part of me actually went into the water. Steam flowed over the edge of the bowl and up into the air.

I heard a clanking sound and felt the spoon hit something solid in the bowl. I blew the fog away and saw a round object sitting at the bottom. A clear stone, about the size of a golf ball, with a hint of blue in it, almost like an ice cube. I reached in to grab it.

"No." Mark grabbed my hand. "You don't want to touch these things."

"Why? What does this one do?"

"This is one of the simplest forms of alchemy, mixing two similar ingredients. My mom tried to get me to make that stone a hundred times before she gave up. All it gives you is a runny nose."

"Show me."

"I'm not touching it."

"Big baby." I picked the stone up. It felt cold and as smooth as ice. It sat on my palm and then flattened out like a scoop of ice cream melting and disappearing into my skin.

"I don't feel—"

Snot ran down over my lip and stopped my sentence. I rushed my hand to my nose and looked at the back of my hand, thinking I might see blood. It looked like water but with more gel to it. The snot continued to drain from my noise.

"Oh my god, it won't stop," I said with my hands flying up to cover my nose.

Mark laughed and shook his head. "I told you."

It ran down onto my shirt. He kept laughing, and I wanted to punch him for it. "It's only supposed to last a minute or so."

I hopped around, pulling at my shirt and stuffing it into my nose. The front of my soaked shirt acted as a poorly built dam, blocking the snot from running further along my body. I felt disgusting enough already. When was it going to end?

I pulled the shirt from my nose and felt the stream turn to a dribble and then nothing. But the damage and grossness had done its job on me. The wet cloth clung to me and I pinched it away from my body, trying to keep it from touching my skin.

"This is so gross."

Mark unbuttoned his shirt. "You can wear this. I have an undershirt." He handed it to me and I placed it on the chair.

He crossed his arms and raised an eyebrow in expectation.

"I'm not taking my top off in front of you."

Mark turned around. "Is this okay?"

"Cover your face."

Mark put his hands over his face.

With one quick glance at Mark, I yanked my shirt over my head. I brushed the dry side over my face, then tossed it to the floor.

Mark looked over his shoulder.

"Hey, no peeking."

I adjusted my bra and yanked his shirt off the chair. It was too big and smelling of Mark, but I slid my arms through the sleeves. He looked over his shoulder again. Did the guy have no shame? Seeing me in his shirt, he turned around.

With the last buttons done, I had to admit it felt good to have it on. Maybe it was just getting my disgusting snot-ridden shirt off, or maybe it was the feeling of being closer to Mark. Such a stupid thought, but there it was. He strutted across the tree fort, staring at my chest.

"You wear that a whole lot better than I do."

"You're unbelievable." I wiped my nose and felt relieved to have a dry face. I stared at the bowl for a while and then turned back to Mark. "This is for real, isn't it?"

"Yes."

"We really jumped back in time?"

"Yes."

I felt nauseated and plopped down on the chair. A stack of books fell to the floor, but I didn't care. The room swayed and I saw Mark moving closer.

"You okay?"

I closed my eyes tight and stopped the world around me from spinning. I didn't notice he had both of my hands in his.

"I'm fine," I said, my words slurring. I couldn't get past the realization that I was some rare alchemist person who could do things that no one should be able to do. Apparently there were more of us, a whole Academy of people like me.

The chair creaked and Mark rose as I sat up.

"Please, show me more." I wanted to learn about every freaking stone in existence. The idea of it swallowed me whole and a tingling sensation through over my entire body. My thoughts ran wild with possibilities.

"I can, but I have to warn you, it's a dangerous road to take. There are people like my mom who search out people like you. The fact that you can make a something like a time stone makes you even a bigger target. There are also dark alchemists who try to take people like you away."

"I can handle the danger. Let's get more stuff to mix. Something cool. Dude, we could do a million amazing things, I bet."

"It's not that simple. Not everything produces results, and I only know so many patterns."

"Then we need to talk to your mom. You said she used to be in some academy, right? I bet she knows all kinds of stuff."

"Allie, no. You don't want her to be involved in this. She'll find ways to manipulate you, create things that who knows what she'll do with."

"Yeah, but she knows how to make these stones. She might be able to help me understand."

"My mom's purpose is to manipulate people with them. I've seen it my whole life. It's something you want to stay away from."

"What do you mean, your mom uses these stones on people?"

"She won't teach you. She'll get you to make a stone, like the time stone or the insight stone. Things that can be used to create a situation of opportunity."

"Insight stone? If we can't trust your mom, then where can I go?"

He rubbed his chin and glanced out the window. "There's the Academy, but I'm telling you that world isn't one you want to get mixed up in. It's filled with greed and deceit."

I ignored the warning with my interest maxed out. I stared at the side of his head, wanting to turn it with my hands and make him tell me more. "Where is this Academy?" I had to know more about these stones and this ability I had. "How do I get in?"

"The Academy watches and listens. Making and using things like a time stone can bring out all kinds of people." He looked at the ceiling and cringed. "I think I've handled you entirely wrong, and I'm sorry. I shouldn't have shown you this stuff. It's just when I'm around you... Listen, with your skills, there'll be some people who will kill to get to you."

"Are there really people out there looking for people like me?"

"If you're looking in the right place, using the right stone, you can find a budding alchemist. My mom found you. How hard do you think it will be for others?"

I hated the idea of someone looking for me, and for what? Because I could make these rock balls?

"Is everyone in alchemy bad?" I asked.

"No. Don't get me wrong. There are ways you can help people. There are ways to do good with it. It's just that too many people get sucked in and consumed by it."

I jumped on the good part. "Why don't we grab some more

stuff from your mom's cabinet? I bet we could make some pretty awesome ones." I wiped my nose. "Maybe even stuff we can protect ourselves with."

"You're not going to give up on this, are you?"

"Not a chance."

"Fine, but tomorrow. I'd like to have another day with you before you go completely alchy crazy."

•

Mark shared my desk the next day. Bridget shot glances back at us if we laughed or spoke loudly enough for her to hear. I couldn't help but look at Bridget differently after what had happened in the chimichanga line.

The time flew by with Mark in class next to me, and then when the lunch bell rang, I lifted a brown bag from my backpack.

"I brought us both lunch today. We can sit at my tree."

The other kids scraped their chairs against the concrete floor and shuffled their books into their packs. Bridget got up and left in a hurry, giving me a glance along the way.

"You don't want to hang in the quad? We might find some people you actually like."

"No, we won't."

"I've only been here for two days and I already can tell you a few people I think you'd like."

"Are you trying to set me up on a date?"

He laughed. "No, let's forget it. I love your tree spot."

I smiled and stood. We walked across the campus, past the art classroom to the large oak tree. I selected a ground-down root as a chair and tapped my hand on the space next to me. Mark sat next to me in the shade of the tree's canopy.

"What did you bring?" Mark asked, gesturing toward my paper bag.

"Turkey sandwiches. I snuck the good sharp cheddar out of the fridge this morning." I handed him the sandwich wrapped in cellophane.

I unwrapped mine and took a bite, but I wasn't thinking about food. I hadn't thought about much of anything besides stones, alchemy, and this Academy he'd mentioned. It consumed my thoughts so much, I had to suppress them so I wouldn't look like some freak in front of Mark.

"We should do something cool today," I said.

He held his sandwich with both hands and chewed what remained in his mouth before answering. "I take it you have something in mind?"

"I want you to show me what you and your mom do. This manipulation thing?"

He set his sandwich down on his lap and instantly I knew I'd asked for too much, too soon.

"I don't help her in that kind of stuff. It isn't right to use the stones that way."

I searched for the words. "We don't have to do it the way your mom does, you know? We can just have fun, maybe mess with some people. You're the one who said they don't even know what happened to them." I hugged my sandwich close to my body. "Come on, please?"

"You're so dang cute when you beg." He paused. "Yes, we can find some innocent people and then use them solely for our entertainment."

"When you put it like that, it sounds even more awesome."

•

I told Mark about the sidecar, which he thought was the funniest thing in the world, but he declined to ride in it. It was a short walk to Main Street.

I felt the small sack hanging next to my hip. Having two stones so close to my skin made me nervous, especially since I knew what they did. Mark had shown me how to make them and they were a staple of his mom's arsenal.

He took my hand away from my side and wrapped it around his. "You nervous?" he asked.

"A little. I mean, what if they notice, or what if I drop one?"

"We can turn around right now." Mark slowed down, but I shook my head and kept walking down Main Street.

The Swan looked busier than normal, with at least six people in it. A few customers were at the bar, and a couple was sitting close at the back table. We passed by the window, and I looked briefly into the next place, Bob's Electronics. TVs were displayed in the window, hanging from thin cables. Some sports game was on; football, it looked like.

Mark slowed down and observed the screens before catching back up with me as I stopped in front of the farmer's market. Busier than the Swan, it had clusters of people touching different fruits on display or taking small samples of beef jerky from a jerky cart. It was big enough for a couple of stone wielders like us to mingle through, but small enough that we could witness the disturbances we created.

"How about him?" Mark nodded toward a hefty man examining the beef and cheese cart.

"I don't know. I was thinking about him." I pointed to a man aat the orange cart. His shifty eyes glanced at us and he moved closer to the stand.

I walked over to the cabbage vendor and pretended to pick through some stacks of iceberg lettuce.

"Two for five, miss," the cabbage salesman said.

I snuck more glances at the man in the thick coat, and when I didn't respond to the salesman, he walked back to his chair, mumbling something about teenagers.

"Five bucks says that guy is shady," Mark whispered.

"I don't know. He might just—" Before I could finish the sentence, I saw him stuff an orange into his jacket. "Did you see that?"

"Got a bandit in the farmer's market." Mark smiled.

This was better than I'd thought. I'd had reservations about using these magical rocks on an innocent person, but this little man had just stolen something. He deserved a little bit of pranking.

"He's the one. Which stone should I use first?"

"The one with yellow stripes."

I removed the sack from my pocket and opened it on the palm of my hand. A blue stone with red speckles sat next to a milky one with yellow stripes. I pinched the yellow striped one and walked over to the shady man, who was now standing next to an apple cart. He asked the salesman to grab a jar of apple cider from behind him and used the opportunity to stuff an apple into his pocket.

I moved closer as he rejected the cider. "Never mind. I thought it might be something spicier," the thief said. He glanced at me and moved to the next cart.

I followed, with Mark close behind me. I pinched the stone harder between my fingers and moved in on the criminal. He glanced back at me and narrowed his eyes before moving to the pomegranates. I moved next to him and reached for a pomegranate. I dropped the stone on the back of his hand. He jerked his hand back, but the stone had already dissolved by the time he brought his hand to his face.

He rubbed his palm and glared at me.

"Sorry, just grabbing one," I said, keeping my eyes on him, waiting for the stone to do its thing.

He stopped rubbing his hands and a glazed look washed over his eyes as his hands slumped to his sides. I set the pomegranate back on the pile and waved my hand in front of his face. He didn't blink.

Mark moved next to me and leaned in front of the vacant-looking man. He studied the man's face, then shrugged, reached into the man's jacket and pulled out his wallet.

"Let's see who this guy is."

"How long will he be like this?"

"You made the stone strong enough to last for a few minutes." Mark opened his wallet and looked through it. "Look." He fanned a thick stack of hundred-dollar bills. "Mr. Ralph Lafferty doesn't appear to be starving."

"What should we do with him?"

"I think Mr. Lafferty here should pay for what he's taken, don't you?"

I nodded and looked over at the man sitting behind the apple cart, leaning back with his arms crossed, watching another person pass by.

Mark walked over to him. "Excuse me," Mark said.

The apple vendor stood up from his chair and sighed. "Yes?"

"Sir, the man over there forget to pay for an apple. He's mighty sorry, and he wanted me to give you this." Mark held out a hundred-dollar bill.

The man's face shrank as he inspected the bill. "An apple is only a dollar. I don't have change for a hundred."

"Keep it."

"You serious?"

"As a heart attack."

"Tell him thanks. He comes here all the time, but never buys anything. I just thought he was some cheap bastard." The man regarded Ralph with a wave.

"Listen," I said. "That man's been taking fruit from you and probably all the other vendors for a long time. Mark, give him all of it. Divide it among the other vendors here, okay?"

He shrugged and pulled the stack from Ralph's wallet, then handed it to the skeptical vendor.

"Who are you kids?"

"Just trying to help out. We'd better get going." Mark nodded his head.

"Just don't ever let that man back here again, and warn the others," I said.

The apple vendor pulled each bill from one hand to the other as he counted them. I wasn't sure if he heard me or not, or maybe he didn't care. A couple thousand dollars might buy you a lifetime stealing permit at a farmer's market. He was transfixed by the stack of money.

Mark rushed to Ralph and stuffed his wallet back in his jacket. He laughed and jogged to the street. I caught up in a second and we headed on our way. I took a deep breath and grabbed his hand this time. I couldn't believe we'd actually done something with the stone that felt good. That scumbag Ralph had been stealing from those poor people for who knew how long and for only the thrill of it. What a sicko. I glanced back right before we passed the corner and saw Ralph moving and patting his jacket.

"Will he remember anything?" I asked.

"No, they usually don't even remember the last few minutes before the stone."

"I bet those farmer's market people won't forget."

Mark smiled and swung my hand with his. "Where to now, m'lady?"

I squeezed his hand and pulled on it. "I bet we can use this second one at Mindy's Café."

"Are you trying to get me on a date?" he asked.

I looked away. I hadn't thought of this as being a date. Maybe it was, but being with Mark and using the stones felt like we were on top of the world. We could go anywhere together and succeed. We just needed to create the right one for the right moment and maybe we could change things for the better, one apple thief at a time.

We jogged across the intersection to Mindy's Café. People were bustling around the entrance and the waiting line looked as long as usual. I took the second stone from my pocket and pinched it between my fingers. This would be quick and easy, just some harmless fun.

"This should be good," Mark said.

I jumped over the curb and onto the sidewalk. A few people were smoking outside, while more were crowded near the door holding their buzzers. I searched for a spot past the door. The waiting people parted to let a group leave the café. I used this opening and tossed the stone on the ground. It skipped across the sidewalk and onto the tiled floor of the waiting area. I lost sight of it and wondered if it wasn't working. Mark had said it would crack after a few jumps.

Then I heard the first scream. I shot a look to Mark, but he kept his attention on the crowd. This wasn't right; something was wrong. The moving throng of people turned toward the scream and I squinted, trying to find out what had happened. A young woman wearing flip-flops continued to scream and stumbled out the front door with one large, swollen leg. I stared at her face and recognized her. She was one of the Dolls Bridget hung with, Kerri. She made eye contact with me and the fear and pain in her eyes made me gasp.

She reached down, touched her swelling leg and fell over face-first onto the sidewalk.

I rushed to Kerri's side and examined her leg. It looked as if someone had injected gallons of water underneath her skin. Her chest moved up and down and she mumbled in her unconscious state. This wasn't right; this wasn't supposed to happen. It was a mist stone. It was just supposed to create water vapor mist and freak a few people out. It must have made contact with her foot and now her leg was swollen.

"We'd better go," Mark said.

I stood just as two men rushed to her side, grabbing at her wrist.

"I think she's in anaphylactic shock," one of them said. "Does anyone know what she ate?"

An older couple pushed through the crowd.

"Kerri," the woman said. "Oh my god, what happened?" She plunged to her knees and pulled at Kerri's arm.

"People, give her some room," the man said as he stood.

The crowd spread out and I lost sight of Kerri lying on the

sidewalk as people moved up in front of me to get a better look at the spectacle.

Mark pulled at me, but I pulled back and turned to him. "Can't we do anything?"

"She'll be fine in a little bit. We should go," he whispered.

He pulled again and I reluctantly complied. We walked through the thinning crowd as people's curiosity drew them toward the incident.

"What was that stone, Mark? 'Cause that sure as hell wasn't mist."

"I don't know what happened. It was just a cloud stone. It should have been harmless. Maybe we got the mixture wrong?"

"You sure she's going to be okay?"

Mark looked back at the crowd. "Yeah, the effect usually only lasts for a short period of time on someone."

I breathed in some relief. The last thing I wanted was a person's death on my hands. We cut back onto the road and headed toward our houses. Passing the café from the other side of the street, I saw Kerri sitting on the curb and rubbing her leg.

"That was dangerous, Mark. We could have killed her."

"I told you these things were dangerous. I've seen the things they do to people all my life." Mark kicked at the sidewalk. "You think I wanted to hurt that girl?"

"No, but if we're going to keep making stones, we'd better know what we're making from now on." I stared at the side of his head for a bit and tried to figure out the best way to approach him. I took a deep breath and decided to just jump in. "I think we should talk to your mom. She's been trained. I bet she can teach me all kinds of different patterns and recipes."

"One blunder and I'm no good to you now?"

"Mark, this isn't something we can trial-and-error with."

"You could just stop making them."

I gritted my teeth at the simplicity of the statement. Of course he was right, but I couldn't imagine ignoring this part of my life now. Mark looked at me with a sideways smile.

"I just think she could help me."

"Fine, but I won't let you create a single stone out of my presence. There are some very nasty ones out there that would make that leg swelling look like a holiday." Mark held his stomach as we walked toward our houses.

I'd seen him from time to time grab his midsection, or rub it. "You okay?"

"Yeah, I just got a little worked up about what happened back there." He glanced back.

I kept my attention on his stomach until he pried his hands away from it. We didn't say much for the last few minutes home. We passed my house and went to the next street over to Mark's house.

"We'll talk with my mom, but I want you to just follow my lead, okay?" he said as we walked along the sidewalk leading to his front door. He bounded up the few steps and opened the front door. "Okay?"

I nodded and followed him into the house. The house still felt empty, many of the boxes left untouched and sitting on the floor. Mark walked to the dining room.

"Hey, Mom...." He stopped and frowned.

His mom was sitting at the dining room table, but she didn't move. Her eyes strained to look in our direction. Her hands were lying flat against the table and she looked frozen in place. I don't think she even blinked. I thought of Ralph, but she didn't have the glazed-over look; she looked cognitive.

"Mom?" Mark rushed to her side.

"About time," a voice said from the kitchen.

I gasped at the sound and turned to the man behind it. He was leaning against the counter with his arms crossed. He was wearing a sleek black suit and his black hair was shaved tight to his scalp. His gaze held mine and then went to Mark before he moved away from the counter toward us.

Ms. Duval's frozen state became more worrisome. She didn't say a word to the intruder or us, but I saw her eyes shaking in their sockets as if she was under great strain.

"What did you do to my mom?"

"Nothing that can't be corrected." The man in the black suit rolled a stone across the table. It contacted Ms. Duval's hand and melted into it.

She jumped up from her chair. "How dare you paralyze me?" she said as she pointed at the man.

He pulled a chair away from the table and sat down.

Freaked out, I stared at Mark. I wasn't sure if we should run, attack, or beg for mercy.

The man crossed his legs and motioned to the other chairs.

"I don't mean any harm. The only reason I paralyzed her is so she couldn't warn you of my arrival. Ms. Duval has been known to hide talent she finds." He looked at her.

She huffed and crossed her arms.

"There is nothing to worry about," the man said. "I'm only a recruiter from the Academy. Please, sit down." He motioned to the chair again.

A recruiter? My curiosity outweighed my fear and I stepped toward the man and pulled out a chair. I spun the chair to face him and sat down. Mark stood next to me and kept a wary eye on the black-suited man.

"Thank you for not causing trouble. My only intention here is to test you. If you pass, you may come to the Academy and learn what it is you were born to do. If you do not pass, I will leave. And trust me, you won't remember I was even here." With his gloved hand, he pulled out a pure yellow stone.

I tried to process everything he said, but the thought of a test and going to the Academy swirled around. A whole place where there would be people like me. I wanted to be tested. I wanted to know about this academy. I thought maybe I could learn from Ms. Duval, but what could I learn from an entire academy dedicated to teaching the craft? These stones' potential seemed infinite and if I could figure them out, I could change the world.

"I found her. This isn't fair," Ms. Duval said.

"Really? You think you own her, then?" The man glared at her. Her eyes twitched. "How did you find her?"

"When a person uses a time stone, it sets off a shockwave my tracker stones simply can't ignore. I imagine you had her make it for you?"

She jumped from her seat again and glared at Mark. "You took my...."

"It wasn't yours, Mother. I saved you a lot of trouble getting rid of it."

"I had a buyer already. We would have been set up for life, Mark. For *life*."

"Yeah, until the buyer tried to kill us. I probably saved our lives."

"You know I wouldn't let that happen again."

"This mother/son thing is real sweet to watch and all, but I have a job to do here. So, if you can sit back down and let me do it." The man looked between the two of them before focusing on me. "Okay. Allie is your name, right?"

"Yes."

"This little tester"—he held a yellow stone between his gloved thumb and finger—"wants to dissolve into the hand of an alchemist and *only* an alchemist. I'm going to place this on your hand, but first I want you to summon as much anger as you can. You see, your anger can hold it back from dissolving. The longer an alchemist can keep it from absorbing, the more powerful they are considered to be." He cupped the yellow stone in his hand, out of my sight. "Most of the time it dissolves within a second or two. If it never dissolves, you fail and you don't have the gift at all."

Mark placed a hand on my shoulder and the nerves crept back in place. I wasn't as scared as I was nervous about failing the test. This man was from the Academy. I never fit in at school, or at home ... anywhere, for that matter. Thinking of a place where I might belong was intoxicating. I could learn how to use my abilities properly, how to mix things in the right way. I didn't want to ever have another accident like what had happened with Kerri again.

I extended my hand and summoned my cocktail of anger. He took the yellow stone and placed it on my palm. It felt warm at first, then became cold. I strained, keeping the anger fresh, and my hand shook, but I kept the stone steady. The man in the black suit shifted in his chair and stuffed his hand into his pocket, probably to bring out the memory-wiping stone.

If I failed this test, I wanted my memory of it all gone. I couldn't go back to my stupid house knowing what I knew about the world around me. I hoped he could wipe the entire week away, if I couldn't go. This was the first chance I had ever had to leave the grasp of Janet and her boy. The man now held a diamond-looking stone in his gloved hand.

"Give it a second," Ms. Duval warned.

The stone felt heavy and the thought of it not melting beat out some of my anger. Then it melted into my hand. He stowed the diamond stone and leaned back in his chair.

"Alright, Allie. My name is Darius, and I have an important question for you. Do you want to train in the field of alchemy? Do you want to come back to the Academy with me?"

I shook with excitement. How could my world change in so little time? My hands covered my open mouth, and Mark looked down at me with a concerned expression. He didn't like this stuff. I wasn't sure why he was so apprehensive about it. Maybe it was because he didn't have the ability?

"Yes," I answered. If I could change time without even knowing what I was doing, what would it be like once I knew how to create everything? A sense of power swelled in me like a drug and I wanted more.

"I don't like this," Mark jumped in. "We don't know this guy. How can we can trust him?"

Ms. Duval huffed, but I spoke first.

"This is my decision. I need to know if I can fit in somewhere, Mark. I'm not like you. Everyone doesn't just love me the second they get to know me. I'm different. I've always known that, and now I have some kind of validation. I have these abilities, and I want to learn everything I can about them."

"When would she be going?" Mark asked.

"Now."

Mark let go of my shoulder and paced back and forth. He looked like he was having a conversation with himself. Just as I was about to interrupt, he came to a stop in front of Darius. "Mom, I'm sorry." He extended his hand toward Darius.

Darius furrowed his brow, but his look was nowhere near the utter shock on Mark's mom's face.

"No. No, that's not possible." She shook her head, her voice a distant whisper, and she seemed lost in her own house.

Mark wouldn't look at her, but moved his hand again toward Darius. All the times he had watched me make stones . . . he had never directly said he couldn't. I'd just *assumed* he couldn't. I didn't like the idea of him keeping something like this from me, but I couldn't imagine what his mom felt.

Darius plucked the same type of yellow stone from his bag and placed it in Mark's hand. The ball dissolved in an instant and his mom let out a screech.

"All these years, you've been lying to me?"

"Mom, these damn rocks ruin our lives. I didn't want anything to do with them. I was trying to save us." He had tears in his eyes.

"All the things I've done for us . . . for you. You don't even know." Ms. Duval glared at Darius. "I need to talk to Allie for a minute."

"We really must get going—"

"I wasn't asking," she snapped.

I jerked at her tone and stared at Ms. Duval. She eyed me and then motioned for me to follow her out of the room. I glanced at Mark as she pushed me into the next room.

She stood next to me in what might be considered the family room, but only a few boxes occupied the space. Ms. Duval fidgeted with her hands and mumbled something about time.

"Yes?"

She jumped at my voice and grabbed my shoulders. I pulled back in surprise, but she held me firm.

"I have weeks of stuff to tell you in one minute." She glanced at the doorway. "Remember how I told you there was a way to help Mark?"

"You were going to tell me, yes."

"The Academy has something he needs to stay alive. I've been searching the whole country to find someone like you who can get into the Academy and do well enough to get one."

"Get what?"

"A life stone. The president of the Academy, whoever that may be at the moment, will either have one, or will have access to the ingredients to make one. You need to get this stone if we have any chance of saving Mark."

My mouth hung open and I searched for the punchline. Her eyes twitched as she watched the doorway and me.

"Is it that serious?"

"It won't be long before he starts feeling the stomach pain again, and I'm afraid there isn't anything I can do to stop it this time. What used to work doesn't have the same lasting effect now because he's grown resistant to it. Most of what I do is to keep him alive when every doctor said he'd be dead before he reached the age of two. Please, you can't tell him about this." She glanced back at the doorway. "The life stone is the only thing that can cure him completely. You have to get it." She shook me.

My heart lumped up in my throat as her words soaked in.

"And you can't tell Mark. He has no idea how bad it is. If he knew...." She looked panicked and pleading with me. "I can't believe he has the gift."

"It's been more than a minute," Darius called from the dining room.

"Get the stone and get out of there." She must have seen the total panic on my face. "Listen, I've met many young men and women around the world, so I can say with total certainty, you're something special and they'll notice very quickly." She chuckled. "You're going to move up very fast and get access to the president."

"What do you mean?" I asked.

Darius stood at the doorway. "We need to get going."

Ms. Duval pulled me closer to her and whispered in my ear, "Please help me with this. Help *him*."

I didn't know what to say, so I just nodded in agreement. If I could find something to save Mark, I'd find it. Ms. Duval let go of my shirt and motioned for me to go.

Darius waved me over and I followed him back to the dining room. Mark looked at the floor before looking up and locking eyes with his mom.

"I'm sorry. I didn't want to become an experiment to you. I wanted to be your son," he said.

Ms. Duval took in a deep breath. "I don't know what to say."

I stared at Mark, looking at his body and trying to figure out the illness his mom had mentioned. He glanced at me a couple of times. My blank stare did little to keep his gaze on me, but it gave me a chance to look him over, to study this new person standing in front of me. He had the same gift I did, but he'd kept it hidden from all of us until now. Why come out now?

"I want to go with her," Mark demanded.

"I wouldn't have it any other way," Darius said.

This couldn't get any better. Not only was I getting away from this hell, I had Mark coming with me. I bounced next to him with excitement.

"So, do you have a bus? Oh, are we flying? I need to pack." I blurted the words out and realized how much I hated traveling. I hadn't been on a plane since I was a little girl.

"Where we're going, you can only reach by portal stone."

Ms. Duval jerked from her stupor and rounded the table. "Why a portal stone? When I was there, it was a simple trip by car."

"Things have changed greatly over the last few years, Ms. Duval. We take great precautions now with our locations."

"Dark alchemists?"

He nodded.

She turned to Mark with tears in her eyes, studying him with a quivering chin. She moved forward and hugged him. "I forgive you, my boy. I'm so proud of you."

I watched the exchange and thought of my dad. He might not be so understanding about me going to a mysterious academy almost no one knew even existed, but I hoped I could be back by the time he got home in a few months. I'd have to get a note to him or call him after I got to the Academy. I thought of Spencer and Janet for a second, and it was a second more than they deserved. The only reason they would ever know I was missing was that they wouldn't be able to fill their daily quota of hatred. I wouldn't miss them at all, but someone might notice I was gone.

"Darius, what about my stepfamily?"

"We will notify them that you have been accepted to a private academy for the rest of the year."

I laughed. "Well, that will piss them off real good. If they think I'm enjoying myself, they'll do everything they can to stop it."

Darius rubbed his chin. "I will visit them personally to make sure they don't take notice of your absence." He paused. "Are you two ready to go?"

"Yes," I said.

Mark nodded and stood next to me. Ms. Duval held his hand and kissed it. "You be safe."

"I will."

Darius rummaged through his sack and plucked out a purple stone with black streaks. "I wasn't expecting three, but the stone will still work. We just all need to touch it at the same moment." He took one glove off and held out his hand, flat and palm up. "Place your hand on the edge of mine."

I put my hand, sideways, next to his. Mark did the same. I watched Darius's gloved hand drop the purple ball into our formed hands. I yelped as I felt as if I was falling through the floor. My hair wisped around my face. All three of us crashed together on a hard floor.

"Get up. We're here," Darius said.

CH.7

My head swayed and I stumbled. Mark grabbed my arm and helped me stay on my feet. I looked around the small room. The ceiling felt low. I could touch it if I wanted, and there was only a small wooden door on one of the four walls in the square room.

"Expecting something with more grandeur?" Darius said, seeing my confusion.

I wasn't sure what I'd been expecting, but it wasn't some tiny room with a door.

"Seems about right," Mark said as he scraped the ceiling with his hand.

He and I had different expectations of the Academy. I guess I'd thought of a university campus or something similar. I wanted to get out of this room. There had to be more.

"Let me explain a few things to you." Darius' tone had changed from the softly spoken words back in Mark's dining room to this stern tone on the verge of demanding. "You are here for one reason and that is to make stones. We will teach you everything you need to know and provide you with all the materials. You will not be coddled. Nor will you be treated nicely. You will need the hate, the anger, to create these stones. Priscilla will decide which side you'll be on. Once your side has been determined, you are to do everything in your power to anger the other side. You will be doing them a disservice if they don't hate your guts. Do you understand?"

I breathed in deep and felt my heart in my throat. I'd thought about grand halls and camaraderie with my fellow gifted people. What he had just described sounded like one side torturing another for the sole purpose of creating stones. He had to be exaggerating. It couldn't be that cruel.

Mark held me with one arm and leaned in to whisper in my ear. "I won't let you out of my sight."

It actually made me feel better and I was glad to have Mark next to me ... a familiar face. "Thanks," I said.

"You have to stay here until Priscilla can make her rounds." Darius opened the door.

"Wait. We have to stay in here? What if we have to go to the bathroom?"

"I don't care. Hold it, piss yourself, whatever. Oh and welcome to the Academy." Darius slammed the door on the way out.

Mark rushed to the door and pulled on the black steel handle, shaking the door.

"Great," he said, pacing next to the door. "I knew I had a bad feeling about this place. The way the guy looked at you back home, as if you were a thing."

I hadn't caught that look, but I hadn't been looking for it. "I'm willing to give this place a chance, Mark. It can't be that much worse than home."

He laughed. "I told you that you were going down a dark road with this stuff. I've seen how it controls every action my mom makes. It consumes her."

"Me? What about you? You lied to your mom, and you lied to me. You have the gift just like I do."

Mark sighed and ran his hand through his hair. "Everything I did was to protect her, to protect myself. I've watched her use up people in the past. I didn't want her using me up. I think the only reason she even had me was to have an alchemist in her grasp."

"How did you hide it?"

"It's not easy. Oh, and Darius is lying about something."

"What?"

"He talks about anger and hatred as if they're the only way to make these things. It may be the easiest way, but there's another way. Any emotion ... happiness, jealousy, love, compassion ... is just as powerful, but harder to control and push into the mix."

"Yeah, well, I don't think I'll be summoning love into my mix."

"You'd be surprised. I think about my dad sometimes."

I thought about my mom. All I had left were whispers from another life. I'd thought I was happy then. I was sure my dad was, but I didn't have an overwhelming sensation of love. There were hints of anger and questions. *Why did she leave me when I was just a young girl? How could she do that to me?* I needed her.

Breathing heavily through my nose, I put my hand over my mouth. I took in the small room and even gave a go at the door. There didn't appear to be any way out. How long would they keep us in here?

"For what it's worth, I'm glad we came together," Mark said.

"Yeah, me too. I'm a bit claustrophobic and if you weren't here, I think I'd be freaking out."

"You can lean on me anytime." He smiled.

I looked at the floor and felt the heat in my stomach again. Being alone with Mark, in this strange place, made me look to him even more for support. It was just me and him. I wanted to hug him right then, to wrap my arms around his waist and place my face against his chest. I'd let him hold me, and then we could face the Academy together. But I didn't hug him. I just stood on the other side of the room and looked at his profile, waiting for this Priscilla person.

A knock on the door interrupted my staring. I straightened up and tried to look proper, not knowing who was going to be on the other side.

The door opened, revealing a small woman. Her black, straight hair brushed her shoulders, while her firm look landed on each of us. I swallowed and looked away from her gaze.

"I'm Priscilla. Come closer, young man." She twisted her finger at Mark.

He raised both eyebrows and walked closer to the petite woman.

She grabbed his hand and rubbed one of her fingers over his palm. "You haven't worked a day in your life, have you?"

"I like to think I keep soft hands for the ladies." He winked at her.

She smiled and curled his hand into a fist before pushing it back to him. Her attention turned to me as I backed into a corner of the room, holding my hands behind my back. She motioned for me to come closer. I looked to Mark, and he shrugged. Moving forward, Priscilla took my hand and rubbed the line creasing across my palm. She spent much more time inspecting mine than she had Mark's.

"This is difficult," Priscilla said. "Darius said this one"—she pointed at me—"rated a nine on the test." She faced Mark. "While you rated a one." She tapped her finger on her chin. "We rarely have pairs, and if we do, we split them up. But I think the two of you in the same house would be most prudent, most prudent indeed." She shoved my hand back to me and I rubbed it, holding it close to my body.

"I'm not going anywhere without her," Mark declared.

"I agree. I think you should be with her. It may increase the productivity of both of you here. You will be in the house of Red."

"Okay, great. What does that mean?" Mark said.

"Your house leads with explain everything to you, or they will just mess with you. I don't know and I don't care."

"That seems to be a theme here," I remarked.

Priscilla smiled. "Good. That kind of thing is exactly what gets the other side going. You may do well here."

"When can we meet the president of the Academy?" I glanced at Mark's stomach.

Priscilla laughed and then bunched her face up in a question. "A student has never asked that before we've even left the portal room. She will see you, if you're worth seeing, and that is all there is to it."

I nodded and watched the woman leave the room.

"You coming?" she said from the adjacent hall.

"Come on," Mark said, and I followed him out of the door.

I thought maybe outside the room would be a grand hall of sorts, or at least something besides a tight hallway. The ceiling seemed a bit higher, but the space felt even more closed in with it being so narrow. I couldn't even stretch my arms out if I wanted. Cracks ran down the rock walls and I tripped over a raised paver in the floor.

Mark turned while still walking behind Priscilla. "Not exactly the Taj Mahal."

I gave a small smile and tried not to think about the ceiling crashing in on us. Lamps hung on the walls and lit the hallway. I kept my eyes on Mark's back and knew we'd eventually have to get somewhere that wasn't a freaking coffin.

I felt a breeze before seeing the doorway. Behind it looked like open space and I wanted to push Mark and Priscilla out of the way to get to it. I nudged Mark and he tripped forward, narrowly recovering before crashing into Priscilla. He looked back at me and walked sideways. He took my hand and held it in his.

"A tad claustrophobic?" he asked.

I shook his hand from mine, not wanting to feel more restricted in any way. "No, I just don't like small spaces." I looked past him to the opening at the end of the hall.

Mark stopped and allowed me to rush past him through the doorway. I took a deep breath. The room was huge, and the ceiling was lined with beige tile work. A street ran down the middle of the long space, divided by a wooden fence. On each side, three stories of windows with doors lined the walls in even increments. Houses were built into the walls and touched the curved ceiling above. Each house connected to the next, and the only difference from one side of the street to the other was the color of the doors. On one side, the doors were painted red, and on the other, blue.

A few people were loitering around the fronts of the houses, but steered clear of the fence, choosing to hug the wall on their side. As soon as people noticed us, they walked closer, forming a small crowd. I eyed the Red side, studying the people who were about my age. They were wearing regular clothes, but each had a piece of red cloth somewhere on their bodies. Many were wearing it on their wrists, while others were wearing it around their necks. The group on the other side had the same thing, but were wearing blue cloth.

Priscilla stood still, looking from one side to the other, trying to create drama. I'd seen Bridget pull this same kind of stuff when she walked into class and stood at the front, like she wasn't sure where her desk was, while really she was presenting herself. The thought of never dealing with the Dolls again made me euphoric.

"We have a nine," she said as she gestured to me, "and a one."

Chatter filled both houses and most eyes were on me and then Priscilla.

Priscilla raised both hands and stared at the Blue houses. "They will both be going to the house of Red." Priscilla marched toward the Red side.

The Blues hissed and booed while the Reds cheered on our arrival. A young woman bounced over with excitement. Her gaze lingered on Mark for a while. She'd probably be swooning over him next. I rolled my eyes, thinking it was hard to get away from high school crap. But I was wrong. She ran toward me, brushing past Mark to grab my hands.

"The second I saw you exiting the hall, I *knew* you were Red all the way. I'm so excited to have you in our house!" She jumped up and down and squealed.

Mark looked at us with a big smile, shaking his head.

"Hi, I'm Allie and this is Mark."

"Oh, how rude of me. I'm Jackie, house leader, and it's so nice to meet you, Allie." She walked past me a couple of steps, toward the Blues.

"See what we've got here, Blues? A true Red. You can all suck it!" She gestured to her crotch and screamed so loud my ears crackled. Then she gave the Blues double middle fingers.

Adjusting her hair, Jackie came back to me. "Follow me." She nodded toward the Red houses.

"She's got issues," Mark whispered to me as we followed her.

"Don't use any hate on another house member, Mark. That's one of the big rules here." Priscilla glanced back at him.

"Yeah, Mark," I teased. "Don't be so hateful."

"There you go, Allie. That's right, you save all hate for the Blues or the stones, never another Red. You are brothers and sisters on this side of the fence," Jackie said.

Priscilla walked next to us. "Well, I'm sure Jackie will take care of you now. Good luck, you two." She left and walked down the fence line.

"Thanks?" Mark said to her back.

"She's a strange one." Jackie pointed at Priscilla. "Don't worry, her kind go to the Black house. The lifers, as we call them."

"The professors?" Mark said.

Jackie laughed. "Some of them call themselves that."

I saw Mark taking in everything around him and I tried to match his curiosity. Each floor of the buildings had similar windows, but many had different blinds or decorations on them. I followed the line all the way to the end, about the length of a football field. At the end, it appeared to open up into a larger space.

"Come on, let me show you to your place."

We walked next to each red door and I wondered which one would be ours, or mine. Did they keep the boys and girls apart?

I looked across the fence and saw a few Blues walking at the same pace as us. They studied me with hate in their eyes. It felt no different than when I would walk past the gym bleachers and the Dolls stopped whatever it was they were doing to give me a stare. I'd been foolish in thinking I could get away from such people. I guessed they existed everywhere you went in life.

Jackie opened one of the red doors and walked in. I looked to Mark for a second before following her. A few doors were scattered around the entrance on the first floor. A wood staircase wrapped in a circle to the floors above.

Jackie stood next to the staircase, her hand resting on the railing. She smiled and seemed to be waiting for something.

"Hey, Jackie," Mark said. "Where are we?"

"You're in the Red house." She raised an eyebrow as if she was wondering how smart Mark was.

I sighed and glanced out the window, across the street to the Blues. It was sinking in that they'd always be there, hating me because of the house Priscilla had put me in. What kind of place pitted two sides against each other like this?

"No. I mean, where are we in the *world*?"

Jackie laughed. "As far as I know, somewhere in Russia. But we did have a shift recently, so we could be anywhere."

"What, are you telling me this whole place moves?" he

asked.

"Of course. How else do you think we keep safe?"

"I don't care about where we are," I interjected. "I want to know what the deal is with this Red and Blue crap."

Jackie huffed and crossed her arms. "Who snatched you two up?"

"We were thrown in here by the recruiter," I said.

"Darius?" Jackie said.

"Yes."

"Why did you agree to come here?"

"I really want to learn about stones."

"Well, you definitely came to the right place. They'll give you your fill of creating stones, that's for sure," Jackie said with wide eyes. "How about we get you to your rooms first?" She took a few steps up.

"Okay, thanks."

Jackie led us to the third floor, where the underclass lived. I didn't mind that, because my room looked out over the street, and I liked being up higher. I could see the Blue houses across the way. They gave Mark a room next to mine. I asked about the coed thing, and Jackie shrugged. It felt weird sharing living quarters so close with Mark. He seemed amused by it and kept giving me a mischievous look.

"We do have a house uniform of sorts. I present you with your Red band." She handed me a piece of red cloth. "Keep it on at all times. Wearing that means you belong with us but it also means the blues will do what they can to get to you."

"Thank you." I pulled it around my wrist.

Jackie tossed one to Mark, who rolled his eyes and put it on.

"Your first class will be in a few minutes. Priscilla has you scheduled to be in her class."

I'd barely had a chance to touch the rough sheets when my attention swept back to Jackie. "Oh, like, now? Great. How do we get there?"

"Follow the spoke. Sorry, that's what we call this hall. Anyway, follow the spoke all the way to the hub and you'll find a class to the left, marked thirty-two. That's Priscilla's."

"Okay, thank you."

Jackie turned to Mark. "It's a good starter for new people, especially those who are weak in the gift." Her face crunched up like she was delivering hurtful news.

Mark shook his head and stared at Jackie. "Thanks for the warning. I'll try to keep up."

"It's good you have spunk. We can use your type in certain battles against the Blues."

"I can whip up some mean macaroni art with deep political satire that will surely rile up those vile Blues."

Jackie laughed and looked at me. "I see why you're around him. He's funny."

"Yeah, well, he has his good points," I told her.

Jackie led us down to the front door and pointed us in the direction of the hub and our first class.

A few Reds nodded to me as we passed them. Mark nudged me farther away from the Red house and closer to the fence in the middle of the spoke.

He leaned close to me and whispered, "This place is nuts."

"It might be a bit premature to be saying that, don't you think? Besides, I like that Jackie girl."

She was actually one of the few girls near my age that I did like. She was bubbly and had given a double bird to a hateful group. Jackie seemed like my kind of people.

Mark looked at the ceiling. "This isn't anything like what my mother described. Either stuff's really changed here, or my mom is a massive liar." Mark looked behind us before looking back at me. "This place freaks me out, and it isn't just the sick games they're playing." Mark pointed to the Blues.

Some Blues took notice of him and walked to the fence line.

Mark ignored their stares and kept his eyes on me. "Something doesn't feel right. I don't think my mom would be this wrong."

"Dude, your mom didn't exactly seem like the most honest person."

"You don't know her. She just let this stuff get the best of her. But I can tell you this: I won't let them get to you the way they did my mom. This stuff messes with your head, the whole power of it. It just doesn't seem natural to me," Mark said.

I raised an eyebrow. "Unnatural?"

"We had some fun with the stones, but doesn't it feel off to you? Like, should we really be able to do this stuff?"

I stepped back from Mark, shaking my head. I sucked at music class, I couldn't climb the rope in gym class, or dodge a ball.

I couldn't draw worth a damn in art but this stone thing I got.

I hadn't noticed how close I'd gotten to the fence line until a Blue grabbed me by the shoulder and pulled me against the slats. Then pain and panic hit me. I pulled hard, but more hands reached over the fence, tugging my shirt tight against my neck. They squeezed so hard, I couldn't breathe.

CH.8

In the midst of chaos, I found a breath and began to scream. A quick burst of whistles sounded, and I thought one of the teachers would be coming to break it up.

"Get your hands off her." Mark grabbed at their fists, but there were too many.

They pulled at me and my head was pressed against the fence. I saw many faces on the other side, but one guy with blond hair had his hand near my neck. He looked manic and filled with hate. More Blues rushed to the fence line and grabbed at Mark as well. He fought off their clutching hands and hit the ones holding me. I screamed again.

They shook my body back and forth, slamming it against the fence. Mark yelled and pulled a hand from my shoulder. Another arm grabbed me and Mark opened his mouth and bit down on it. The Blue cried out in pain and pulled their hand back.

Another person whistled, but this one was on our side. In a moment, I felt a wave of bodies on the Red side grabbing at me. They screamed profanity at the Blues as they freed me from the fence line. I fell backward and landed on my butt. Mark freed himself in the chaos and rushed to my side.

I couldn't catch my breath and my hair hung over my face in sweaty clumps. Pain radiated out from the side of my head and body. A few scratches marked my arm, but I didn't feel any serious damage.

The Reds pushed against the fence and both sides yelled at each other in an incoherent rant.

Mark wrapped me in a hug. "You okay?"

I winced a bit from his grip around my bruised shoulder.

"Yeah." He helped me to my feet and I brushed some of the dirt off of me. "What the hell is wrong with those people?"

Jackie pushed through the crowd, breathing hard. With a red face she said, "Oh my god, are you okay?" She snarled as she glanced back at the Blues.

"I'm fine, just a bit banged up."

"What the hell is going on here? Why would they do that to us?" Mark asked. He kept glancing back at the mob of Blues on the other side of the fence.

"You got too close to the fence line. It's a neutral zone of sorts, and anyone who goes within arm's length is fair game."

"Those people were crazy. They wanted to kill us." Mark

pointed to the Blues.

"Yeah," Jackie said, as if it was obvious. "Look what Priscilla just gave us." She gestured to me and I shook my head in confusion. "She gave us two people and one is a mother-loving nine."

"There'll be a retirement soon, I bet," a guy in a white T-shirt said.

Jackie nodded. "Yeah, you're right. The lifers will want to adjust things so they're numerically even again."

I watched Mark fuming next to me. He rubbed his mouth and eyed the Blues. I knew he wanted to go over there, jump the fence, and beat them to death. But I wouldn't let him commit suicide. The spectacle had gathered large crowds on both sides of the fence.

All of this, just to make better stones? I didn't want to hate the Blues, but I did. And what's worse, I didn't know a single one of them.

People on my side waved toward the Blues and said things like, "Bring it," while the Blues marched closer to the fence with a large number of guys near the front line. The flimsy wood fence seemed like an arbitrary barrier, and I looked for a quick exit just in case. A guy with blond hair stood in front and stopped near the fence, eyeing Jackie before turning around. The Blues took a few steps back.

"How do we keep them from getting to us? I mean, they're right there," I asked.

Some of the people around me laughed and Jackie smiled. "You're a Red now. We've got your back and you never have to worry about them hurting you. If they do, they'll have the entire house of Red falling on them." Jackie shook with rage and I saw some of the double-middle-finger attitude in her again. "You hear that, Blues? You touch her again and the *whole* House of Red will come crashing down on you."

The Reds around me closed ranks, filling the space between me and the Blues. I'd had a few moments before where a person might have said, "Leave her alone," or "Be nice," but having a small army standing beside me was something I had never imagined would happen in my life.

Jackie leaned close to me. "But don't ever go to the neutral zone again. You got that, Mark?" She looked up at him. "Can you make sure she gets to class safely this time?"

"Yeah," he replied with his jaw muscles bulging in and out.

I breathed deeply and felt a bit of the tension lessen. The Reds and Blues began to disperse. Once the crowd had thinned and Jackie had said her goodbyes, Mark and I continued our walk. We made sure to stay toward the Red side this time, far away from the fence. A few Blues kept pace with us, but I didn't look at them.

I listened to Mark's heavy breathing as we walked. The adrenaline was still feeding my beating heart and chills were running through my hands and arms. I'd never been in a real fight before. When Mark wasn't looking, I felt the bruises.

"Thanks for helping me back there," I said.

"Don't thank me. I wanted to kill them, you know?"

"Well, you can use that hate to make stones." I looked at his shaking hand.

"I can, but that doesn't make it right."

The end of the fence approached and the Blues, who had been following us, stopped and trailed back to their houses.

As we approached the hub, I saw a huge, circular room. The ceiling towered high above with tile work lining everything. Large lights lit up the space. The area felt like being outdoors with its great expanse. The floor sloped slightly toward the middle, where a large statue stood. The woman, taller than a house, held what looked like the earth on her shoulder.

"Who knew Atlas had a woman counterpart?" Mark said.

"What are you talking about?"

"The statue." He pointed. "You've never seen the male version?"

I stared at it and thought hard. I'd seen one, a man with a grizzly beard, holding the earth, but I'd never known its name. A few people were lingering around the statue and even Blues and Reds were mingling nearby. I breathed a sigh of relief. I didn't want to be thinking someone might kill me wherever I went. This hub must be a safe zone.

We walked to the left of the entrance of the huge room. The wall wrapping around the expanse held a door every hundred feet or so. I didn't see any other halls connecting to the hub. The spoke must be the only one.

"You notice there are no windows, like, anywhere?" Mark asked.

"Yeah, what's up with that?"

"They don't like us looking outside," a voice said from behind us.

I jumped and turned to see a petite girl standing behind us. She cowered away from my gaze, but after a second, she glanced up.

"Who are you?" I asked.

"I'm Carly," she said and smiled. She squeezed her shoulders together and kept looking at Mark. Finally, someone was looking at him. I thought it was the strangest thing ever that none of the girls had shown the slightest interest in him yet. I mean, the guy was hot.

"Nice to meet you, Carly." I was intrigued by her openness. "What do you mean, they don't want us looking out?"

"They don't want us knowing where this is," she whispered, and looked around. No one was near us, yet she moved closer and whispered even quieter. "They think they'll find us if we do."

"Who? Who will find us?" I asked.

She looked around and I wondered if she had heard me.

"This isn't good," Carly said. "The two of you. We'll have a retirement for sure."

"Retirement?"

"When we retire, we get sent home. Some people believe it, but I don't think they're going home at all." She mostly talked to Mark, and for the first time I started to feel like I was back in Summerford High, being a shadow on the wall.

Mark bent over to the diminutive Carly. "What exactly are they teaching here?"

Carly looked past us. I turned to see what she was looking at.

A Red walked by, eyeing me. She nodded to me as she walked by. I responded with the same motion and went back to talk to Carly, but she was already thirty feet away and walking fast.

Mark's brow crunched up and I was starting to pick up his emotions. His look was more of a thinking face than angry. If I could crack open his head, I knew I'd find a million wheels turning, trying to process this place. His mom must have fed him some kind of Utopian bull crap, and now he had to tear it down layer by layer until he solved the mystery. I wasn't as skeptical. Sure, it was freaking strange to pit two sides of the Academy against each other, but at least it was for a purpose.

"Come on, Mark." I touched his arm.

"I keep saying this, but I don't like this place. Nothing feels right."

"Our class is the first door on the left. Let's check it out. What do we have to lose?"

"We have a lot to lose." He paused, looking at me with those eyes.

I felt my heart beating faster. He didn't look away. "Maybe, but let's check it out," I said, thinking about how I needed to show my skills. I wanted to be so impressive that the president of the Academy would want to see me and I could get the life stone for Mark.

He nodded and we walked farther into the hub, hugging the curved wall to the door with the number thirty-two inscribed across it.

"I'm not letting you out of my sight," Mark said.

"You need to chill."

I opened the door and the class went silent. Priscilla was standing near the door, in front of a chalkboard. She motioned for us to come in.

"Take a seat. Reds on the left."

Like I needed a reminder. The students on one side of the room had red accessories while those on the right side were adorned in blue gear. I looked at the red scarf wrapped around my wrist and scanned for an open desk on the Red side. I spotted two in the far back and walked toward the large divide in the middle of the room separating the two sections. I walked down the middle but hugged the Red side, keeping an arm's distance from the Blues. Mark walked right down the middle, staring at each Blue.

Mark and I sat next to each other in the back and I strained to see what Priscilla had written on the board. I didn't mind. I wanted to sit in the back. Having people behind me bothered me. I always felt their eyes on the back of my head, like they were judging me, and I couldn't even see them. The anonymity of the back seat had great appeal.

The metal chair creaked under my weight and I ran my hands over the wooden desk. Pulling at the edges, I realized it was one of those flip-top desks. I lifted the top and saw an assortment of vials, one bowl, and a wooden mixing spoon. When I closed the top, Priscilla was standing directly in front of me.

"Did I instruct you to open your desk?"

"No." I looked to Mark. I was going to get in trouble before my butt had warmed my chair.

"This is your one warning, Allie."

"Sorry," I muttered.

Priscilla turned and walked back to the front of the class. I'd be lying if I said I didn't want to open the desk back up and get into the kits. I wanted to make more of those stones and find out what they did.

"We're all alchemists, but we're not equals. Some of us are born with a greater ability than others. I know that isn't fair, but that's the way of it. Allie, can you please come up here?"

I froze in shock. Not only had I been scolded in the first minute of being here, but now she wanted me to be at the front of the class? I glanced at Mark and he shrugged. I rose from my seat.

"Today, please."

I moved quicker and got to the front of the class. Priscilla clanked a bowl on her desk and pulled out a yellow liquid, placing it on the desk before going to retrieve another item from her drawer. Next, she had a handful of what looked like oak leaves. She crushed the leaves in her hand and dropped them into the metal bowl. Then she grabbed a spoon from the drawer and slapped it against the desk.

"Show us."

I waited for more instructions, or some kind of clue as to what she wanted, but all she gave me was a raised eyebrow and crossed arms.

I took the yellow vial and pulled the lid off. It reeked of sulfur. I winced and moved it away from my face.

Some of the Blues snickered, but they all had their attention on me. I glanced over the class and they were leaning forward in anticipation. I'd never seen a group of teenagers more engaged. Back in high school, half the class would be on their cellphones, or thumbing through books. Here, the whole class was staring at me. I sucked in a breath and picked up the spoon next to the bowl.

The smashed leaves were in a small pile at the bottom of the bowl. I wasn't sure how much to pour in and I could tell from Priscilla's annoyed face that she wasn't going to be of any help.

I closed my eyes and gripped the spoon. I thought of the people pulling me into the fence line and their hate-filled faces. The thoughts raged in my mind and when I shook with anger, I spilled the entire vial into the bowl.

Priscilla stepped forward and reached toward me as I poured, but stopped and put her arms back in their crossed pattern. I didn't care what she thought, and the idea of her making me come up in front of the class filled me with more anger. I stirred the deep yellow liquid, watching the oak leaf bits rise to the surface and melt into the liquid. The concoction steamed and soon I couldn't see into the bowl any more. The mixture became thick and rancid, but I pushed the spoon through it, thinking of Janet and her stupid skinny face, mocking me. The mixture became easier to stir just before I heard it: a clanking sound, as if someone had dropped a stone in the bowl. I knew I had mixed whatever it was she'd wanted.

I felt perspiration on my forehead and glanced back at

Mark, who seemed to be concerned. It took me a second to realize all of the kids looked like him, Blue and Red alike, with their mouths hanging open. I turned to Priscilla, who approached the bowl with skepticism.

She blew the mist away. A green rock with thick yellow lines was sitting at the bottom.

"You used the entire vial. That was for a dozen stones." Priscilla put on a glove and carefully plucked the stone from the bowl, then placed it in a small box lined with velvet.

Had I done something wrong? I wanted to ask, but I felt that if I said anything I would get myself in trouble. I'd had no idea I was supposed to use a small amount. It wasn't like I had been given any instructions.

"I'm sorry," is what I settled on saying.

"Why? You just created a very powerful stone."

That hint of praise raised my spirits and I looked back at Mark with a smile. "Oh, good. I thought I messed up."

"You have no idea what you just did?" Priscilla said.

"No. What does it do?"

"At the dose you made, it could…." She looked to the class and cleared her throat. "Go back to your seat, Allie."

I lowered my brow and walked back to my desk, looking back several times, hoping for an explanation of what had just happened. Each of the people I walked by stared at me. I wasn't sure if I had just done the worst thing or the best thing. I assumed the worst.

I plopped down in my seat.

"Okay, class, come up and get your mixing assignments for the day."

The class groaned in much the same way my old class might have, but I was excited to do something with my power. I jolted out of my seat and made my way back up to Priscilla's desk. I looked over the shoulder of the girl in front of me, trying to see what I would get to mix next. What would it do? I really wanted to know what I had made with that yellow and green stone.

The students in front of me hunched over and dragged a bowl, spoon, and vials off her desk. I might have thought they weighed a ton, but I knew the slump of the unmotivated all too well. I pushed my shoulders back and looked on with enthusiasm.

"Come around the desk, please," Priscilla said.

I made my way around and looked for my assignment.

"You won't be mixing anything in here." Priscilla moved closer to me and whispered, "You clearly don't belong in this room. I'm sending you straight to room twenty-eight."

"I don't understand. Did I do something wrong?"

She frowned quizzically at my comment. "Wrong?" She shook her head. "You just made something that none of these Malkis could even dream of," she said in a whisper filled with disgust. "You should be making stuff we can actually use. I bet you'll be a top-tenner before the month's out."

I didn't know what most of that meant, but I knew I was moving up. Good, closer to learning something and meeting the president.

"Okay, what about Mark? I'm not leaving without him."

She sighed. "Darius's report showed him a hair above these Malkis. I'd be putting my neck out letting him go with you."

"Please. He knows more about this stuff than I ever will. He can help me."

"Fine, but if he can't produce, he'll get moved back down to room thirty-two and there isn't a thing you can do to stop it." She looked past me. "Mark, come up here."

The Blues booed as Mark walked to the front.

"Mark," Priscilla said in a slow way. "Allie is going to take you to room twenty-eight, okay?"

He frowned at her tone. "Only if she holds my hand the whole time. I gets lost real easy."

Priscilla shook her head and waved her hand. "Just go."

I glanced back at the class. As they watched me and Mark leave the room, I saw the envy in their eyes. They wanted a ticket out of there as well. What could be so bad about mixing stuff up and creating those stones?

I closed the door and stepped into the hub. To the left, the circular wall bent inward and I saw the door numbers lowering as they went across. A few people were mingling around the statue. A huddle of Reds eyed us as we walked past room thirty-one.

"She called you a Malki. What is that?" I asked.

Mark sighed. "It's what they call alchemists who are weak with the gift, like my mom, and I guess like me. It's derogatory."

I bit my lip. I'd known it meant something mean. I would never call someone a name with hate behind it.

"What did I make back there? Why was she all weird about it?"

"It wasn't what you made as much as the potency. The more ingredients you use, the greater risk of failure. You poured the whole damned mixture together and still made a stone."

"Yeah, but what was it?"

"I think it was a mist stone."

"Like the one we were supposed to make?"

"Yeah."

A group of three Blues walked by, and I kept my head low as they passed. Mark glared at them, but they didn't engage.

"Here's room twenty-eight." Mark pointed at the wooden door with the number carved in the front.

"Should we knock?"

"Did you knock at Summerford High?" He opened the door and we walked into the room.

I didn't like it, but the first thing I looked for was the color people were wearing on their wrists and necks. I let out a long breath when I saw that every person in the room had red on. They looked up with weary eyes from their frothing bowls. I gave a small wave in an attempt to greet them, but they quickly went back to their mixing.

"Ahem." A man standing behind the teacher's desk looked at us. He was wearing a white lab coat, and his black hair was slicked back with a small pouf in the front. His polished black shoes held the large roll-up on his pants. "What are you doing here?"

"Priscilla sent us," I said softly over the clanking of mixing spoons hitting glass bowls.

"Did she, now?" He raised an eyebrow. "I'm Professor Dill.

There are two desks in the back available. Here are your materials until lunchtime." He pulled out a milk jug and what looked like a bucket of wood shavings.

"Professor Dill ... oh, you probably knew my mother," Mark said. "Sarah Duval."

The man frowned and shook his head. "I don't think I remember a Sarah Duval."

Mark looked down and crunched his eyebrows together.

I eyed the back of the room and saw the tables, glad to be in the back again.

"Come on." I scooped up my supplies and Mark did the same. The bucket of shavings smelled just like pencils, a smell I enjoyed. I breathed it in and felt comfort in the one familiar thing in the room. I placed my supplies down on the last desk and pulled the chair close. I glanced over to Mark with a big smile, but he didn't seem to have the same enthusiasm. He pinched some of the wood shavings between his fingers and smelled them.

I leaned close to him and whispered, "What does this make and how much should I use?"

"I'm not sure, but if these are wood and milk, I think it's a growth stone."

"Like, I'll get taller?" I wouldn't mind a few more inches.

"Maybe, but this is stuff you would use on trees or plants. You know, to grow crops faster, like fertilizer."

I rolled my eyes and looked at the milk jug and wood shavings. Fog and fertilizer weren't exactly the groundbreaking feats of alchemy I thought I'd be making, but I'd make do.

In the safety of looking at their backs, I watched the other students and their process for mixing. The room was filled with the sounds of clattering bowls, pouring milk, and the hiss of stones being created. The guy sitting in front of me kept grabbing and pinching his thighs, muttering to himself. He seemed to be cursing, and when pinching wasn't enough, he started hitting his leg and rocking back and forth in his chair.

"Barry?" Professor Dill said. "Have you created one yet?"

"No, but I've gotten a lot of steam from this one. I'm almost…."

The teacher walked toward him and the class kept mixing, taking careful glances at the situation arising. I didn't have any qualms about expressing my curiosity.

Dill stopped at his desk and lifted his bowl. He inspected the contents and swirled the muddy-looking remains. Dill tilted the bowl and poured the muddy contents onto Barry's lap. The room erupted in a flurry of mixing as everyone seemed to hug the bowls in front of them. I couldn't look at anything but Barry's shaking hands and tear-stained face as he glanced around the room. What kind of teacher dumps a bowl of muck on one of their students?

"I'm sorry, Professor Dill. I'll keep trying. I'll get madder, I promise."

"It's not your fault, Barry. It's my fault for not giving you proper motivation. Tell me, what is your trigger?"

Barry glanced around at us. He shook his head and his mouth opened and closed. I wanted to speak up and tell Barry we didn't need to hear his trigger, whatever it was.

"I don't like to think about it. I haven't seen her in a long time."

"You want to lose again, Barry?" Dill pointed to the front of the class at something.

Barry shook his head violently.

"Then you better consider your trigger."

Barry looked around. "My sister has Down syndrome, and it's when I hear people use 'retard' to describe her. Please, don't tell the Blues."

"But your sister *is* a retard."

My mouth hung open. Barry's fists clenched tight as he laid them on top of the desk. I stopped breathing in anticipation as Barry pulled back one hand. I glanced over to Mark and found him sitting in his seat, arms crossed, looking at the materials on his desk. I turned back to Barry and Dill.

"Retard?" Dill said as he hung over Barry's desk. "I think that word is too good for your sister. To call her a retard would imply she's a human of sorts. But she isn't, is she?"

Barry stood up from his desk, both hands white as he squeezed his fists and sneered at Dill.

"But you know the truth? She likes it when I call her 'retard.' She wants me to call it out every time...."

"Just stop it, man," Mark said, loud enough to make me jump in my seat.

Similar words were in my mouth and I was glad someone had spoken up. I was thrilled to see Mark stand up for this kid.

I wanted to cheer him on and push the teacher away. Thoughts of regret spread through my mind. Maybe I had made a mistake in coming to the Academy.

Barry turned to look at Mark at the same time as Dill.

"I know you're new here, but don't ever interrupt a buildup," Dill threatened. "In order for you to make a stone, you have to pour your emotion into it. It's my job to get Barry to find that anger and now you've interrupted the process. Are you a Malki?"

All eyes were on Mark, and the whole room went silent. I could hear my heart pounding in my chest. I wanted to blow out the tension in the room and make everyone chill.

"I'm not a Malki," Mark stated.

"Then don't act like one," Dill said. "Barry, use your sister as fuel and mix me up a damned rock right now. Time's running out."

Barry's lips thinned as he sat back down. In a few seconds, he had distributed a small amount of shavings into his mixing bowl. The class still hadn't moved, and Barry took center stage. His spoon shook as he poured a small amount of milk into the mix. After a few moments, it steamed and hissed. A white stone with brown splotches appeared and rolled around. Barry lifted the bowl and stared at what he had created. His face filled with pride as he tilted the bowl for the professor to see.

Dill nodded. "You see? You just needed to find the trigger. That goes for the rest of you as well. You have to be able to pull out the things that scare you, the things that make you angry ...

hysterically angry. This is the only way we can win. Now think about the thing you hate most in this world and pour it into the bowl. Go on, put it in."

Barry used a cloth to pick the stone up from the bowl, then scurried to the front of the room and dropped it into a wooden box next to the professor's desk. A number on the wall changed from twelve to thirteen.

"First to a hundred. You people had better get moving."

The sound of mixing erupted as everyone rushed back to their bowls. This was the craziest class I'd ever seen.

Barry turned back to me, smiling. Had he already forgiven the things that had been said to him, or was he grateful for the buildup? I knew then that I never wanted to fail at making a stone out of fear of getting a buildup.

I shook my head and stared at my bowl, thinking about my triggers. My stepfamily was an easy one, but if I dug deeper, I could find all kinds of stuff. It seemed that my well of anger was bottomless and I could access a bucket of it at any moment. I studied the ingredients.

"Ahem," Dill said.

I looked up and noticed him standing directly in front of my desk. I hadn't failed yet, and my breath quickened as the thought of exposing myself to the class.

"Make a stone, Allie."

"How did you know my name?"

"We communicate with each other," he said bluntly. "Now mix a stone. I need to see this."

Annoyed by the callout, I pinched a few shavings into the bowl and stirred as I poured small amounts of milk into the mix. In a second, the bowl filled with white steam and then I heard the distinct sound of the rock rolling around in the glass.

"Very impressive. Are you of similar talent, Mark?"

Mark huffed out and I could tell he wanted to play it cool, but I saw the corners of his eyes crunch down. He was nervous. I was curious as well. I hadn't seen Mark make anything yet.

Mark dropped a small amount of shavings into his bowl, his face turning red as he stirred in the milk. The bowl steamed, but I didn't hear the clunking sound of a stone solidifying. He kept mixing the muddy liquid.

"Just stop," Dill said. "This is painful. If you can't improve, I'll have to send you back to room thirty-two."

Mark didn't look up at this threat. He kept his attention on the bowl in front of him, staring at the milky brown liquid.

Dill shook his head and walked back to his desk. He plopped down on his chair and rubbed his forehead. Raising a hand, he pointed to a digital number displayed above him.

"Back to work."

A girl with straight black hair sitting diagonally across from me turned back, looking at me. "You need to put your stone in the box," she said, urging me on.

"Okay." I shrugged and used a black cloth the size of a napkin to pull the stone from the bowl.

It felt heavy, and having one so close to my skin gave me goose bumps of excitement. I wanted to make more. I wanted to make fantastic ones, like the type Mark had showed me. I stepped up to the wooden box with a round hole in the top, just big enough for a stone. When I plunked it into the box, the number above changed to fourteen.

The students went back to their work and I heard a few comments about some Malki, but mostly they just kept their heads down and kept working.

"Nice work, Allie," Dill said.

"Thanks." I smiled all the way back to my desk.

Mark sighed. I knew he wanted to tell me something, but he bit his lip and turned back to his bowl. He had cleaned it out and looked as if he might be having another go.

The black-haired girl turned back to me. "If you can make the stones that easily, we have a chance of winning today. For once I would love to win." She said the last bit through gritted teeth.

"Win what?"

"We beat the Blues next door to us. The first to a hundred wins the right to—"

"Quiet back there. Get back to mixing."

The black-haired girl quickly went back to her work.

"What's your name?" I asked.

She turned back long enough to say, "Ira." Then she rushed back to her work.

I leaned close to Mark. "This place is freaking weird."

"I know, right?"

"Keep talking back there and I will personally tie you to the fence."

I looked at the number fourteen on the wall. First to a hundred? I wondered how many of these stones I could create.

In less than a minute, I had created another one. I walked to the front with it in my hand, and the rest of the class watched. I saw the awe in their eyes as I dropped it into the box. Fifteen. Another person dropped theirs into the box and a few more as well. Soon we were up to twenty.

The class seemed to be hyper-motivated. The sounds of mixing didn't slow, and the line to wash out the bowls grew as the attempts at creation increased. I didn't need to wash my bowl out as each time, a stone plopped into my bowl. I was churning them out like a beast.

I walked my thirtieth stone up to the box. I hadn't seen anyone even come close to my production and with each drop a few of the Reds cheered.

Ninety-two displayed above.

Dill smiled, and when he looked up at the number on the wall, optimism crept into his eyes. I really wanted to get to a hundred. As I walked back, the faces which had once looked beaten and depressed now held a spark of hope. Many glanced at the big number on the wall before getting back to work.

"Have you ever won?" I whispered to Ira.

"No, at least not since I've been here."

I went back to my bowl. I wanted to give my team a victory. I had never been involved in a team before, at least beyond small work groups back in high school, and those had sucked. I always ended up trying to do the project while the others just sat there with dumb looks on their faces waiting for me to do the work. This was different; I wanted the win. I wanted the class to know I had gotten it for them. It felt great to be the driving force behind something bigger than myself. I had to win.

I dropped another one in the box. Ninety-seven.

I turned and bumped into Mark holding a stone in his hand. I beamed at his creation, but he didn't seem happy at all. It was difficult to understand how he couldn't get behind this win with enthusiasm. We were about to beat the Blues.

Mark dropped it into the box. Ninety-eight.

I ran back to my desk as I saw another person drop a stone into the box. The class went silent as everyone stared at the number.

Ira turned to me and slapped her desk. "Go for it, Allie! Make the last one." She slapped her desk again and kept doing it in rhythm. The rest of the class joined in, and soon all eyes were on me as they slapped their hands on their desks in unison. I breathed hard and pinched the last of the wood shavings into the bowl, then poured in the milk. Steam filled the bowl and I heard the distinctive clunking sound of the spherical rock forming.

The class erupted into applause and I covered my face. One girl near the front was in full tears as I passed her. She nodded and mouthed *thank you* as I walked by. Wow, these people had really needed a win. What did we win, cookies? I stared at the stone, smiling, and realized I hadn't summon the anger to make it. I had felt so elated with all the attention, I had made it with another emotion.

"Put it in the box," one yelled out.

As I neared the box, the room plunged into silence. Everyone leaned forward. When I dropped the stone in, everyone looked up to see the number change to one they hadn't seen before—one hundred.

Everyone in the room cheered and bowls spilled to the floor as some of my classmates jumped up from their desks. Many of them openly sobbed in joy as they embraced. The expression of sheer elation in front of me sent chills through my whole body. A few people rushed toward me and thanked me. I didn't know what to say.

My classmates were happier than I had ever seen a group. It was as if their favorite team had just won the championship. I felt like I didn't deserve the accolades coming my way because of the ease I had making stones. It was just stirring stuff in a bowl as far as I was concerned, but Mark could only make one. Maybe it was hard for others? He was sitting in the back with his arms crossed, shaking his head. Why couldn't he celebrate my victory?

Dill stood up from his desk and held a bowl high above him. He hit the bowl with a mixing spoon and the celebration slowed to a murmur.

"Please, Allie, stay up here."

I stopped my retreat back to my desk and turned to Dill.

"We owe this win to you," he said to me, and then looked over the class. "Since this is the first win for many of you, I will state the rules before we head over. No permanent marks, and no touching under clothes."

I frowned at the rules, not understanding, but my classmates rubbed their hands and talked closely with each other. I had no idea what these rules meant, but they morphed the expressions of joy on everyone's faces to looks of mischief and malice. What had I actually won for us?

"Okay, let's go," Dill said and opened the door out of the classroom.

CH.9

Dill held his hands up to quiet down the racket and waited until near silence had spread over the group. He grasped the handle of door twenty-seven and pushed. The fifteen students around me held their heads high and chests out as they walked into the classroom.

Mark and I stayed in the back.

"This place is all wrong," he said into my ear.

"What do you mean?"

"It's purely a hate factory. Did you learn one thing back in that class? All we do here is create stones for them."

We edged closer to the room.

"I see your point." I thought about it a little. "But I kind of like the competition. And did you see how many stones I made?

I won this for the class. Did you see their faces?"

"Yeah, like a bunch of jackals running for a kill."

We walked past the door.

The room looked similar to the Reds', but the students' necks or wrists were adorned in Blue. All their hands lay flat on the desks in front of them and none of them moved. Were they real? I pushed my way between two Reds and got a better look at them. They were frozen in place, locked in paralysis like wax figures.

"Go ahead and get it over with," the Blues' professor said as he rubbed the top of his balding head.

"Okay," Dill said. "Class, show them the same courtesies you've been given."

"There's that bitch, Jill," Ira said, and stomped over to her desk. She hesitated, shaking her hands and grunting as if trying to decide what to do. She reeled back and slapped her face hard enough to make a cracking sound. Ira then screamed a long stream of profanities, directed at Jill's appearance, skills, and breath.

The rest of the Reds each rushed to a Blue. It was clear that each classmate had a particular person they wanted to berate, smack, or downright violate. Some of the Reds simply yelled in the Blues' faces, while others went into physical attacks, smacking and knuckling the tops of their heads. Barry climbed on top of a desk and began humping a Blue's head, smashing his crotch against her face. Mark rushed over and pulled the guy off the girl, towering over the small guy. He scurried away to find another Blue to attack.

I felt ill. This was our victory?

"How do you like it, Jill?" Ira screamed as she repetitively slapped the girl's purpling cheek.

How long had the Blues been doing this to them? This kind of manic hate seemed to have been built up over weeks or months, if not years. The Dolls had harassed me for a long time, but I was nowhere near this level of venom. The stoic Blues took it; they had no choice. I tried not to judge. Who was I to judge their pain? This was their moment of payback.

I couldn't help it, though; I felt for the Blues, and wanted to scream and make it stop. My mouth hung open and I couldn't breathe. I felt tears building in my eyes. Ira continued to berate the girl in front of her while Mark darted around the room, pulling the most egregious offenders off their victims.

This was how the school worked? I was going to be sick.

A whistle blew and Ira glanced back. She slapped Jill once more before getting off her desk.

The Reds left their counterparts and headed for the door. Some were sweating, and wiped the clumping strands of hair stuck to their foreheads. Others glided to the door, as if on clouds.

Mark and I stayed back, transfixed by the train wreck they left behind. I hadn't even noticed the student on the floor, still in a sitting position with his palms flat out. The Blues' eyes twitched in their sockets, and tears were falling down many faces.

"I take it you were the difference?" the bald professor asked me.

I couldn't reply; the words choked my throat. I was still in shock from what I had seen. How could anyone treat another person so badly?

"Don't feel bad for them," the teacher said. "That will only ignite a fresh anger, and during the next competition, they'll have a lot of hate to work with. I bet you won't be around to carry them next time."

Mark pulled on my hand and I let him guide me from the room.

Dill closed the door as we entered the hub. He smiled at me and nodded his head. The Reds roared with cheers and surrounded me. I had never had so many people hugging me and thanking me. More tears flowed and I didn't know what to say or do.

"Class, you can take off the rest of the evening."

They cheered again and dispersed, with most walking toward the Red houses.

Mark placed his hand on my shoulder and turned me to face him. His face was contorted with all sorts of emotions, but the most obvious was worry. "We need to talk, somewhere private."

"We can go back to our living quarters."

"Fine. I don't like being out here anyway."

I glanced back at door twenty-seven. My mom had always told me never to judge another culture, but this didn't seem right on any level.

"Thanks, Allie," a guy said before smiling and walking away.

Another girl rushed up to me. "You rocked it so hard, making those stones. We owe you big time." She reached out to me and I went to shake her hand, but she gripped my hand with both of hers before bouncing and running off toward the House of Red.

I watched her catch up with a few others. They huddled close together, jumping in unison. Even with the horrible stuff they'd just done to the Blues, I bet it would pale in comparison to what they had endured. Those particular thoughts made me more comfortable, and I felt warm inside, like I was actually part of something. The only people who'd cared to give me any notice at my old school were the Dolls, and that was for a completely different reason.

We left the hub and walked close together past the first section of Red houses. I recognized a few people from room twenty-eight. They made sure to wave enthusiastically as we passed, calling my name.

"You're a damned celebrity on day one," Mark said.

"They're just happy we won."

"I don't know if that's what I would call it." He put his hands in his pockets.

I wanted to defend myself for a second, but he was right. It was definitely not a *win*. Both teams were losing, any way you looked at it.

"You even picked up a stray."

Behind us walked Ira.

"Hey," I called to her.

She stared at the ground before looking at me.

"What's your name again?" I asked. I already knew, but it seemed like a good conversation starter for the nervous-looking girl.

"Ira," she answered.

"Ira. I like that name. And it's good to meet you outside of that class." I extended my hand. She shook it with a limp grip, fingernails painted black.

"Nice to meet you." She looked down and her hair covered some of her face.

"I'm Allie and this is Mark."

Ira regarded Mark for a second through her bangs, but didn't say anything.

"I take it you really didn't like that girl?" Mark commented. "Jill, was it?"

"She's done … terrible things to me for almost a year now." Her face crunched up; she was fighting not to cry.

I looked at Mark and then back to Ira. "You've been here for a year? Overall, how do you like it?" I asked.

She looked up with her mousey face. "I hate it here." She kicked the ground and stumbled forward. "Today was different, though. Today *we* won because of you." She touched my arm with both hands and made eye contact.

"Okay, well, I'm glad we won. We're going to our house now, but it was really nice meeting you," I offered.

Ira pulled my hand back, her limp wrist turning into a vise. "I need to know something about the outside world."

"What do you want to know?"

Ira looked around at a few Reds mingling nearby. "Can we go to my room? This will only take a minute, and it's right here." She pointed to the red door ten feet away.

"Sure," I shrugged.

She let out a quick breath and smiled.

Mark and I followed her into her room.

"It's a little messy, sorry," Ira said as she flung a few article of clothing into a basket.

A black theme ran wild through the room. Black sheets were hanging over the windows and the floor looked marred with black streaks running across the wood planks. I spotted a book on her nightstand and squinted to read the spine.

"Do you have any books on alchemy?" I asked.

Ira picked up another heap of clothes and dumped them into a hamper. "No, there aren't any as far as I know."

A scratching sound came from the back of the room, like nails on cardboard. Ira cleared her throat and rushed up next to me and Mark.

"I just want to know if you've heard anything about my dad. Right before I left, we found out he'd been taken prisoner in Iran. He's a freelance reporter, and his name is George Parker." Wide-eyed, she waited for my answer.

I searched for the name, but came up with nothing. I looked to Mark and he gave me a slight shake of the head. "I'm real sorry, Ira. I haven't heard anything."

She sighed and pulled on her red scarf. "I thought maybe

there would be news of his release, or...." She closed her mouth and sighed.

Another scratching sound came from the back of the room, followed by a squeak. I gazed around behind her, trying to find the source of the noise. A few items of clothing lay scattered around a dinette table. Above the table were drawings of circles with symbols mixed in with them. Finally, my eyes landed on a cardboard box just as it moved with the same scratching sound.

"What've you got back there?" Mark asked and took a few steps forward.

Ira went pale. "You can't tell anyone. We aren't allowed to have pets here. They'll take him away from me." She rushed to the box and knelt down to pull off the lid.

"He's really friendly," Ira said.

I walked over and peered into the box. At the bottom stood a ferret, clawing at an edge. Ira reached in and pulled it out, holding it against her chest as it smelled her face.

"You won't tell anyone, right?" Ira asked.

"No, we won't tell," Mark said.

"What's his name?" I smiled and petted its soft, furry back. It cocked its head and I pulled back my hand.

"Sir Joffrey." She smiled so big it brightened her whole face. I realized how beautiful she looked without the sulk and slump. "He gives me a reason to keep moving on, and when I can find an excuse to not go to class, he and I have so much fun in this room. Don't we, Sir Joffrey?"

The ferret nuzzled against her nose and she giggled.

"Well, I wish we had good news about your dad, but we'd better get back to our place," Mark said.

"I understand," Ira said and looked away.

"Maybe I can come back and visit with you and Sir Joffrey?" I offered.

"Oh, would you?" She lit up again and her beauty shone through.

"Yeah, of course." I knew her better than I wanted to admit. I saw the loneliness in her eyes, the hurt. I wanted to wrap her up in a hug and tell her things had a way of getting better over time, but I wasn't sure how true that would be here. I knew I would make sure she had another victory during the next class competition. The thought of Jill violating her, or whoever it might be, sent my blood pressure shooting up.

"Thanks, Ira, for showing us your pet. We promise, not a word." Mark locked his mouth and threw away the key. "Come on, Allie."

"Bye, Ira."

"Wait. Sir Joffrey wants to say goodbye." The ferret stood on her shoulder and waved both of his tiny, furry paws up and down.

I wanted to snatch that thing up for myself. "So, so cute. I'll see you in class tomorrow, okay?"

The smile left her face. "You won't be there next time," she said so low I didn't know if she had really said it. She sank her head and Sir Joffrey ran into her lowered hands.

We left her house and started walking back down the spoke

towards our place.

"Uh, I feel so bad for her." I turned and glanced back at her door.

Mark's eyes followed. "She's a mysterious little thing, isn't she?"

"I kind of like her."

He looked at me. "Me too."

I greeted a few Reds I didn't know as we passed down the rows of houses.

Jackie pushed a guy out of her way and rushed up to us. "I heard you led the victory for room twenty-eight today?" She bounced with excitement.

I smiled. "It was a team effort."

"Please, that class hasn't won a damned challenge in ... well, I don't know how long. They want to throw you a party tonight."

I looked at the high ceiling with no windows. "How do you even know when it's nighttime?"

"They dim the lights and then turn them off, kind of like a sunset. You'll get used to it."

"Wait, we never go outside?"

Jackie opened her mouth and was about to say something when she moved closer. "There's an observation deck, but we can't go up there."

"I'd like to see it."

"It *is* an option for reward, but nobody ever picks it. Stop worrying about the lame stuff. We have a party to plan, and you're the guest of honor. You'd better be there." Her excited face didn't offer "no" as an answer.

"Of course. I'll be there."

"Good. I'll see you later, then." Jackie skipped away.

Many Reds made eye contact with me as we walked to our house door. I saw they wanted to talk to me, but I gave them a brush-off. If I stopped because of each person's inviting face, I didn't think I'd ever be alone with Mark.

Watching him walking next to me, I noticed that his brows moved closer and creased the space between his eyes. He was still studying everything and everyone around him. I'd grown to like his concentration face.

"What are you looking at?" he asked, and smiled.

"Just watching you think."

He laughed. "If we're relying on me as the thinker, we're in trouble."

"Hey, Allie," Barry called.

"Hello," I said and kept walking, leaving Barry and his raised hand behind me.

Several more people I didn't recognize greeted me, and one touched my shoulder as he did so. I started to think being popular might not be all that great. I lowered my head and walked more quickly.

I followed Mark up the spiral staircase to the third floor. When we reached my door, Mark opened it and we entered my room. As if on cue, the outside lights dimmed, casting long shadows from the bed and chairs.

The wood floor held deep scuffs and the finish had long

since disappeared. The raw wood had never seen any weather, so all the wear would be from the countless feet walking across it.

"How old is this place?" I pulled a wooden chair out from the dinette and sat.

"I don't know. Old." Mark ran his hands through his hair and I saw on his face that he had no intention of talking about antiques. "I don't like this place at all."

"Yeah, it's pretty weird, but don't you think they have a reason behind it all?"

"What, like torturing people to make those damned stones?"

He paced nearby and I adjusted myself on the chair to face him as he moved. "Did I mention how much I appreciated you rescuing me from the fence today?" I plucked an apple from a fruit bowl on the table.

He stopped midstride and looked at me. "That's my point. What kind of place breeds such hate between people? It feels volatile out there. Even within our own color, people give me hateful looks. Did you see how the Reds treated those frozen Blues in class?" He moved closer to me. "They were humiliating and even *violating* them. Some of those bastards should be arrested. They took it too far."

I sighed and thought about the kids in the room. Mark didn't get it; he'd likely never been on the receiving end of a bully's anger. Those people in the class had finally gotten their revenge. Would the Blues have been any different than the Reds, if they'd won?

"You remember the way the girl in the front of the class was crying when we won?" I asked.

"Yeah." He crossed his arms.

"She went right to the guy I'm sure was her tormentor and slapped his face silly. She spat on him and called him every horrible name in the book. That kind of hate isn't something you'd understand. How many times have you had your face rubbed in the mud?"

"This isn't about revenge, Allie. This is about this crazy-ass place. Do you really think it's a good idea to brew all this hate? They're going to burst out there. Some of them already look broken. I think we need to leave."

"Do you want to leave because it's weird? Or maybe it's not what your mom said it would be." I leaned back and crossed my arms.

"No. Well … actually, yes. I don't think we should be here. This place is going to warp us."

I took a deep breath. "For the first time in my life, I *am* someone. They're counting on me out there." I laughed and pointed at the window. "They're having a freaking party in my honor."

Mark rubbed his head and looked at me with concerned eyes. I held his eye contact and they softened. It quickly became obvious that we were in a bedroom together, with no parents, no supervision of any kind. I looked at the door and back to Mark. I had to say something before it became awkward.

"Why did you come with me?" I asked. "You kept this secret

from your mom for years. Why expose yourself now?"

He walked closer and sat at the tiny dinette table, scooting his chair near mine. "I think you know why I came."

I felt a heat in my gut and even though I hadn't experienced it much, I thought he was flirting again. "I have no idea why."

"You're going to make me say it?" He touched my knee.

"What's wrong with saying it?"

"Fine. I came here because of you. I didn't want to lose you. The thought of you going somewhere for a long time without me was unbearable. So I played my cards."

I tried to hide a big smile and lowered my head. "Well, I'm glad you came."

"You sure? A Malki like me might just hold you back." He pushed on my leg under the table.

The room darkened. The soft glow of the simulated moonlight lit the room just enough for me to see his face.

"Please." I rolled my eyes. "You could never hold me back."

"Is that a challenge? Because I can start pulling you in all kinds of bad directions."

"I don't mind some bad." My lips parted. I'd never thought this conversation would've turned out this way, but I didn't want it to stop. The second we got to the Academy, it had felt like it was Mark and me versus the rest of the world.

"One perk." He looked around the room. "We're alone here. No parents, no rules. Nothing to get in the way."

Oh, goodness, he *was* flirting with me. I couldn't stop smiling like an idiot, my nerves sending waves through my body. Why wouldn't he look away? I lowered my head until his hand left my knee and touched the bottom of my chin. Lifting my face, he moved close, kneeling between my legs.

"Is it okay if I kiss you?" Mark whispered.

"Yes." I didn't think I could want anything more.

I closed my eyes as he approached. I felt him against me, his hands moving across my shoulders and grazing my neck. His lips brushed against mine and I quivered. I wanted to grab his face, explore his mouth, touch his body.

He brushed against my lips again, but this time he pushed forward. He felt so warm and soft. My mouth opened and he tilted his head, deepening our connection. I was in danger of melting into the chair. His arms were the only thing holding me up.

I grabbed his hair and ran my hands down his back, over each stiff muscle. Holding tight, I tried to keep from falling into a deep abyss. He backed away to take a breath. In the faint light, I saw the need in his eyes. I stood, but he stayed down, arms wrapping around my thighs ... locking me in place.

"I've got you," Mark whispered, tightening his grip around my butt. He rose up, lifting me off the ground. He was much taller than I was, so I wrapped my legs around him and slid down to his hips. Face to face, we kissed. He backed up until his knees hit the bed, then leaned over and laid me on the bed. I made sure he came down with me.

"Allie."

"Yes?"

"I didn't say that." He pushed himself up and looked toward the window.

I rolled to my stomach and heard my name being called outside. Then it happened again, but many more people joined in. Soon it became clear and loud, after they'd gotten their timing down. They were chanting my name.

"I think your fan base is calling you."

I smiled and ran to the window. It couldn't be true. But the street was filled with Reds, looking up and yelling out my name. When they saw me, they cheered. Some waved for me to come down, while others yelled it out.

"Better get down there," Mark said.

I strutted to him with a failed attempt at a sexy walk. "Will you come with me?"

He smiled, and it lit up my world. Then he hunched over, grabbing his stomach.

"You okay?" I rushed to him and put my hand over his.

"Yeah, it's just something I ate, I think." He took my hand and laced his fingers with mine. I wanted to kiss him again. Hell, I wanted to forget the party and get lost in him. Unfortunately, he took my hand and pulled me from the room. I glanced back at the rumpled blankets before the door shut.

We walked down the stairs and through the group of Reds at the bottom. The mob rushed forward, vying for space next to me. They shook hands, patted me on the shoulder, or high-fived me. Many introduced themselves, but I knew I could never remember all their names. I hadn't even made it to the door yet.

I glanced back at Mark for help, but he held up both hands and smiled.

"Leave her alone, you damned heathens," Jackie said, pushing her way through. She was wearing a small black dress that showed a lot of cleavage and legs.

"Hey, Jackie."

"Come on." She grabbed my hand and pulled me outside. The second I was out, they cheered again. It was really all too much, and I buried my face in my hands.

"She's shy," Jackie announced. "Tonight we're celebrating Allie, for delivering the first victory to room twenty-eight in a long time. 'Cause we know you poor, stupid bastards couldn't have done it without her."

They hooted and hollered, looking at me with waiting eyes. Tears fell on a few faces as I scanned the crowd.

"I don't know what to say. You've all made me feel very welcome. So, thank you."

They cheered again.

"Great speech, Allie," Jackie said, shaking her head. "Well, let's get this party started!" She started dancing with her arms held high. There wasn't any music, but I didn't think she needed any. She was the type of girl who should be with a guy like Mark.

Mark slid up next to me and clasped his hand over mine, then brought it up to kiss the back of it.

I was looking up at his face when I noticed an object flying across the sky. "Look out!" I called, but Jackie kept dancing.

The stone flew toward her until a guy jumped and caught it in his bare hand.

Jackie spun and saw the guy collapsing to the ground. His hand was stuck in front of him and he didn't move. The Reds gasped.

"No, no. What did you do, Peter?"

A group of Blues were standing near their houses with smug looks as they watched.

"What kind of rock was it? Did you see it?" Jackie petted his hair back.

"It looked like a paralysis stone," Mark said.

"Like you would know, Malki," someone chimed in.

"No, he's right. He's as stiff as a board," Jackie said.

Another stone landed next me, an orange one with yellow streaks. It rolled next to my foot and everyone stepped back from it as it rolled back toward the fence and dropped into a hole.

"Really?" Jackie got to her feet and left frozen Peter on the ground. She stomped toward the fence. "That could kill someone."

A Blue with bleach-blond hair walked toward the fence. "I know, and I'll keep—"

Jackie quickly drew her gloved hand from her pocket and sent a stone flying over the fence. He reeled back, but it struck him on the cheek. Grabbing for his face, he fell to his knees.

I watched him through the thin slots in the fence as he coughed and touched his neck. He heaved out a green liquid and it splattered to the street around him. One more cough, and he vomited again.

A line of Blues formed near the fence, giving their friend space to spew whatever he had left in him. One of them tossed a stone over the fence, and in less than a second, twenty more followed. I dodged one, but another struck my chest and fell to the ground. It rolled toward the fence and down a slot in the middle.

Another stone struck a person next to me and her hand swelled up and turned red. She screamed in pain and ran toward the house.

Mark pulled me back as stones flew. The Reds regrouped quickly. Several Blues were frozen from Jackie's efforts, and she strutted next to the fence line, screaming at them to "bring it on" like a crazy person. She kept throwing stones and batting theirs away. She let loose a train of obscenities that blended together as one word.

"We've got to get out of here," Mark said, glancing up at the sky.

Damned Blues … they'd ruined my party.

A loudspeaker crackled to life and a buzzer sounded in two quick bursts. I sighed with relief, figuring the teachers were putting a stop to this. The stones stopped flying and everyone stayed still, waiting for something.

"All students are required to attend a retirement ceremony for—" The woman talking over the speaker paused, and everyone seemed to lean forward, waiting for the last words. "Costas Vance of the Red house."

The Blues roared in excitement. The Reds slumped and many eyes turned to a guy who was maybe eighteen. He rubbed his hands and looked at his housemates.

"I guess it's my time to go back to the rubes." He smiled. The Reds around him patted his shoulder and whispered to him. Everyone started walking toward the hub.

My adrenaline was still firing as I kept watching the Blues, waiting for one of them to throw another stone. But they all seemed to forget the full-blown fight we'd just been in. Reds and Blues alike walked toward the Hub.

Carly walked near me and I grabbed her wrist, bringing her attention to me. "What was that all about?" I pointed to the Blues.

"We have wars with them all the time. We aren't supposed to have our own stones, but it isn't exactly like they enforce shit here. I think they like it. It keeps us hating each other, especially if someone gets hurt bad."

I took a deep breath and watched the Reds and Blues walking toward the hub, giving the fence a wide berth. The Reds for the most part kept their heads down, while the Blues hurled taunts over the fence.

"I hate them," Carly said and walked away.

I knew what she meant. It was so easy to hate someone who had attacked you the way they had. I had been a victim at the fence not long ago. I fingered the soft bruise under my hair.

"You okay?" Mark asked.

"Yeah. Just a bit freaked out after our first stone war, I guess."

The Reds moved past us toward the hub.

"Guess we'd better start sneaking stones away if we're going to have a fighting chance here," he pointed out, taking my hand in his. "Did you hear Costas? I think he's getting out of here. This could be our chance of finding a way out."

CH.10

Once we crossed into the hub, the taunting and swearing stopped. Everyone kept silent and formed a mass of people around the huge statue of the woman, whose name someone told me was Clymene.

I'd been to many assemblies and pep rallies, but this took on a whole different vibe. With the Reds around me, sulking and mostly looking at the ground or the ceiling, I didn't expect a cheer squad to come out and get things started, but there were definitely two teams involved. The hub didn't have a fence, but there might as well have been one. A solid twenty feet separated the Reds from the Blues, making a clean line across the hub to a set of double doors.

The large wooden doors opened and the professors emerged,

each wearing a black suit or dress. A dozen or more of them formed a circle around the statue. Only a few coughs and rustling feet broke the silence.

A woman with blonde hair pulled into a tight bun stood at the edge of the fountain. She took a white stone from a sack at her hip and dropped it into the fountain. It struck the water, sending ripples through the shallow circle. The water bubbled and steamed, shooting up Clymene's legs and reaching her chest. The blonde woman then pulled out another stone and hurled it into the water, which froze over the statue, encasing it from the chest down.

The blonde took off her glove and handed it to Priscilla. Behind her, the globe opened in sections, like a sliced orange. One of the wedges lay on the floor next to the woman.

Even from our considerable distance, her bright smile was a beacon as she held her hands out. "Will Costas Vance please come forward?" she asked.

Costas walked past me and made his way through the crowd. The Reds shuffled out of his way, not making eye contact with him. He reached the clearing near the fountain and stopped, wiping his forehead with a shaky hand. The Blues on the other side of the fountain clapped and grabbed each other as they pointed at him.

The woman stepped down from the fountain and greeted Costas with a big smile, her hand landing on his shoulder. "Costas, the Academy and I would like to thank you for the years of service you brought us. I know you'll carry the memories of what you have learned here, and perhaps you can make the world better than the way you left it," she said.

I noticed Ira next to me, staring at the floor.

"Who is that?" I whispered.

"President Verity," she answered so low I thought I had misheard her name.

The president. The very person I had come here to find.

"What's all of this about?"

"Just watch, if you can," Ira said.

I turned and watched. Verity pulled Costas up onto the edge of the fountain. The Blues cheered and a few Reds politely clapped.

"Are you ready for your retirement?" Verity asked.

"Uh, I guess. I haven't seen my family in a long time."

"Good. I bet they can't wait to see you."

The boy kept looking at the open globe. Verity took both of his shoulders and steadied him. "Costas, I have sacks carrying one stone each. Once you have been accepted by our goddess, you will open the sacks and combine the two stones. There isn't any light in there, but I'm sure you can feel your way around a bag, yes?"

She didn't wait for an answer. "Good. Now, up you go, and tell your mom 'hi' from us."

Costas held the bags in his hand and glanced back at us with a small smile. He then stepped onto one of the slices and walked up the ramp onto the flattened part at the center of the globe.

"Are you ready?" Verity asked.

Costas didn't say anything as he looked at the bags in his hand.

"Great. Then let it begin." She put her glove back on, jumped onto the edge, and tossed a stone into the fountain. The frozen water liquefied and fell ... some splashing out and washing onto the Blues' feet.

They didn't seem to mind as they stared at Costas. The slices of the globe retracted and Costas ducked down as they closed over him. The sound of the metal clunking together resonated through the hub.

The room fell silent again and even the teachers looked up at the globe.

I leaned forward in anticipation and wondered what it was we were waiting for. Was Costas going to sprout wings and fly?

The whisper of a scream emanated from the globe before bright slivers of light shone through the gaps. The bright light lasted for a few seconds and then blinked out.

I swallowed between quick breaths and wondered what it meant. I didn't remember any bright lights when Mark and I had portaled into the Academy, but maybe we couldn't see it because we were on the inside.

A clanking sounded, like a ball was rolling around on metal. Verity stepped into the fountain, thigh deep in water, held her hand near the boot of the woman holding the globe and placed a bag there. The ball continued to rattle down the statue until it dropped into the bag. Verity cinched it up with a drawstring and held it high over her head.

"Another retirement."

The Blues cheered and the Reds gave a smattering of polite applause.

"What happened to Costas?" I asked Ira.

"He was sent back home."

"And the stone?"

"It's supposed to be a culmination of what he learned while he was here. On retirement day, you're given two stones to create something new. We don't know what the results are, because she never lets us see what drops from the boot."

I didn't get it, but I looked over at Verity, who had stepped down from the fountain and started walking toward the double doors. I sidestepped, pushing through the Blues, trying to make it to her. I heard Mark apologizing behind me, keeping pace as I rushed to her.

I reached the edge of the crowd of Blues just in time to watch her approach. When she was only ten feet from me, I noticed the slight creases at the corners of her eagle-like eyes.

She passed me and her hazel eyes met mine. I slowed down, thinking she was going to say something as her mouth opened, but she closed it and moved on. With a smile plastered across her face, she left, and soon all the teachers had gone into the hall behind the double doors.

Mark brushed against my arm, looking at the empty space left by the teachers. Ira had followed me as well, and was rocking side to side, looking at my shoes.

"What the hell was that about?" He pointed at the globe.

Ira opened her mouth, but Mark interrupted.

"I heard what you said before," he said to Ira. "But what really goes on in there?"

Ira shook her head and looked at the floor. "I don't know."

Mark brushed his hair back and looked at the people walking around us. "I don't think that's the way home." He raised an eyebrow at me and pointed at the globe.

Some of the Blues could be seen laughing and hollering at a few nearby Reds.

"Why are the Blues so happy?" I asked.

"Costas used to be a great stone maker. He won quite a few battles for us, back in the day."

"What happened? He stopped making stones?"

"The elites push themselves hard and burn out quickly. It's hard to hate forever. You become desensitized. Being numb is a big fear here."

Ira looked past me and I turned to see Jackie walking against the traffic.

"Ira, I hope you aren't spooking our new team members." She kept her eyes on me.

"I just ... no, Jackie." Ira rushed away as Jackie watched her with a big smile.

Once Ira was far enough away, Jackie leaned in and said, "She's sort of different, but we love her, as we do all the Reds."

"Yeah, well, this whole place is sort of different. I mean, what the hell was that all about?" Mark asked, pointing to the statue.

Jackie took a deep breath, which made the smile she maintained seem strained. "We always have to make room for the new." Again, she just looked at me.

"But—"

"Another loss for ya, Jackie. Pretty soon I'll be winning in every room." The bleach-blond guy said from his side of the hub. He was surrounded by other Blues.

"Please. Costas was as numb as your nuts," Jackie said. She wrapped her arm over my shoulder and pulled me close. "This little lady, here, is worth ten of him."

The guy rolled his eyes and shook his head. "I bet she's a quick fuse and burns out by the end of the week. Then I'll be right back to where I was, kicking your ass."

"You're going to eat those words every day."

He chuckled. "We'll see." Lingering, he stared at Jackie for a moment before heading toward the Blue houses.

"What a dick," Jackie said, watching him leave. She took a deep breath and turned to me. "Leader of the Blues, if you couldn't already tell. The sad truth is, he's been kicking our asses on the reg for some time now." She smirked. "But now we have you."

I shook my head. "I'm not sure I'm comfortable being considered a replacement for Costas."

"I'm not going to lie to you and say I won't miss Costas, but that's just part of the deal here. Besides, that globe is the only way a person leaves this place." Jackie looked at me. "If you're as special as I think you are, I'd like to get to know you better. Would you have dinner with me?" She glanced at Mark and then back to me.

My stomach rumbled at the mention of food, and I wanted nothing more than to sit down with someone and discuss this cuckoo-land academy.

•

"It's always empty here after a retirement. People just want to go back to their houses," Jackie said as she looked around. "That's why I like it."

Rows and rows of tables filled the large cafeteria. A woman in an apron was sitting on a stool behind a glass case of all sorts of meats and containers designated more by color than actual contents. I forked the mashed potatoes, smeared them over the Salisbury steak and broke off a piece. It had gotten cold from my spending most of my time answering all the endless questions Jackie threw at me.

What celebrity is dating who? What won best movie? How were the Super Bowl commercials? What are the hit songs right now and can I sing them?

My mouth hurt and my shoulders slumped. For everything I asked, she came back with quick, one-word answers and then went back to pop culture questions.

"So no Google, Facebook, cellphones or anything here?" I snuck in a question.

"Please. Like they want us communicating with the outside world. Besides, I doubt they have internet where this place is. I wasn't much of a tech geek anyways." She laughed. "But some of these kids come in here and go into freaking withdrawal over losing their digital tethers. We had to talk a girl down just a few months ago from the edge of her window. She kept screaming about getting a charger for her phone. Crazy bitch."

I tapped the phone in my pocket. The battery was long dead and I'd never had a moment of cell coverage since arriving here. The idea of not being connected edged me a little, but the things around me filled my every thought, drowning out my need to update my status.

"One person here asked us about her dad. Do you have anyone back home you're waiting to get back to?" Mark asked.

Jackie took a deep breath and stirred the whipped cream on her plate with a spoon. "No."

The double doors to the cafeteria swung open and I whipped around to see a new face. I recognized her as the girl who had stared for a while at Mark. She was cute in a way, but she'd be much cuter if she didn't have a resting bitch face. I didn't think she was upset as much as she was in deep thought.

"Hey, Carly," Jackie said with little enthusiasm.

"I was wondering where you hid them," Carly said and sat down at the long table, right next to Mark. She pulled her small purse onto the table. "Hogging the newbies all to yourself?"

"We were just getting to know each other, sharing stories."

"If we're sharing, I say we make this interesting." Carly tapped the bag on the table.

Jackie leaned back and blew out a long breath.

"What do you mean?" I asked.

"You know about truth or dare?"

"Yeah." Not that I had ever played it.

"Well, this is like that, but when you touch this stone, you'll have to tell the truth whether you want to or not." Carly opened the bag, used a black cloth and placed a crystal stone with pink speckles on it on the table.

Jackie crossed her arms and looked away.

"Are you serious? You guys will have to answer anything I ask?" All the questions that had been in my head a moment ago had disappeared. I scrambled to think of more.

"Yes, but with each question it gets weaker, until it's nothing but a pile of dust," Carly said.

"I can't believe you busted out the truth stone," Jackie said. "You guys don't have to play."

"No, I want to," I said and glanced at Mark.

"I don't," he said. "I think there are some things we keep to ourselves for a reason."

"Big surprise coming from you, Mark," Jackie said. "I'm down."

"Okay, good. I hate small talk, and this is the fastest way to learn about someone." Carly smiled and clapped her hands. "So, each of us just place one finger on the stone." She pushed the rock to the middle of the table, leaning against Mark as she did.

Jackie reached over the table and put a finger right next to the stone. "Don't be a pussy, Allie, with the questions. It would be just like you to ask what my favorite color is."

Now that she mentioned it, I *was* interested in that question and wanted one of them to ask me. I wasn't really sure what my favorite color was, and with the stone, I'd have to answer truthfully. I leaned close to the stone and placed my finger next to it.

Carly cleared her throat. A smile kept creasing her face before she fought it back again. Jackie kept one eyebrow up and looked from me to Carly.

"Your rock, Carly. You answer the first question," Jackie said.

Mark scooted down the bench for a better view, or maybe just to get some space from Carly.

"Okay." Carly pressed her pointer finger on the stone. "Now I have to answer any question honestly."

"Why you been acting weird lately?" Jackie asked.

"I thought you were acting weird, so I started acting weird," Carly said. "Now you two have to touch it."

I pressed my finger to the side of the stone at the same time as Jackie. The imperfections in the stone stood out, small fracture lines and ridges.

"Why have you been so weird?" Carly asked Jackie.

"I've been under pressure a lot lately to make the stones I used to be able to make. I think I'm losing some of my abilities."

Carly took a deep breath and nodded.

"Have you slept with Mark?" Jackie asked.

"No, we haven't done that kind of stuff." I blurted out the words almost before I could even think of them. I covered my mouth with my free hand.

"You can ask us something now," Carly said.

"Where are you two from?"

"Richmond, Virginia, for most of my life." Jackie shook her head. "I knew you'd be a pussy."

"I'm from Carson City, Nevada," Carly said.

"Couple of state capital girls," Mark said.

Jackie turned to him. "Unless you produce a touching finger, you aren't allowed to say a word."

"I have another question," I said. "What happens in the globe during retirement?"

"I don't know," Carly said.

"One way or another, you leave," Jackie said. "Better, Allie."

My finger slid down the stone but stayed pressed to it. I searched for Jackie and opened my mouth to ask a follow up, but Carly spoke first.

"Allie, are you a dark alchemist, or have you ever worked with them?" Carly asked.

Jackie froze and stared at me, waiting for the answer.

"No."

They glanced at each other.

"Why?" I asked.

"I—" Carly said.

"We…." Jackie added.

Carly finished, "We think there are dark alchemists looking for this place. And when we get someone like you, we're suspicious of who you are and your intentions."

"My intentions are noble," I said.

"Good. Why don't you ask another question?" Carly offered.

"Is there another way out of this place, besides the globe?"

"I've searched through many of the secret places, but I've never found a way out unless you use portal stones," she answered.

"Boring. You think we'd be sitting here if we knew a way out?" Jackie huffed. "Carly, if you could have sex with one person in the Academy, who would it be?"

"Mark."

Jackie laughed. "This is getting fun. Carly, have you ever used a stone improperly?"

"Yes."

"Now we're getting somewhere." Jackie brushed her hair back and stared at her. "What did you do?"

Carly's jaw muscles flexed and her eyes twitched. "I've been holding onto a time stone for a few weeks now," she blurted out, then took a deep breath. "I made it in the house lab. And when I saw Mark today, I knew I could do whatever I wanted to him and then just use the time stone to go back a few minutes. No one would be the wiser."

"You sick bitch, what did you do?" Jackie asked.

My mouth hung open and I couldn't blink or think. I only stared and waited for whatever putrid thing she'd done to spill all over me and Mark, soiling us possibly for life. Mark leaned way over, getting a better vantage point to see Carly's face.

"First, I froze him and Miss Perfect here." Her gazed darted to me. "Then I dragged his stiff body to the lobby and into my room. I proceeded to take off his clothes and found, to my surprise, that some things still work even when they're frozen.

That was when you came in, Jackie."

"Me?" she said with a big grin and pointed at herself.

"Yes, you marched in with fire in your eyes, but something changed when you saw Mark naked on the floor. You joined in and we took turns on Mark like he was a twenty-five-cent grocery store ride. After we had ours, I used the time stone, and nobody ever knew what happened."

Carly pulled her finger off the stone and held her hands over her mouth. She glanced back at Mark, and I'm sure I looked as shocked as he did. He glanced down at his lap.

I couldn't speak. This couldn't be real, but her finger had touched the stone, so I knew it was. My anger built up, my face twitched and my hand clenched up in a fist. I took my finger off the stone and found the spot on Carly's sick face I'd gouge out.

Jackie put a hand up, stopping my assault. "I have to admit, I *have* used a stone in an improper way." Jackie lifted the stone off the table and tossed it in one hand. "It was the time I asked Carly to come in here and pretend this stone made you tell the truth."

Carly lowered her hands to reveal her big smile. "We got you."

Jackie laughed, but I didn't think any of it was funny. I smacked the table hard with my palm. The table rattled, and that sent Carly and Jackie into more laughter.

"You really thought we tag-teamed Mark?" Jackie laughed. "Oh my god, I can't breathe."

Carly grabbed at her stomach, laughing. "I'm sorry, but this is just too much. Have you two really never hooked up?"

"Her finger was on the truth stone, so it must be true," Jackie said. "You newbies will believe these things can do anything."

Mark stood. "Come on, Allie. We don't have to put up with this."

I sat and crossed my arms. "I don't think what you two did was funny at all."

Carly took some deep breaths. "I'm sorry, but we only get to do that joke every few months, and this was one of my favorites. Please, we like you, Allie, and Mark too."

"Yeah, it was just a joke, guys. Mark, sit back down." Jackie got up from the table. "I'll go grab some ice cream shakes from Beatrice. Hey, Beatrice." The woman behind the counter moved. "Four chocolate shakes, please."

I tried to control my breathing, but Carly had put a picture in my mind I couldn't get rid of, even if I knew it was all a fabrication. It still felt real.

Jackie returned with a tray of four shakes in tall glasses.

I grabbed a glass and pulled it close, inspecting the contents. I put my mouth on the straw and kept my gaze on Carly. She watched me as I dropped the straw from my lips and stared at the brown contents of the glass. "This isn't a shit shake, is it?"

Jackie spit her shake out onto the table and laughed. "No. What the hell?"

"Well, I don't know how far this pranking is going to go," I said.

Mark walked around the table and sat next to me. He eyed the shake and licked his lips.

"You want some?" I pushed his over closer to him.

"No." He shook his head.

"So, what's the real deal with you two?" Carly said.

I looked to Mark and watched his gaze move to each of us. "We're a couple." Mark glanced at me for confirmation.

"Yeah, a couple." It felt incredibly weird to have a label put on us. I liked being around Mark, and I think he liked being around me, but more than that seemed presumptuous.

"Are you two, like, high school sweethearts?" Jackie asked.

"I bet they're the *it* couple." Carly rolled her eyes.

"No," I said. "We're not the *it* couple. We just met a few days ago."

Jackie leaned forward with narrowing eyes. "A few days?"

"Yeah. What's with the inquisition here?" I asked.

Jackie laughed. "We get so bored with our old, worn-out news, when someone comes in here, we thrive on their news, their rumors, and with two of you…." She waved her hand forward. "We can't control ourselves."

"Well, it's creepy," I said and took another drink of the shake. "You two have anyone in here you're seeing?"

Carly grimaced. "No."

Jackie leaned back and looked to the door.

"What about you, Jackie? All the time you've been here and not one guy?" I asked, happy to be asking the questions for once.

"No," she said, but she kept looking away.

"She lies. I see her sneaking around sometimes at night," Carly said.

"Shut up."

"I do. You sneak around."

"Just exploring this place."

"I bet you're exploring something."

Jackie leaned back and crossed her arms.

Carly opened her mouth, but the sheer will of Jackie's glare forced it closed. The temptation to push it farther swelled in me, but I fought it down.

"I think I'm going to go to bed," Jackie said as she stood.

"Yeah. We should do this again tomorrow. I like you guys," Carly said.

I raised an eyebrow. "No more shenanigans?"

"Maybe just a little." She winked.

Mark stood as well, and I shimmied my way off the bench seat. "Later, Jackie," I called out to her back.

She raised a hand and kept walking.

Carly walked next to me and we watched Jackie leave through the door. "She had a guy. They were inseparable, but shortly after I got here, they retired him. It was a retirement we'll never forget. Jackie and Ned wouldn't let go of each other, and eventually the lifers pried them apart and all but shoved Ned into the dome. He cried out something, but I was too far in the back to hear it. She made some real whoppers of stones after that."

"Why doesn't she just get retired?" Mark asked.

"I don't think she believes we really go home in there. I have my doubts as well."

I was beginning to have some doubts too, but I never liked

to judge things based on other people's opinions. People seemed to look at things through warped prisms, or maybe I just wanted to see everything for myself. If the dome really didn't send the students home, then what did it do? Where did they go? This whole place felt magical and terrible at the same time. The hate they instilled and perpetuated felt as if it had a purpose, but if in the end this dome thing did something to you other than send you home, then this entire place was a lie. Either way, I had a mission, and this day I hoped had brought me one step closer. Tomorrow, I'd push even harder.

CH.11

Lying in bed, I stared at the ceiling. Closing my eyes didn't work because the thoughts came too quickly when I did. Looking at the dimly lit ceiling gave my mind a resting space. I needed to think of something besides the truth around me.

I rolled to my side and looked at the door. The hand-carved wood seemed too intricate against the plain floors and walls. But I wasn't really thinking about the door; I was thinking about the guy who was just beyond the door. The guy who, just a few hours ago, had been with me on this bed.

It was terrifying and exciting how I had been willing to do anything with him. I'd felt some heat for boys in passing, but I'd never had a moment like the one I'd shared with Mark. How far would I have gone if not for the interruption?

The door handle moved. I stared at it and heard a faint click as it turned all the way down. The door crept open and my heart began to race, thinking it must be Mark. I felt confusion slamming against me in a split second. Not knowing what I would let him do, what I wanted to do. I still had my shirt on, but I had taken off my pants before I got into bed. The door opened all the way and a person too small to be Mark glided into my room. I was about to scream when I saw Jackie's face in the shadows.

"You awake?" she asked.

"Yes."

"Good. Remember the Blue who grabbed you today at the fence?"

"I don't think I'd forget that."

"How would you like to play a little prank on him?"

"Hell, yeah," I replied. It was more about doing something other than lying there, thinking about stuff, but it did sound interesting. "Can you turn around? I'm not wearing pants."

She crossed her arms and turned a tad. I flung the blanket off and walked to the armoire.

"I wish they gave us panties like that," Jackie said, staring at mine over her shoulder.

I sighed at the privacy breach. I didn't think they were anything special; they had a hint of pink with a red floral pattern on them. I opened the armoire and pulled my jeans from it.

Jackie pulled the front of her pants down a tad to show the top of her panties. "Before long, this is what you'll be wearing." She snapped the elastic band of her plain white undergarments.

They could have been guys' underwear.

"They don't look bad."

"Yeah, well, they give us okay clothes, but the underwear is a constant complaint from the women here."

I slid my legs into the jeans and wondered what I was going to wear tomorrow. If I had thought about it more, I would have gone back to my house and packed.

"How long have you been here?"

"Three years."

I sat on the bed, dumbfounded. "And you've never left?"

"Nope." The fake moonlight lit enough of her face for me to see the hurt. She tried to smile, then looked away.

"Can't you ask to be retired?"

Jackie laughed. "It's not so simple. Listen, you're a day one girl. You don't need to hear about my problems. We have a Blue to get back at." She winked.

I did want to hear about her problems, but I didn't push it any further. I put my black boots on. They reached just past my ankles and I clasped the leather straps.

"Those shoes are amazing."

"Thanks." I stood up from the bed and looked at Jackie. "So, what are we going to do?"

"First, we need to make a few stones, if you're up to it."

"I am. I should wake up Mark and get him." I was more excited about making stones than getting back at the Blue.

Jackie frowned. "No, he looked awfully tired. Why don't we let him sleep?"

•

We tiptoed down the stairs and into the entryway. Nobody was in the main room. Jackie turned to the door under the stairs and opened it. She motioned for me to follow and we entered. A small hall opened up into a large room where several people were working with bowls and vials.

Ira looked up from a bowl and quickly looked back down as we made eye contact.

"You guys make your own stones here?"

Jackie smiled and slid a finger across a highly polished table. "Let's just say it's a well-known secret."

The few other people in the room stopped whatever they were doing to give me their attention, or at least Jackie's, as she raised her hand.

"Reds, I'm sure you know who this is by now, but her name is Allie. She's the new girl who's going to help us take out the stupid Blues."

The introduction seemed awkward. I didn't know if I should say something, so I just stood there and gave a small wave.

"Allie, I heard from the room twenty-eight Reds that you were somewhat of a specialist at making stones."

"I guess. I don't really know what I'm doing."

"Good. Ignorance actually helps the process. The more you think about it like a science project, the less it works." Jackie looked me up and down. "How much reserved anger do you have in this body?"

"Plenty."

"Good, because I bet everyone here could use your help in making stones. That's what this room is about, helping each other."

"Jackie," a guy sitting at a desk said, and cleared his throat. "I'm having a bit of trouble making this falling stone." He pointed to the bowl and the materials sitting on the desk.

"Do you need a buildup, Walt?"

"I think it could help."

Jackie walked toward the guy, but turned back to talk to me as she did. "Something the teachers won't tell you is that there are other ways to make stones. For some stones, different emotions are needed ... as with this particular mix."

"What's a falling stone?" I asked.

"It's like a nightmare stone. It gives you the sensation of falling. Your body and mind are certain you're are falling, even though you're not. It's really a terrible feeling and can last for a minute or even an hour or two, depending on the alchemist. A perfect stone to give to a Blue."

It seemed like a nasty prank, but the Blues probably deserved it, especially after the way they had grabbed me and thrown stones at my party.

Walt faced forward as Jackie walked behind him. He kept trying to stuff a huge grin away, but failed miserably.

"You ready to make that stone?" Jackie whispered in his ear as she massaged his shoulders.

"I need a bit more than that," Walt said.

"I haven't even started."

Jackie grabbed the sides of his head and ran her fingers through his hair. She bent over, tilted his head and licked his neck. Then she moved to Walt's side and grabbed one of his hands, guided it over her neck and down her arm. He grabbed her and reached for a kiss on the mouth, but Jackie deftly dodged it and worked on his neck for a moment longer.

"Mix it," Jackie said with a heated breath.

Walt tentatively used both hands and mixed the ingredients as Jackie whispered into his ear. His lips parted and his eyes rolled up. He looked like he might pass out, but he kept the spoon in his hand and stirred. He spun the spoon around with the limpest of wrists, swaying in his chair as Jackie slid her chest against the side of his face.

A stone clunked around in the glass bowl.

Jackie shot up and pushed Walt's head away. "You have B.O.," she said with a disgusted look.

I looked at the door, wondering what the hell I was getting into.

Walt didn't respond, just breathed deeply and focused on a spot on the wall.

With a cloth in her hand, Jackie reached into the bowl, grabbed the rock and wrapped it up. She dumped it into a tiny bag and pulled the string tight, then held the bag high and admired it.

"This is really going to freak him out," Jackie said to me.

Walt looked as if he wouldn't be standing anytime soon,

which creeped me out. I turned slightly to block him from my view. Everyone else seemed to take it as something normal.

"How are you going to get that stone to him?" I asked, trying to get past what I'd just witnessed.

"Don't worry, we'll help you get it over there."

"Me?" That would mean going into the Blues' houses. A while ago, I was merely standing next to the fence and they'd gone bonkers. What would happen if they found me in one of their houses?

"But this isn't the stone I wanted to show you." Jackie stuffed the bag into her pocket. "I have a special stone, something I've been trying to make for a long time. Do you think you could give it a go?" Jackie pointed at a table.

"I can try."

"I'm sure you can." Jackie pulled out a chair and placed on the table a small box filled with what looked like salt, but the grains were a bit larger than table salt and clearer. A flask of brown liquid sat next to the box. A glass bowl with a wooden spoon topped off the trio of tools all the alchemists here seemed to use.

I sat in the seat and scooted forward. Jackie moved in behind me and I tensed as I thought she might start doing to me what she'd done to Walt. Jackie was cute, but I was sure I wouldn't have the same reaction Walt had had to her tongue.

"You'll have to summon some real hate for this one. Thankfully, from what I hear, you don't seem to have any trouble making stones."

I took a deep breath and looked at the ingredients near me. Everyone else in the room had stopped mixing their stones and was staring. Even Walt looked past Jackie to me.

"What does this make?"

"It's a secret. If you can make it, I'll tell you what it is."

I didn't really understand not being able to make a stone. Every time I had tried, I'd been able to make one. It didn't seem like a major feat of strength.

The salt-like crystals were as coarse as sand. I pinched some of it into the bowl. Jackie leaned close behind me, next to my head. I turned to her and she backed away, taking a place next to me at the table, leaning on it with her hand, watching.

They were all watching.

"Is this enough?" I pointed at the salt stuff in the bowl.

"It doesn't matter much. Whatever your gut tells you is the right amount."

I took a small bit of the salt crystals and looked at Jackie as she frowned. I dipped in and pinched a larger portion and Jackie's eyes narrowed. "I really don't know what I'm doing, Jackie. I mean, I don't even understand how these stones are made. What makes you think I can make something you haven't been able to?"

Jackie took her hands off the table and laughed. "This isn't something you learn." She pointed at the bowl. "It's something you're born with. If anyone says they understand exactly how we make these stones, they're liars."

"Yeah, but you all know what the hell you're doing, and I

don't."

"That's one of the reasons we can't do it as well as you. We've become so used to making stones, we've lost the edge. When you summon the anger again and again, you become desensitized to your triggers. I bet you don't think about your trigger much, do you?"

"I don't...." I wanted to say I didn't think I could ever get used to Janet's comments, or Spencer tearing up the letter from my dad. The thought of not being mad terrified me. It would be like forgiving all the people who had done wrong things, forgiving the Dolls for their years of hate and crappy looks. "I shouldn't have a problem."

"Okay, but make sure you use your biggest trigger on this one. It's a special stone."

All the people in the room had left their tables and formed a small circle around me. What in the world was I making, and why had no one else been able to make it?

Going off my gut, I poured more of the salty substance into the bowl. Walt raised his eyebrows at my move, but I didn't care. I had already started thinking about something that always got me angry, something which made me hurt so much, I rarely went to it.

My mom's face had once been a sharp memory, but over the years I'd had to use pictures to cement it back in my mind. But pictures weren't memories; they were a snapshot in time, and I felt my heart beating hard in my chest as I struggled to find that stark image of her. I hated that my mom had left me as a child.

She had hurt me deeply and it wasn't even her fault. I hated the fact she hadn't seen me grow into a woman. But what I hated most of all was not being able to forgive her for dying.

I lifted the brown liquid up into the air. A deep mixture of emotions filled me and I had trouble steadying the liquid over the bowl. Jackie leaned in close, her rapid breath pulsating near my ear. The wood spoon struck the sides of the bowl, and I winced at the sound breaking the silence.

"Allie, stop!" Mark yelled.

I jumped at the interruption and dropped the container on the table. Jackie snatched it and kept it from spilling more than a few drops.

Mark was standing in the doorway.

"Great. Thanks for the interruption, Malki," Jackie seethed.

"I can't believe what you were having her make." He stormed past the doorway to the edge of my desk.

The wind he'd created blew against the perspiration on my face. The anger slipped from my consciousness and I looked to Mark for an explanation. Jackie crossed her arms and scowled.

"I don't know—" Jackie began to say.

Mark raised his hand toward Jackie's face. She gasped, and I didn't like it much either. I didn't like this angry Mark who wouldn't explain himself.

"That is a memory stone." He glared at Jackie. "Right?"

Jackie looked at the floor. "Yes, but—"

Mark interrupted her again. "That kind of stone, in the wrong hands, can do a lot of harm."

I looked at the salt in the bowl and wondered what a memory stone did. "Like, it removes memories?"

"Exactly."

"How would you control something like that?"

"You don't. It could wipe the last ten minutes of your life from your memory, or much longer, depending on the potency. And from the look of the diamond dust in the bowl, I bet it would have been much longer."

I stared up at Jackie and rose from my chair. She wouldn't look at me at first, then met my eyes.

"You were planning on wiping a Blue's memory?" I asked.

"Everyone out!" Jackie yelled, and glared at everyone in the room. Mark crossed his arms and stood like an unmovable stone.

The other people in the room darted out, leaving just the three of us.

Mark staggered toward my table and leaned on it with one hand. His other hand clutched at his stomach. His face contorted with pain and he struggled to stay standing. I rushed to his side. He righted himself and gave me a weak smile.

"What's wrong?" I asked. "And don't tell me it was something you ate."

"It's nothing. I just get these stomach pains sometimes."

"You're sweating. You don't look right."

"You look like hell," Jackie added.

"Thanks. It's just something that comes and goes. It's been happening my whole life. I just get used to it most of the time."

I took in a deep breath and gazed at the perspiration on his forehead. My stomach wrenched in pain as well. He wiped his face and within a minute, he had smoothed out his face in an attempt to look normal, but the corners of his eyes were creased. Before I could ask him about it, he glared at Jackie.

"I don't like you using her like this."

Jackie crossed her arms and huffed. "Please, you Malkis all use us to get by. You couldn't create a simple growth stone, from what I hear."

"This isn't about me, and you know it." Mark moved closer to Jackie. "She's special, and people like you want to suck her up, drink her down, and piss her out. I won't allow it."

I thought Jackie might have tears in her eyes, but I must have been mistaken. She pointed at me. "Allie won't have it in her forever to make these kinds of stones. The anger fades over time. I *need* that stone."

"Why?"

"Don't you get it? I've seen too much. I've been here too long, and I'm numb to it all. I have rages, but they burn out like quick fuses. I've almost lost all of my deep anger, no matter what I do."

Being numb to the hate seemed foreign to me. I couldn't imagine getting used to, or even forgiving, the things people had done to me. Most of the time, I felt as if I was suppressing the anger versus trying to summon it. I had felt it for so long, it was a relief to finally find a way to express it. Making the stones let me take the cap off the bottle. The rage jutted out and seemed bottomless. I lowered my head, staring at the diamond dust in the bowl. Maybe it wasn't bottomless. Maybe if I let it pour out long enough, I too would empty out.

"You think you can wipe your memories and get back the hate you once felt?" I said.

"Yes. It's my only option. Will you help me?"

Part of me wanted to help her, but the other part stared at Mark's shaking head. "I don't think I'm ready to make this stone. I haven't even learned anything here yet. I mean, this place is really nothing like I thought it might be."

Jackie frowned and looked at the floor. "I think I'm going to be the next one to retire, if I don't get back what I had."

"I'm sorry."

"Don't be. By tomorrow I'm sure you'll be moving up to the middle classes. You can learn all about alchemy and how to make stones for these assholes. Then, if you can find it in your heart to make a simple stone for me, please let me know," Jackie spat. She stormed out of the room, slamming the door behind her.

I put my hand on Mark's shoulder. He studied me.

"Don't give me that look. What's up with your stomach?"

"It's no big deal. Don't worry about me." He glanced back at the door. "These damned people want to sink their claws into you. That's who you should be worried about."

He told me not to be worried, but he didn't know what his mom had told me about his condition. What had she done to keep him alive in the past? How much longer did he have? I gritted my teeth and wanted to get back to Ms. Duval and tell her Mark had regressed, and needed whatever it was she did for him.

"I can't help but worry." I rubbed his arm, and he shook his head with a smile.

"I think you're going to get us into a lot of trouble in this place."

"Well, we've had one hell of a first day."

"Listen," Mark said.

I wanted to sigh because I felt a lecture coming.

"You have a thirst to figure these stones out. I get that, but these people see you as a tool to be used. I want to be at your side no matter where they put you. If you're in another class, you need to demand I go with you."

"And what if they won't listen?"

He smiled. "I have a feeling you're going to be very popular here. They'll do what you want, as long as you can make those stones for them."

I chuckled at the thought of being popular … the girl who sat under the oak tree at lunch, alone. Yeah, I wasn't not the popular type. If too many people started liking me or even worse, were fake to me, I didn't think I could take it.

I yawned. "What time is it in this place?"

"I don't know. I'll walk you to your room." Mark cupped his hand over mine and led me to the door.

We made it to the staircase, where a waiting Priscilla was standing, looking agitated. She moved away from the wall and crossed her arms. Her fingers tapped on her forearms.

"Hey, Priscilla," I said.

"I need to talk with Allie, *alone*." She glared at Mark.

He paused. "I'll be right upstairs, within screaming distance, if you need me."

I nodded and glanced at Priscilla. I was probably in for another lecture, and I searched for what I might have done wrong during the day, but there weren't many rules to break.

"I came to fetch you."

"What did I do?" I looked back at the door under the stairs.

She sighed. "I know you guys make stones in the back rooms, and while I frown upon such activities, it's not the reason I'm here." Priscilla straightened out her black jacket. "She wants to meet you."

"Who?"

"President Verity."

CH.12

The spoke contained a couple of Blues on the other side of the fence, looking on with interest—probably their on-duty guards. Priscilla nodded to a Red as we walked by. I didn't recognize the girl, but she stared at me. I gave a fast wave as we passed her. She lit up with a big smile and matched my wave.

We entered the hub, walking straight through the middle. I slowed a bit to admire the giant statue. Costas had been in there earlier for his retirement. The water, once frozen, now looked as still as bath water.

I sped up my steps to catch Priscilla. "Why does Verity want to see me?"

"You'd better put 'president' in that name. She'll throw you right out of her office if she catches you doing that."

"Okay, but what does she want?"

Priscilla stopped at the double doors and turned to me. Her eyes narrowed, trying to figure me out. "What do you know about the Academy?"

"I've only been here a day, and in that time I've learned how to mass-produce growth stones and watched a stone battle between the Reds and the Blues. Oh, and I saw some guy get retired in the globe thingy."

Priscilla stopped and turned to face the statue. "That's Clymene, mother of Atlas. Some of us like to believe her to be the mother of alchemy. Some thought of her as a god, but the world doesn't like what they can't understand, so the rubes killed her entire city." Priscilla smiled. "Some think all of us alchemists are her descendants."

I shook my head, looking at the statue. "So I'm a demigod who's now kissed a relative."

She smiled but ignored my comment. "President Verity wants you, and you'll be respectful and compliant to whatever it is she wants. You may find yourself in the upper classes sooner rather than later." She shoved the double doors open, stopping the barrage of questions waiting to spill out.

The doors opened to a large hallway with stone arches towering high into the ceiling. Doors flanked each side of the lengthy hall.

"Is this the teachers' quarters?"

"Yes."

She marched down the hall toward another set of doors.

When we reached them, she placed her hand on the handle and took her time turning it. When she nudged the door open, the hinges squeaked under the belabored pace.

Just open the damned door, woman! Finally, the never-ending process was done and Priscilla motioned for me to go in first.

The flooring transitioned to wood. My boots clicked on the surface and the sound echoed around the wood walls and ceiling. My gaze landed on a long wooden desk with President Verity sitting behind it.

The door creaked behind me and closed. Priscilla had left me, and it was kind of like landing in the principal's office. When I had built up the courage, I looked at Verity and swallowed. Ms. Duval's stern expression felt soft and friendly compared to Verity's. Her thin frame accentuated her narrow face and pointy nose. Her thin black blouse clung to her, while her fashionable jacket was a size too big. Our eyes met and mine grew as silence ensued.

"It's rude not to introduce yourself," Verity reprimanded me.

I cleared my throat and approached her desk. "Hello, I'm Allie." I extended my hand over the desk. Verity hesitated but took it in a rushed shake. Then she pulled a drawer out and plucked a small bottle from it, pumped a clear liquid into her hands and rubbed them together. I smelled the alcohol. It figured she'd use hand sanitizer.

As she was closing the drawer, I snuck a look at the contents inside, but didn't see anything resembling a life stone. I fought the urge to plead with her about giving up the stone and letting me save Mark. Her expression didn't leave any room for pleasantries, let alone charity.

"Pleasure," she said. "I am President Verity."

"Good to meet you."

She sighed and stood up from her desk. "I understand you have a gift with stones."

It didn't feel like a question. "I guess."

"Who is your mother?"

Taken aback by the question, I stammered, "Catherine Norton."

"Norton." She tapped her chin. "And that is her maiden name?"

"No, it's Magnus."

She stopped and stared at me, searching for my sincerity. I had never put much thought into my last name, let alone my mother's.

"Very interesting names. Both have a long history in alchemy. You surprise me once again, Allie." She moved in front of me and leaned against the desk. Reaching into her pocket, she fumbled around with something, her eyes narrowing as she moved closer. "Your mother is dead?"

"Yes, since I was eight."

"And your father?"

"I ... he's in the Navy. I haven't seen him in a while."

"Practically an orphan. Do you remember anything about your mother?"

"Yeah, a few things, here and there."

"You remember a particular Christmas, though, don't you?"

I blinked a few times, searching for what she wanted. The

last Christmas I remembered had happened a few months before my mom had died. She had sat on my bed on Christmas Eve and asked me if I could have anything in the world, what would it be? Living in Summerford, a white Christmas wasn't possible, but I asked for one that day. She smiled and said she'd see what she could do.

The next morning, I woke to my mom and dad laughing in the backyard. I ran down the stairs and through the patio door, and slid on the icy concrete. I couldn't believe it. Our backyard had turned into a winter playland. My mom and dad threw snow at each other. When they noticed my arrival, two snowballs hit me consecutively. I laughed and joined in.

I hadn't thought about it until Verity asked.

"My mom used some kind of snow stone, didn't she? She was the alchemist?"

Verity nodded and leaned back against her desk. "I hope this isn't too difficult of a question, but how did your mother die?"

"Car accident."

"You have more thoughts on that, don't you?"

"I don't like talking about my mom." I slumped in the chair and rubbed my forehead, trying to think of any other times something unusual had happened in my childhood. It was hard to filter magic from my youthful memories, as I hadn't been told magic didn't exist. Everything felt magical in my foggy childhood memories.

"I'm sure she was a wonderful woman who would be proud to see where you are today."

"I suppose."

While Verity stared at me, I used the awkward silence to study the many paintings of ancient-looking men and women on the wall. I stopped and squinted at one I recognized. "Isaac Newton?"

"Very good. He was a man of many talents. Sadly, he didn't have the gift. He may have been a Malki like your friend Mark, but we don't believe he ever created a single stone."

The jab at Mark sent me to the snippy side. "Then why display his picture?"

"The world watched him blunder in alchemy before he moved to chemistry and physics, helping produce the sciences that sent alchemy into the history books. He helped us become invisible to the world of science. But a history lesson is not why I brought you here."

She unfolded her arms and the corners of her mouth crept back in a soft smile. "How was your first day at the Academy?"

I thought of the many horrible and awesome things I'd witnessed in one day and didn't know how to answer the question. I had so many questions I wanted to throw back at her. Like, why couldn't we leave? What the hell had happened to that Costas guy? But the biggest question was, where was the life stone?

"Fine, I guess." The response was automatic, probably a trained reaction instilled in all teenagers: the simpler the answer, the better.

"I spotted you during the retirement. You looked like you'd

seen a ghost."

"It's a lot to take in. Is this why you wanted to see me? To talk about my day?"

She gave the slightest shake of her head. "No." Turning, she walked to a large cabinet behind her desk and pulled a necklace over her head. A small key dangled from the chain. She took the key and slid it into the cabinet's keyhole.

I took a few steps left to get a better view of the contents. The life stone had to be in there.

With the cabinet door open, Verity concealed her next action, but from the motions she made, it looked like she was gathering something from within the cabinet. She used her knee to close the door and when she turned around, she was holding an alchemist's mixing bowl and a few containers.

She placed the objects on the desk and wiped her hands with a towel. "There is a curve for stone makers. When you start out, your learning and ability grow exponentially until you hit a plateau. That is where an alchemist can make their greatest work, but it comes at a cost. The more you draw from your inner self, the more you exhaust it, and the downward trend begins. I make it my personal goal to guide special students at the plateau, which is why I brought you in tonight."

"You think I've plateaued?" The idea seemed incredibly insane. I wanted to scream at all these people and tell them I had no idea what I was doing.

"I don't know, but I haven't seen such creation of stones in a long time. It comes easily to you. Darius said you created a time stone?" She raised an eyebrow.

"I just mixed stuff together. I'm not sure what I made." I danced around the truth. I knew what I had made because Mark and I had used it to save Bridget's feelings. Well, mostly Mark used it. Bridget seemed so far away now. How had my world grown so big in the space of a day?

"Maybe, but what flows through you and into the mix is what differentiates an alchemist from a rube." She set the wooden spoon in the glass bowl and twisted off the caps of the two containers.

Each container contained a vial. Verity took her time in lifting the vials from the containers, then placing them near the bowl.

"You want me to make another time stone?"

"So you *do* know what you're doing."

"I just remember these ingredients from Ms. Duval."

Verity perked up at the information and I wondered if I'd shared too much.

"I wondered how she had procured the ingredients. Such things are not easily collected." She slid the vials closer to me. "In a decade, we might make one time stone, if we're lucky. If you can make one, it would greatly help the Academy in getting closer to understanding them."

I sighed and could hear Mark's comments bouncing around in my head, telling me not to help this woman. Verity's face left little to be discussed and the impatience of my pause made parts of her face twitch.

"I can try, but like I keep telling everyone, I really don't know what I'm doing." Saying it aloud was like a safety blanket wrapped around a lie. Verity didn't respond to my words. It was clear I knew exactly what I was doing, even if I didn't understand the science behind it. I was beginning to wonder if anyone did.

I stepped up to the bowl and took the two vials. Everything in my body told me not to make this stone. My face shook in false anger and I pushed the blood to my head, hoping it gave me a red complexion. I emptied one of the vials into the bowl and steam filled the space. Verity leaned forward, staring into the mist. For a second, I thought maybe I'd still make the stone. Maybe I didn't need any anger to make these stones.

After the mist settled, Verity took the bowl and swirled the contents.

"You failed," she said, and narrowed her eyes. "I hope you gave it your full effort. Those ingredients were very valuable, and now they're worthless."

"I'm sorry," I lied. "I think I'm just tired. It's been a long day." I produced a yawn to back it up.

"Yes, well, to say I'm disappointed in you is an understatement." She set the bowl down on the desk with a thud. "Regardless, I'm moving you to room ten," she announced.

"What's room ten?"

"It's a place for the more advanced students."

I waited for her to add more, but she sat back in her chair and gazed at me as if waiting for me to speak.

"Uh, I do have a request. Mark, the guy who came with me. I need him in room ten with me."

"Need? Such a strong word. From what I understand, he has little innate ability and was recommended to room twenty-eight."

"He helps me make stones. Without him, I don't do as well."

Verity raised an eyebrow. "Does he arouse you?"

My face flushed a bit and I nodded. I couldn't leave Mark to the attacks the room would be receiving when I was gone. Maybe if I made stones for them in advance to turn in….

"Fine, he can be with you in room ten, but I expect results." She raised both eyebrows as I stood there in silence, rocking back and forth. "Is there something else?"

I didn't want to ask, but thinking of Mark and his condition, I didn't want to leave anything off the table. She might have life stones piled up in the cabinet behind her.

"I have a sick friend, and the only thing that can save him is a life stone." I blurted out the words before I even realized it.

A wicked smile spread over her face and she leaned back in her chair. Great. She had something on me now. Something she knew I wanted badly, but I didn't care because I *did* want it badly.

"The ingredients for such a stone are much more costly and difficult to work with than the time stone you just failed to make. If you can show me you can make any stone put in front of you, I will help you make a life stone personally."

I took in a deep breath and nodded.

"Good. Now get back to your room."

"Good night, Verity."

"*President* Verity."

"Oh. Yes. Sorry."

The double doors swung open and I walked down the teachers' hall. Looking for Priscilla, I found the hall to be empty. The doors behind me slammed shut and I winced at the sound echoing through the empty corridor. I took a few steps, studying each door I passed. The teachers probably had piles of books on alchemy stuffed in their quarters. What I wouldn't do for just one book on the subject. I stopped next to a door unlike any of the others, a plain, painted door with no markings. It stood out like an albatross among pigeons. Had it been there before? Surely I would have noticed it. I ran my hand over the smooth finish and moved to open it.

The handle creaked and the door swung open. It seemed to want to show me what was inside. I stood there, waiting to accept its picture show. In my dreams it might have been a library, but I stared with my hand over my mouth at a tunnel, maybe wide enough for a gold cart, extending as far as I could see. Stepping into the endless hall, I saw it slightly curve, just enough that I couldn't see where it ended. I pulled the door closed behind me. The air smelled different here; it had more humidity to it than in the rest of the Academy. It almost tasted stale.

I turned around and grabbed the handle, but it wouldn't move. I pushed down on it with my full weight, but it held. I lifted my hand and stopped short of slamming my palm against it. There had to be another door farther down the hall, and I intended to find it before the walls moved in on me, or the lights went out.

Freedom always felt like nothing more than breathing air until the moment someone choked it from you. I had the freedom to take a single path. The hall's stone floor didn't change and after a few minutes of walking, I started to fear there was no other exit. I dreaded going back to the teacher's door, hitting it and screaming until someone came to my aid. But anything was better than being stuck in some back hall.

Fast walking turned into a light jog, which turned into a run. The stone pattern on the wall and floors repeated as I ran, but still, no door. The path behind me looked identical to the path in front of me. Maybe I had gotten turned around, or maybe the hall was a trap formed by stone magic, a place to keep the exploring kids from ever getting back to their houses.

I ran, staring behind me, wondering if the flickering light I had just passed was the same light from a few minutes ago.

I never saw her coming, and I don't think she saw me, or she would have yelled a warning. I crashed into her and we both fell to the floor. Pain shot into my chest and legs from the impact. The girl I'd collided with moaned underneath me. Rolling to my side, I took a good look at the person in the hall with me.

"Carly, what are you doing here?"

She lay on the floor, clutching a book in her hands.

CH.13

"I just knew you'd fall for their door trick. You see, if you don't know this hall, it will eventually take you back to the teachers' door. They wait until they hear you screaming for help before they rescue you. It's just one of their tactics for enraging you."

"Thank you, Carly," I said. "But how exactly do we get out of here, 'cause I feel like I've run a mile."

"This is the place Jackie mentioned. I found the back door to these halls a few months ago. I can show you the way out."

"Can we get back to the teachers' hall using this tunnel?" I looked back.

"Not without breaking the door down and causing all kinds of ruckus." Carly narrowed her eyes. "Why do you want to go back to the teachers' hall?"

"I need something for Mark." I put my hand over my mouth.

"What about him?" She moved closer.

I looked to the floor and wondered how much I could trust Carly. Would it even matter if the teachers found out? Verity would probably figure out soon exactly who I'd meant, and once Mark started getting worse, everyone would know.

"Mark's dying, and if I don't get him a life stone...." I trailed off, not wanting to put it into words. "That's why I'm here."

She looked shell-shocked. "But he looks like he could split lumber for twelve hours straight!"

"I thought the same thing, but his mom told me she's been helping him his whole life. Nothing is working, and I already see him getting worse. He keeps his hands on his stomach all the time now."

"I saw that." Carly took in a deep breath.

"Oh, please don't tell him. He thinks it's not serious."

"Mum's the word. So, what's the plan?"

"His mom told me the president would have access to a life stone. I need to get close to Verity and get into her office."

"She comes into our class sometimes," Carly said. "But she doesn't really interact with us."

"President Verity has me going to room ten tomorrow. Do they make that kind of stone there?"

Carly laughed. "You're going to room ten? I've been here for over a year and I just got to room ten." She grabbed my wrist and pulled me down the hall a few steps before walking into the wall.

At least I thought it was a wall, but when she entered it, I saw a small space that led into a different hall. I looked back before she pulled me into the darkness. Thankfully, she kept hold of my wrist as we plunged into complete darkness. My shoulder rubbed against the wall and I adjusted my position to what I thought was the center of the hall.

I bumped into Carly and she put a stiff hand on my shoulder. "You hear that?" she whispered.

In total darkness, my enhanced hearing picked up the noises. There was distinct giggling and talking between two people. Carly took her hand off my shoulder.

"This is the only way back to the spoke," she whispered.

I placed my hand on the wall and looked back at the darkness behind us. Near the end, I thought I saw a faint hint of light. I wanted to turn around and go to the light and get away from whoever was making the sounds. Their laughter continued and I counted two distinct voices, one male and one female.

"We should get out of here," I whispered to my guide. I couldn't see her face or hear her. She might have been a mile away by now, leaving me in the darkness alone. Maybe this was her sick game the whole time, another prank by her and Jackie.

"Carly," I said louder.

The laughter ahead stopped.

"Quiet," Carly said, and touched my arm. The laughter started up again and got closer. The stone hall echoed the noise all around me and I had trouble defining how far away they were.

"Go," Carly said, and pushed me back in the direction we'd come from.

I used the wall to guide me through the darkness, scraping my fingertips along the jagged walls. The laughter grew louder and Carly pushed me harder. A glow of light down the tunnel gave me the confidence to speed up.

The sounds behind me grew and Carly kept pushing me along. The female voice sounded familiar.

"Get into the hall," Carly said.

I jolted past the last few turns at the end of the hall and stopped. Carly slid out behind me and stopped at the opening. She tilted her head and listened.

The whispers of laughter flowed into the hall and grew. Carly frowned and glared into the darkness. "Get against the wall," she whispered before grabbing my hand and pulling me past the dark hall. She leaned her back against the wall and nodded for me to do the same.

We stayed flat against the wall, ten feet down from the dark hall.

"What—"

"Shh," Carly said.

"Like you ever say no to anything," a playful, kind of whiny voice said.

I knew that voice, but couldn't quite place it.

"Good, 'cause I have some things I'd like to try," a male voice said.

The female voice laughed. "Why wait?"

The two people emerged from the hall. The man backed out

first, with both arms wrapped around a girl. They kissed as they backed into the wall.

I gasped, and they both turned to face us. "Jackie?" I said.

Carly bounced off the wall toward them. "Freaking *Leo* is who you've been sneaking around with?"

The leader of the Blues was with Jackie? Was she sneaking him down here for some diabolical reason? I stared at their ghostly white, shocked faces and knew otherwise. They had just been caught red-handed and were staggering back from the approaching Carly, still holding each other.

"We...." Jackie struggled to talk. "You can't tell anyone."

"Tell?" Carly waved her hands around, veins popping in her forehead. "No one would believe it, even if I had pictures. How could you do this, Jackie? He's a *Blue*. The *leader* of the Blues!"

"I don't know. It just sort of happened."

Leo added, "Yeah, you can't tell anyone. It would hurt us both." He grasped her hand and she moved closer to him.

"Jackie, you make me sick," Carly said. "Is this your slutty love hall? How long have you been fouling my halls?"

Jackie looked at the floor. "A few months."

"Months! The whole year I've been here, you've done some despicable things to the Blues and even Leo directly. Just today, you hit him with a vomit stone. Please tell me this is some sort of plan, some sort of evil plot against him."

They held each other for support. "I like him, Carly, and he likes me. So what if we escape together for a few minutes and find a place to be happy? You think I wanted to fall for this Blue douchebag? Things happen."

"Yeah," Leo said, and kissed the side of Jackie's head. "I caught her sneaking around near the portal rooms a few months back. It was like magnetism. We're just sort of attracted to one another."

Carly grunted and turned to me. "I can't stand looking at them together for another moment." She took my hand and pulled me into the dark hall. I glanced at Jackie and Leo one more time before turning the corner.

Carly kept a brisk pace through the dark hall, holding my hand.

"I can't see a freaking thing. You know where you're going?"

"Yeah. Don't worry, I won't let go."

Her grip loosened on my wrist and I sucked in a breath. The lit hall we'd just left had felt confined, but this hall in complete darkness was much, much worse.

"What's up with Jackie?" I asked.

"This has to be stemming from Ned. He had a similar look to Leo and all the same kickass, bad boy swagger." She grunted again. "I should have known, but there's no way I would have actually believed it."

The Blues had been nothing but horrible to me and just the thought of being with a Blue romantically repulsed me. Her voice was what struck me, though. I had barely recognized it because that was Jackie's happy voice. It was filled with girlish charm.

"She seemed happy," I admitted.

"Yeah, that was the most disgusting part. I almost wish we'd move right now, and let them get lost in the tunnels."

"What do you mean, move?"

"When this place moves, these tunnels change a little bit. I bet I'm the only one who knows my way around the different variations," Carly explained.

She stopped in front of me and I bumped into her.

"We're at the back door to the portal room. We have to move quickly through it or risk them portaling a person inside of us. Just follow me through the room, okay?"

"I still can't see a thing."

"Don't worry. When I push open this door, you'll be flooded with light. Here we go."

I wanted to protest, but Carly already had the door open. The light hurt my eyes and I squinted as she pulled me into the small room, the same room I had arrived in with Darius.

Carly slammed the stone door behind us and I glanced back at the hidden door, camouflaged by the surrounding stone. To think I had been in that room not long ago with a secret door I had no idea existed.

The wooden door offered little resistance as Carly shoved it open and pulled me into the hall.

She breathed hard and leaned forward, clutching her folder. "That room freaks me out. I can't imagine someone portaling into me."

I snickered at the thought and she glared at me. "Sorry, but the way you said it…."

Carly shook her head and smiled. "You stick around here long enough and I guarantee someone will try portaling into you."

It had been so long since I'd had anything close to a conversation about boys. I laughed, and Mark crossed my mind. My eyes went wide at my own thoughts and I looked away from Carly. It didn't make sense, but I couldn't look at her for fear of her reading my thoughts. She seemed to like Mark, which made it all the more uncomfortable.

"Do you have someone special waiting for you back home?" I asked.

"Yes," Carly said. "Mr. Snugglebottoms." She said without a hint of a smile.

I, on the other hand, struggled to stop my laughter. "You snuggle his bottom?"

"He's a cat."

"My stepmom won't let me have pets. She says they're vile, filthy creatures who wallow in their own poo."

"And my mom always told me to beware of people who hate animals."

"Smart woman. I bet you can't wait to get back to her."

"Yes, her and Mr. Snugglebottoms," she added with a smirk. "Jackie thinks there's a way out, somewhere in those tunnels. I agree with her, for once."

I looked back at the portal room door. If not for Carly, I would have been pounding on the teachers' door, begging to get out. She had saved me from the humiliation. "By the way, thanks for getting me out of there."

"Anything for a special like you," Carly said. She already seemed over the whole Jackie-Leo thing and smiled. "We'd better get back to our rooms. That Priscilla woman is prowling the corridors tonight. I'm guessing she's waiting for you not to show so she can go back and be your triumphant hero." Carly walked down the hall.

"Are there curfews, or rules of any kind? Because it seems like near anarchy here."

"That's just surface stuff. And, yeah, you can get away with quite a bit, especially if it's directed at the opposing side. But if you do the wrong thing, you'll know it, because you'll just be gone one day. No retirement or fancy ceremony, just *gone*."

Like Ms. Duval, I thought. "Well, I'd better be on good behavior."

"Please. A special like you could get away with murder." A hint of Carly's snark came back. "But don't mention what I did for you. No one really knows about that hall."

"I won't tell anyone."

"Good. And forget about seeing Jackie as well. If word got out … well, let's just say people might not be as accepting as we are."

"Of course."

We reached the edge of the hall overlooking the spoke. A number of hours ago, I had stood in this same place, looking at the same colored buildings. But now it looked smaller. Some of the wonder had left.

"She's gone. Let's go," Carly said.

The guards who patrolled the street didn't look back as we

glided to our house door. Carly opened the door and waited for me to go in before inching it closed. With it closed, she leaned against it and let out a long breath. "I hope I don't have to go rescuing you again."

"Me either."

"Are you really going to room ten tomorrow?"

"That's what Verity said."

"Good, because as much as I hate to admit it, I'd love to stuff you down their throats." She glared at the Blue house through the window. "I hope you make them weep and beg for mercy," she bit out, almost frothing at the mouth.

"Do you guys have a competition, like in room twenty-eight?"

"Oh, yeah, we compete. And with Costas gone and Jackie faltering, they would have crushed us tomorrow." Her eyes narrowed. "I know this kind of goes against what I've been saying, but tomorrow, for one day, I want to make the Blues lick their tears and swallow their vomit. For one day, I don't want you to hold back, even if we're just sweatshop stone makers."

"If there's one thing I seem to be exceedingly good at, it's making these stones."

A wicked smile crept over Carly's face and I wondered if I had gotten her wrong. She didn't seem like the passive person I'd first met. She was really the bloodthirsty type. I wondered how much the Blues had done to her to cause such hate.

I wanted to push the edge with her a bit more, so I said, "Did I tell you Mark is coming to room ten with me?"

"Shut your face."

CH.14

Mark took the move to room ten with some trepidation, but I reassured him that getting closer to the top people in the Academy would be good for us. We would learn how to make the best stones, surrounded by the best people. At least that was what I thought.

In room ten, Jackie and Carly sat on either side of me, while Mark sat in front. He looked back so often that I almost asked him to turn his desk around so he could just face me at all times. A few other Reds rounded out our half of the room. Much like room thirty-two, on the other side of the room sat the Blues. They looked contentious and mostly stared at me and Mark. I was sure they'd heard rumors of my exploits and wondered about the hype. I aimed at giving them a show for Carly.

I caught Jackie sneaking a glance at Leo on the other side of the room. She noticed my catch and glared at me. I rolled my eyes--like I'd go telling people about her depravities. I had more important things to do, and this upper class was a step closer to getting there.

"I am Professor Deegan," the portly man at the front of the room said. He stood up from his chair and gazed at the class. "I see we have a few new faces here today, so I think it's a good time to go over what this room is all about."

I leaned forward in my chair.

"This is an advanced placement for talented young alchemists, and not the factory floor of the other classrooms. Here, you will learn the advanced methods and ingredients to complete the most complicated of circles. So please forget everything you've learned, because it will be far easier for me to teach you the proper way."

Deegan turned around and drew a circle on the chalkboard. He drew in a few lines going to the center of the circle. It looked like a bicycle wheel until he drew in a few symbols at the sides.

"Do any of you know what this circle defines?" he asked.

Jackie raised her hand, and Deegan pointed to her. "Ingredients ... pitch, sulfur, and universal solvent. Result ... nightshade stone." She leaned closer to me and whispered, "It makes a person go blind for a while. A terrifying stone for many."

"That's correct, Jackie." The teacher turned back to the chalkboard and wrote another symbol in the circle. "We add just one more item and we get a very different result. What are we making now?"

Jackie raised her hand again. "Someone gets touched with that stone and they'll have a fate worse than death. Suspended animation."

Chatter spread through the room.

I leaned over to Jackie. "Like the frozen stone?"

"Worse. You can feel and hear, but you can't move, not even your eyes. Your body temperature drops and your heartbeat doesn't register on medical equipment, it's so weak. A doctor would pronounce you dead. There's a rumor—"

"Please, Jackie, speak up so the rest of the class can hear you. Tell us about this rumor," Deegan interrupted.

She sighed and looked at the Blues. "It's said there were two alchemists, Blane and Evers, so obsessed with transmuting gold that Evers used a suspended animation stone on Blane out of fear that he was getting closer to it than Evers. Except he didn't know exactly what effect the stone would have, and when he patted the back of the man's neck with the stone, Blane apparently fell over dead. He was put in a coffin and buried alive. The theory is, Blane is still alive, four hundred years later, stuck in his tiny coffin ... living every second of his endless nightmare with no chance of dying or escaping."

My mouth hung open. I knew why she had said it was a fate worse than death. Just thinking of being trapped in a coffin sent chills through my body.

Deegan nodded and walked around his desk. "Interesting story. Like most stones, they can be used by people with good or bad intentions. Can someone think of a good way to use it?"

I looked around the room at the blank faces. They'd seemed to jump on every other question, but this one stumped them. Every way I thought of using the stone ended in malice and vengeance. I even briefly thought of using it on Janet.

Mark raised his hand and Deegan pointed at him.

"If you were dying of some disease, you could use the stone to put a pause on your life until they found a cure, or astronauts could use it on a long-term space mission."

"Very good, Mark. What about when you want to get out of the stupor?"

The class rumbled with chatter. Jackie and Carly leaned over my desk to discuss their theories.

I raised my hand and Deegan nodded to me. "A life stone."

He raised an eyebrow. "Yes, a life stone should work. It looks like our two new students have the wits to be here."

I glanced at the Blues' sneers. Good, let them hate me. I would show them what I could really do, for Carly and for the rest of the Reds dealing with their crap.

"Can we make this life stone?" I asked.

Deegan smiled. "Ambitious. That's good. But to create a life stone, you have to take a life, and I doubt we have any volunteers for that."

His words hit me right in the stomach, and my jaw felt unhinged. I stared at the back of Mark's head and I saw him leaning forward, clutching his own stomach. He'd tried to hide it while walking to class today, but I could tell he hurt. I didn't want to take the life of another to save Mark; at least I didn't think I wanted to. There had to be another way.

"Since it's challenge day, we're creating only this one single stone." Deegan pointed to the chalkboard. "First team to make the stone gets to pick their reward from the Scroll of the Victors." Deegan walked to the corner of the room and pulled back a curtain wrapped around like a quarter-circle shower. He shoved the curtain to the wall and revealed an arrangement of alchemist supplies.

"Reds first, since they answered the questions today."

Jackie bolted from her seat, followed by Carly. I stayed seated and felt sick to my stomach from the realization about the life stone. It was all I really wanted to make. My eyes went wide as I thought about what Mark had said. If I could put him in suspended animation, I could spend years trying to get the life stone made. I closed my eyes and felt a headache coming on.

A hand touched mine. I looked up at Mark's smiling face.

"You okay?" he asked.

"Yeah." I wanted to grab him and tell him what kind of danger he was in and how I would spend every waking second trying to save his life, but Ms. Duval was right. He didn't need to know, and I'd find a way to save him before he even knew how much trouble he was really in.

I watched Carly, Jackie, and a few others mulling over the best selection of equipment. Jackie led the way, thrusting items into the waiting arms of the Reds.

Jackie would be my answer. She knew the questions and

probably knew a great deal more about stones than any of the other students. If she knew a way around the life stone, I'd find it through her.

Carly plopped a bowl in front of me and I jerked back. Jackie and a few others piled materials on my desk. I glanced over at our rivals, who were huddled around the head of the Blue house, Leo. I met eyes with him and narrowed my lids. *Yes, I know your secret.*

"You're mixing, Allie. I hope you're up to it," Jackie said.

I looked around at the faces surrounding me. Carly seemed confident with a wicked smile on her face and Mark looked on with his usual concerned expression. I was sure he hated me making a single stone for the Academy, let alone something as hardcore as this stone. Jackie crossed her arms and raised an eyebrow at my lack of action.

"What do I do?"

A few of the Reds groaned.

Jackie took a vial of black goo and put it in front of me. "We have enough materials for about ten attempts, but I don't want to make more than a few. Leo over there probably won't need that many." She gazed at Leo. "So you need to summon your trigger for each process, but save your worst for when you mix in the solvent." She pushed a vial of pure blue liquid toward me. "So put in the pitch, then the sulfur." She moved a vial of putrid yellow powder toward me. "Mix in this blood and —"

"Wait." I stopped her words, but she continued to slide over the vial of deep red liquid. "Whose blood?"

"I don't know. Just a donor. It has to be very pure blood, though."

"So they couldn't use yours, Jackie," Carly said.

"Yes, well, yours I'm sure would be black with conspiracies and contempt," Jackie said. "But please, they're already mixing their first attempt." She took a deep breath and continued. "Mix in the blood and the solvent at the same time." She tapped her finger on the blue and bloody vials.

I went through her instructions and took the vial of black pitch.

"It's really more like bitumen," Carly said.

Jackie stared her down. "Sorry. Just do your thing, Allie."

The black liquid moved like thick ketchup in the vial. I summoned a few angry thoughts as the liquid took its time pouring into the glass bowl. With the thick black goo at the bottom, I took the sulfur and poured it in. I already felt my triggers coming up, my mother leaving me and Janet and Spencer tearing apart that letter from my dad.

I took deliberate breaths through my nose as I took the last two vials in my hands and held them over the bowl. Everyone around me leaned in and I felt their breath on my arms. I didn't like to be crowded, and I used it like a fuse to get myself to my rage point. The anger flooded into me as I thought of my past. My hands shook with rage and I dumped the two vials in.

Then I grabbed the spoon and yanked it around the bowl. The mixture resisted my stirs, but my anger pushed through the thickness. The top of the bowl overflowed with a steamy mixture that smelled like rotten eggs. Air pockets popped as I mixed, and I felt the spoon spin in my hand when the mixture solidified and condensed into a stone. I let go of the spoon and waited for the sound.

The stone clunked against the glass bowl and the Reds around me gasped. Jackie rushed forward and blew the mist away, revealing a black ball with yellow and white speckles.

"*Yes!*" Jackie yelled.

The loud sound made me jump in my chair.

"No way," I heard from the Blue side.

Deegan walked over with a skeptical expression. He gazed into the bowl and then furrowed his brow as he stared at me. I caved under the pressure and looked away from his stare. He picked up the bowl as if he was carrying the most delicate of china dolls and took it to his desk. Wearing a black glove, he scooped the stone out with a cloth and placed it in a small bag. He dropped the bag into a drawer in his desk.

"Reds win." He seemed burdened with a heavy load. "Choose your reward." Deegan pointed to the wall with a scroll running floor to ceiling.

It listed many things, and I wondered what Jackie might select. Probably the balding or the nightmare stone. Something to punish the Blues, I was sure.

"We couldn't have won without you, Allie. You choose," Jackie said, out of breath.

They cleared a space for me and I walked closer to the list, taking in the different options. Then I saw it.

"I choose the observation deck."

The Blues laughed and clapped at my choice. They gave each other high fives while the Reds looked at me, confused.

"Roof it is," Deegan said. "Blues, you can go back to your houses now."

I moved back to my desk and to Mark's smiling face.

"Good choice." He looked at the ceiling. "I can't wait to see where the hell we are."

Deegan took a keychain from his pocket and opened a locked drawer in his desk. He pulled out another set of keys and started walking toward the door.

"If you have a sweater, you might want to bring it. Come on, let's go."

Carly grabbed me by the arm. "Why didn't you turn their sewer privileges off for the week?"

"Yeah, or make all their balls fall off?" Jackie said.

"I didn't see that option," Carly said, looking back at the list.

"I just made it up, but it would be a pretty good one," Jackie smirked.

Mark jumped in to take my side. "It just seems like we've had enough hate. This is something we can maybe enjoy that doesn't result in anybody's balls falling off."

"I'm with Mark. I think it's a good choice. I've been curious about where we are," Carly said.

Deegan, carrying a coat over his arm, flung the door open. We chased after him. He stood by a door a few doors down from room ten. It didn't have any unusual marks on it, beyond the typical carvings of circles and symbols most of the doors had. He fumbled with his keys until he found one he liked and slid it into the door.

It didn't work.

"Been a while. I think this is the one." He slid the next key in and the door clicked open, revealing a small room. Then he motioned for all of us to pile into the tiny space.

The floor moved up and down a few inches as each person walked in. Deegan squeezed in last and pulled the door closed.

I pressed my body hard against Mark's and felt his arm wrapping over my shoulder and down my back. I didn't want to think of being packed into a small room, so I looked at his excited face. It was the first time I could remember since arriving at the Academy that he'd had a genuinely happy expression.

"This elevator will take us all the way to the top. If I can just find the next key…." Deegan struggled as the air became damp and used, and the temperature of the confined space rose to sweltering levels.

"Hurry the hell up or I'm going to freak," Jackie said.

Sweat built up between me and Mark, but I didn't mind. His arm felt hot on my back, and I hoped he didn't mind getting a bit sweaty with me either. His face told me he didn't.

"Ah, here we go." Deegan pushed the key into a slot and turned it. The elevator moved up in a jolt.

The ride lasted a minute before at the elevator came to a stop. When the door finally slid open and a gust of frigid air swooshed in, it felt like daggers against my sweaty skin. Deegan moved out of the elevator and Jackie jumped out behind him.

I broke away from Mark and stepped outside.

The icy wind told me how far away we really were from home. My first breath blew out in front of my face in a cloud and the inhale felt like needles in my chest. A thin layer of snow crunched under my feet as I walked across a tiny roof no larger than my bedroom.

"Below thirty, I bet," Deegan said.

The bright sky shone down on us and I thought if I looked only at it, I could be anywhere in the world. Seeing the blue sky made the whole trip worth it. I lowered my gaze and took in the pure white landscape beyond. The stiff winds stirred up a bit of snow from a nearby mountain and swept it down to the valley just twenty feet below us. The flakes pelted my face and stung my cheeks. White covered everything, including the small section of the Academy oddly jutting out from the frozen tundra below. Even a plane flying directly overhead would probably have a tough time making out the structure.

"Antarctica?" Jackie asked.

Deegan nodded.

"No freaking way." I couldn't believe my eyes. How could we be at the bottom of the world? People didn't live down here, only the penguins. The supply drops to support all the people below would be staggering.

I walked to the edge and looked out as far as I could, squinting at the horizon. They had to be wrong. A fresh gust of wind blew more bits of snow into my face.

Mark moved behind me and rubbed my arms. "We'd better get inside. You're going to freeze out here."

"No, this can't be right," I said.

"Allie, I've seen enough, and so have you. Let's get off this roof, for real."

I paused briefly before complying and then walked sideways toward the door, staring at the white landscape. A gust of wind pushed against me, feeling like frigid razor blades against my face. I'd never been in such cold weather, not even close.

I wasn't really sure what I'd expected, but it wasn't this. Even if I got the life stone and healed Mark, where would we go? We would be dead in minutes out in that frozen landscape.

"Everyone in? Good." Deegan closed the elevator door.

Mark gave me a comfortable spot to nuzzle up against. My whole body shook against his and he rubbed my arm and held me tight. The elevator descended for a minute and then stopped. Deegan opened the door and the warm, stagnant air swept in. We got out, rubbing our arms, still shivering.

"Well, that's it for today. I'll see you all tomorrow." Deegan hurried back to room ten.

"Thanks for the ice roof field trip, Allie," Jackie said.

"Maybe she should have let the Blues win," Mark said as he stepped in front of me.

"At least we know where we are," Carly offered.

"Yeah, for now, and then we'll move again and be who knows where," Jackie said.

"Move?" I asked.

"Yeah, every few months they freaking move this whole place."

Carly had mentioned that the halls moved, but she couldn't have meant the entire building. I didn't understand. The building had to weigh millions of pounds. How could they transport it to and from Antarctica?

Mark asked the question first. "How do you move this place? What stone?"

"Portal stone. Or, should I say, a master portal stone. We just boost it until it's enough to move us all," Jackie said.

"Let me guess. Verity has this master stone." He rolled his eyes.

"Yep," Carly said. "Her stone absorbs others and we jump. It sort of feels like we're falling for a few seconds and then the world firms up and we move on."

"Why do we move? I don't get it."

Jackie sighed and crossed her arms. "Am I the freaking Academy wiki here? Wasn't at least one of your parents an alchemist?"

"My mom's dead, and my dad's in the Navy," I said. "I haven't seen him in months. My mom never mentioned anything about being an alchemist, and my dad sure doesn't know. This crap is all new to me."

Jackie looked at the stone floor. I didn't want her to feel bad that I'd brought up the dead mom stuff, but they needed to know I wasn't some alchemist kid, growing up with a wooden spoon and a bowl in front of me. What I knew about alchemy wouldn't fill a page.

Mark struggled to smile, and he kept his hand over his stomach. I gritted my teeth and took a deep breath. These people seemed preoccupied by the most mundane things, like getting back at the Blues, when they should be trying to figure out the mystery around them. This whole place was under a blanket of snow at the bottom of the world, and none of them seemed interested in that fact.

"Sorry about your mom," Carly said.

"Yeah, that sucks." Jackie stuck her thumbs in her pockets. "When the academy found me, they didn't quite ... explain it right in the brochure."

"My mom fed me similar tales," Carly said. "All the parents did. I bet it was some unspoken rule not to tell us what really happened here. If we knew the truth, we might have stayed home and never become alchemists."

"Same here," Mark added.

"Why do we move, again?" I tried to steer the conversation back to the question at hand.

"Young people are more powerful in the creation of stones." Jackie laughed. "They say we have the raw emotions it takes to make them. So our parents send us here to make rocks in a charitable effort to help the world. Noble, isn't it? Just think, all those growth stones may fertilize land in some poor country. But there are people out there who want to take what we make and control the world, or use the stones for profit. They're always searching for the Academy and every few months, they find it."

I shook my head in disbelief and looked at Mark. He gazed

at me, judging my reaction. How could he not have told me how big the world of alchemy was? There were people who were after us, or me. One of those dark alchemists could have taken me and done who knows what.

The ground beneath my feet shook. Wisps of dust fell from the ceiling and everyone in the hub stopped. They all would have looked frozen in place if they hadn't looked up.

"What was that?"

The ground shook again.

Jackie raised both eyebrows and took a deep breath. "Looks like we talk about the devil and we get the devil. That"—she pointed to the ceiling--"is caused by the dark alchemists."

CH. 15

Two deep buzzer tones blared through the speakers of the building. My heart pounded and I saw the fear on everyone's faces. Well, not Jackie; she bounced and clapped her hands in excitement.

Verity's voice came through the speakers. "All students, report to your classrooms for the immediate making of booster stones. Your teachers are setting up the rooms now for their creation. They seem to be hitting us much harder this time, so we don't have much time. Do your best work, people."

The speakers sounded two more buzzers and then went silent. The hub filled with noise as everyone ran in every direction. Several guys brushed by me, running to their classes.

"What the hell do we do?" I asked, staring at Jackie.

She smiled and pointed to room ten and to the teacher's door. "Watch. They just don't use these stones for making the world better. They use them as weapons and defense mechanisms."

The building shook again, much harder than before. Deegan's door was flung open first. A black ribbon was strung across his chest like a Girl Scout sash, but instead of badges, it held stones. Deegan rushed down the line of doors and stopped at the elevator. With gloved hands he grabbed several stones from his sash, opened a hatch and stuffed them in. It sounded like a vacuum hose sucking up a stone. He waited a few seconds, then sent up another set.

"See?" Jackie pointed. "I don't know what they're sending up, but I bet it's nasty stuff."

"Get to your classes," Verity yelled. Her voice carried over the hubbub. Everyone who had been walking started running.

"Come on," Carly said.

We jogged to room ten just as Deegan showed up at the door. The Blues came in behind us as we entered the classroom. I took my same seat and everyone rushed to their own chairs.

Another explosion shook the building and the lights flickered.

"Get your bowls and spoons ready, kids," Deegan said, and he rummaged through the lower cabinets behind his desk. He plopped a five-gallon bucket on his desk, then went back to the cabinet.

Carly slid a bowl and a spoon across my desk. "Here. I think we're going to need you for this one."

"What are we making?" I asked.

"Booster stones," Deegan answered as he set another five-gallon bucket on the table. "We need to boost Verity's portal stone enough that we can move this entire place. Unfortunately, they have the shelf life of a gnat, so we make them quick and get them out to her."

Everyone rushed around me to get to the two buckets on Deegan's desk. They formed two lines, Blues and Reds, and in an orderly fashion took a scoop out of each bucket, filling smaller bowls. Carly rushed to my side and pushed the bowls in front of me.

One looked like black sand, and the other looked like vegetable oil and reeked like a dead fish. Carly pushed a group of blue vials towards me.

I stared at the mixture and looked up at Mark sitting in front of me. He hadn't gathered any ingredients and no one had brought him anything.

"What do you think, Mark?" I asked.

The building shook again and I grabbed at my supplies, keeping them from crashing to the floor. The sound of glass breaking and the subsequent cursing told me several others hadn't been as successful.

Mark looked to the ceiling and shook his head. "I don't know, but I really don't want to find out who's trying to break in."

"Five minutes, everyone." Deegan held a finger to his ear.

"Five! Jesus, Mary and Joseph," Jackie said. "Let's make some freaking rocks, Reds."

Jackie started mixing in the black sand and oil. Finally she dropped in the blue liquid and stirred. No mist or anything seemed to be happening. She grunted and grabbed the bowl, rushed to the trash can and scraped the contents into it.

"Pick it up, Allie," Jackie said upon returning.

"I've got one," a kid on the Blue side called out.

"Good! Keep it going. Two more minutes."

"Done," Leo said. He smiled smugly as he held the stone over his head, wrapped in a black cloth.

I didn't like getting beaten, especially by some Blue who'd had his hands all over me just a day ago. I felt my anger build. I always felt anger simmering, but I'd spent my entire life it keeping at bay. Here, and with these stones, I didn't have to pretend not to be mad. I could push my rage to its limits.

I dumped the entire container of metal shavings into my bowl while I shook with anger at Bridget's stupid comments about me and what a freak I was.

Carly said something, but I didn't listen as I took the oil and poured it in. My thoughts traveled to Janet and Spencer. The anger enveloped me, like throwing gasoline on a fire, making my hands shake and my vision shrink down to a narrow tunnel.

I thought of my dad and why he hadn't been coming home anymore. It'd been too long. He'd left me, just like my mom had. It was a thought I usually never dared to think, but it skittered across the edge of my consciousness and once I grabbed it, it overwhelmed me.

The half-dozen blue vials clattered as I scooped them up. Blackness filled the edges of my vision and I hoped the blue liquid made it into the bowl as I turned my wrist. But really, I didn't care. I grabbed at the spoon, pulling and yanking it around the bowl. Mist covered everything, like a deep fog had just rolled in. The spoon broke free from its stubborn path and I heard a plunking sound at the bottom of the bowl.

"Holy salt on a cracker," Jackie said, fanning the fog away from me. "You actually made one."

Sweat beaded on my brow and I leaned back, staring at the bowl. A metallic silver stone looked back at me.

Deegan emerged from the fog and leaned over my desk with a concerned expression. He tilted the bowl and watched the stone roll around before leveling the bowl back down.

"That isn't supposed to be possible. Not using that much," he whispered.

The speaker blared with Verity's voice. "All students to the hub, and bring your stones."

Deegan adjusted his sash. I noticed the stone I had made not long ago, the suspended animation stone, sitting in a pocket on his sash. "Let's go," he instructed.

The stone glimmered as it reflected the light from the ceiling back at me. I stared at it until Mark used a black cloth to pick it up.

"That stone is going to hit Verity like a ton of bricks," Jackie said. "I can't wait to see it." She pulled out a small bag from her pocket. "Here, Mark, put that thing in here before you hurt yourself."

He pursed his pretty lips, but complied and handed the bag to me. I clasped it with my shaky hand. The weight of it shocked me. It must've weighed several pounds.

"You guys coming?" Deegan popped his head back in the room.

"Yeah," Jackie said.

The hub was full of motion, everyone moving for positions near the center statue. I followed Jackie and Carly as they led the way through the crowd. The Blue and Reds moved aside as she forced her way to the front. Verity was standing barefoot on the edge of the water fountain. She held her hands high above her and tried to silence the crowd.

"All those with stones, I need you up at the front. Everyone else, back up and make room." She walked on the edge, looking over the groups as they rearranged in priority.

Jackie stayed by my side, as well as Mark.

"There's no way I'm missing this," Jackie whispered to me. "I have no idea how the woman holds a stone for as long as she does. Her anger's the freaking Mariana Trench."

"As soon as I place the portal stone in my hand, nothing can interrupt me, and no matter what happens, you need to keep putting your stones on mine until it's powerful enough to move us."

The building shook again. I looked to the ceiling where a deep crack had formed. Drips of water fell from the crack.

"Get ready, everyone." She nodded to a few teachers. They looked on high alert as they scanned the walls and ceiling. Verity took a deep breath and placed the portal stone on her bare palm. Her face contorted with strain as she kept it from dissolving into her hand.

A person nearby pinched their booster stone with a cloth and touched it against Verity's portal stone. It absorbed into it, and the next person did the same.

Jackie nudged me, wearing a wicked smile. Most of the people had walked in front of me and I got in line maybe ten people back. I watched Verity as she received each stone; the strain grew in her face and she shook. Not just her hands, but her whole body.

Two more people placed their stones on hers. I opened my bag and used a thin cloth to lift the stone. It wanted to slip from my fingers, so I gripped it tight.

Something slammed against the building. I stumbled and Mark held me steady. Bits and pieces of the ceiling rained down. Some screamed and ran from the falling debris. A small beam of light shone through the ceiling. I stared at the light and something dropped through the crack. As it got closer, I saw it was a stone.

Deegan ran toward the falling stone, holding one of his own.

The stone struck the floor and bounced. An instant later, a man appeared in its place. He was wearing a sash much like Deegan's, and he pulled a stone from it. He searched the people around him, looking over the heads of many.

"Dad?" a Blue called out. "Dad!"

"Son—"

Deegan threw a stone at the man, striking him on the side of the face. I recognized the stone, as I had just recently made one like it. The suspended animation stone dissolved into his skin and he fell to the floor. Wait—had he said *son*?

Jackie nudged me again. I turned to face Verity. She shook violently and stared past me, through me. Her look made me take a step back, but there were no more students to add to her portal stone. They formed a half circle and nudged me toward her shaking arm.

As I got close, I heard her teeth chatter and saw in her eyes that she was somewhere far, far away. I took the heavy stone, pinching it with all my might, and placed it against her stone.

Verity's head jerked back and she exhaled a long breath as she fell backward into the fountain. The water splashed around her body.

I gasped as a wave of air pushed past me. I fell through the floor ... at least I thought I was falling. It felt just like the time stone, a feeling of falling. I grasped for the air around me until the ground firmed under my feet once more.

The water sloshed around the fountain, and Verity stayed under the surface. Priscilla rushed to her with a couple of other students and they pulled her out. Her arms and head bobbed around with no muscle control. Her eyes stayed closed as they laid her on the floor.

"Is she breathing?" Deegan asked.

Priscilla put her ear near Verity's mouth and nodded.

"Then get her to her room. I'll handle the intruder," Deegan said.

Priscilla and a couple of other teachers lifted Verity and carried her past me. As she passed by, my mouth hung open.

The woman had sacrificed her body to protect us. I didn't know why I thought it was so weird. I guess I just hadn't thought the woman had it in her. She'd saved us all from the dark alchemists. They were about to start falling from the ceiling, like that Blue's dad.

"You okay?" Mark asked and rubbed my shoulder.

"Yeah, just a bit freaked out."

He and I looked at the kid on the ground, holding his dad, sobbing into his black jacket.

"What did you do?" the Blue asked no one in particular.

Deegan rushed to the boy's dad but didn't answer. I could have answered. I'd made the very stone which had put him in the stupor. I resisted the urge to tell the Blue that his dad had become a modern-day Sleeping Beauty.

"Get him out of here," Deegan said, and pointed to the Blue holding his dad.

The Blue fought and screamed, but a group of Blues pulled him away all the same.

Deegan motioned for the bald teacher and a few others to grab the practically dead man and pick him up.

They discussed something in a hushed manner as they carried him toward the teachers' hall. In another minute, the teachers, the dark alchemist, and Verity were gone. Most of the students stayed in the hub, looking more like zombies than anything else. They staggered around, looking at the ceiling and floors. I felt the same way. Confused and scared, mixed with angry.

Someone had attacked us. Not just someone, but a student's dad.

Carly rushed to our side. She smiled and pulled me away from Mark and Jackie, moving close to my ear. "The halls can change some when we jump. I think we should explore them tonight. You in?"

"Um ... sure." Curiosity overwhelmed my common sense.

Carly smiled and scurried off toward the Red house.

"Well, that was awesome, wasn't it?" Jackie said. "I mean, that dude dropped through the ceiling in a flippin' *stone*. I had no idea a person could do that." She gazed at the ceiling in astonishment.

"Pretty strange, though, you know, with him being that guy's dad and all?" Mark said.

"No. I bet my mom was a dark alchemist." Jackie shrugged.

"You think Verity is okay?" I asked, and glanced at the closed teachers' door.

"Please. That bird is immortal as far as I can tell." Jackie laughed. "I knew your stone would send her to the plunge. Man, she is one tough woman."

"Where are we now, do you think?" Mark looked at the ceiling.

I searched for the hole in the ceiling and thought I saw something, a black hole where everything else was gray. Nighttime, I thought.

"Who knows, and who cares. This event probably just sparked enough in me to keep it going for days."

The hub started to clear out as everyone went back to their houses. I assumed there wouldn't be any more classes. There wasn't a teacher in sight.

Jackie brightened. "Oh my god, I just realized we get to have a jump party now."

I started to feel as if she found a reason to party every night. She bounced around me for a little bit before running toward the Red house. The party didn't interest me, but finding Carly and figuring out where we moved did.

A hand touched my shoulder. I turned to find Mark.

"Don't you think it's weird that that kid's dad dropped in to say hi?"

"Yeah, I think this whole place is pretty strange." I leaned closer to Mark. "Carly wants to go exploring down the tunnels I told you about. She says things change when we jump."

"Fine, but if I find a way out of here, we're gone. Deal?"

I nodded, looping my arm through his.

CH.16

Jackie didn't mess around when it came to a jump party. I don't know how she got it together in less than an hour, but from my window I saw how the entire spoke in front of the Red house had turned into a street party.

The Blues hadn't emerged from their houses … at least not in force. A few mingled near the fence line, probably waiting for a person to get too close.

Mark leaned on the windowsill next to me. I stared at him while he took in the jump party below. He would probably be the life of the party back in Summerford, but he was standing next to a window, an outsider, much like I used to be at school.

I didn't get too close to the window because they called for me each time I did. Part of me wanted to join in and another part of me wanted to stay in the room with Mark.

"I can see you looking at me," he said, not turning his head until after he spoke. "Do I have a booger or something?"

I smiled and took a step closer, inspecting his nose area. "Nope, shipshape! You know I'd tell you if you did."

"A true friend. Thanks." He turned back to observing the party.

Digital music was playing and I peered over the sill to see the bodies dancing.

"You think over time, they just get used to it?" he asked.

"Used to what?"

"Being here."

"Oh, I suppose most people can get used to just about anything."

"I suppose." He rubbed his chin and stepped away from the window.

"Something's bothering you. Why don't you just say it?" I asked.

He turned to me and opened his mouth.

The bedroom door was flung open and Jackie strutted in. "There you bitches are." She walked to the bed, sat down, and proceeded to rummage through my nightstand drawer.

I raised an eyebrow, but she didn't seem to notice.

"Why are you two in this room? I thought you might have been naked when I came in here, but here you are, fully clothed and not at my party."

My mouth hung open. If she thought Mark and I were naked, why would she have just flung the door open? The idea of her thinking we might have been naked warmed my cheeks and choked the words in my throat.

"Please, don't be all shy about it. It's not like I don't see you checking out his junk every chance you get."

I didn't think I could be more shocked. I had never checked out anyone's junk, ever. Great, I'd just checked out Mark's junk.

"What do you want, Jackie?" Mark asked.

She sighed and looked at me. "I need you down at the party, and you can bring your man if you want to. Maybe you can get him to loosen up a bit with a little dancing. Plus, I have a plan for the Blues in a little bit and I know you won't want to miss it."

The words finally loosened from my throat when she led the conversation away from discussing me and Mark. "What plan?"

"I don't know what's up with them, but after a jump we usually have a party, sort of a competition to see who can get louder and rowdier. I win at parties, but they're just sulking in their houses. I aim to raid their stone room."

"You want to go into their houses?"

"Yeah, if we do it as an all-out assault, they shouldn't know what hit them. We could be in and out in a few minutes."

I shook my head and glanced out the window to the Blue houses across the street. What were they doing in there? The last time we had a party, they'd gathered in force outside and everything had ended in a stone war.

"I don't—"

Jackie jumped from my bed and grabbed my wrist. "I won't allow you to be up here, fully clothed, with Mark." She stopped and turned to him. "Unless you were going to get naked. I mean, he *is* cute." She eyed him up and down. "For a Malki."

"We weren't going to get naked." I glanced at Mark and wondered what he was thinking. It wasn't as if I didn't wonder what was underneath his shirt. I felt his hard body from time to time and from what I could tell, he'd look incredible shirtless. More heat entered my cheeks as Jackie pulled me out the door.

"Guess we're going to the party," I called to Mark, and he followed.

We descended the stairs.

"When I whistle once, we'll all be attacking their main house and going straight to their stone room. Cover your face and watch for stones, 'cause they'll be tossing them like crazy and they have some nasty ones. Don't let them get a hold of you...." She looked back and raised an eyebrow at me. "They'll do more to your body than throw stones."

"Why don't we just leave them alone? Maybe that kid's dad freaked them all out or something," I said.

Jackie stopped at the front door of the house. "What?" She squinted and crunched her mouth to one side. "You just don't get it. The second we let up is when they attack."

"I thought we weren't allowed across the fence," Mark said.

Jackie brightened up and a wicked smile hit her face. "This is the beauty of a jump, and that dark alchy showing up makes it even better. There won't be a single teacher anywhere. We can get away with a full frontal assault. Plus, I want to get into their stone room."

She pulled me out the front door and into the thumping party. People cheered as I stumbled onto the street. Many faces turned to me and Jackie held up my arm like a victorious prize fighter. They cheered again.

I felt sick. Did they all know we'd be attacking the Blues?

"Here she is, the finest acquire we've had since ... well, me." Jackie curtsied. "Five minutes, people."

They cheered again and went back to dancing. The music got louder and made it hard to hear Jackie as she leaned closer to my ear.

"Why don't you get stick-in-the-butt Mark out on the dance floor? Maybe moving will thaw him a bit."

I took a deep breath and glanced at Mark. My instant reaction was to defend him, but he'd been different since we'd come to the Academy.

Jackie jumped away and hollered with her arms flailing as she entered the party.

"You want to dance? You know, just to satisfy the masses," I asked. He could use a thaw. He seemed wound tight.

"Sure. But I hope you can keep up with my skills."

"You dance?"

"A little bit." His smile led me to believe he knew a great deal about dancing.

He took my hand and led me into the fray.

I was nervous about my first dance with another person, and my heart beat faster. I'd danced, but I wasn't sure if it counted when you're by yourself in your bedroom. "Freaking out" is what Janet called it when she walked in on me dancing one day. She'd teased me for a month about taking me to the doctor for my "condition."

Mark found us a space. He hovered near me and started moving. He moved along with the beat and kept inching closer to me. I laughed because I realized I couldn't dance, and he really could. The thought of moving my body in any way close to the skill of Mark sent me into another laugh.

"Here, let me help you." He touched my shoulder and stepped behind me. Whispering in my ear, he guided my body along with his. "It's easy. Just move with me. This isn't the waltz, it's club dancing. The sole purpose is getting closer to the person you're dancing with, so the movements are slow."

I controlled my laughing and felt my body sync with his. My breath slowed and I zoned everything out but the music and Mark's body brushing against mine.

"There you go. You're a natural," he said with a hot breath on my neck.

The music stopped. Mark walked around me, looking at the speakers they had pulled into the street.

"What's going on?" I spotted Jackie and realized I had forgotten about her plan. I wanted to yell at her to stop, that I needed more time with Mark, but her hand was already in motion. A stone flew to the four Blues walking nearby, hitting one in the chest and igniting in a green cloud. The group fell to the ground coughing.

Jackie pulled a section of fence open, put her fingers in her mouth and whistled.

The Reds around me jumped and ran toward the opening. They funneled through and ran toward a Blue house door with Jackie leading the charge. Reds pushed past me and Mark as we stayed behind.

The girl with the ferret, Ira, pulled on my sleeve. "Some people will get hurt over there and need our help."

Mark nodded and moved forward. I dragged my feet at first, then caught up to them as the raucous crowd pushed through the narrow fence gap. Once on the other side, everyone spread out, running toward the Blue house.

I felt as if I was running into a battlefield when I crossed the fence. I was on enemy territory. Ira was right, though; if we could help, we should.

Jackie and a few others breached the Blue house door and stones flew out around the Reds who were entering. She led the charge and dodged a few stones while entering the Blue house. She covered her eyes and threw a stone to the floor. It exploded in a bright flash. She screamed in laughter as as many Reds as Blues fell to the ground, grabbing at their eyes. Jackie disappeared deeper into the house. I shook my head. We'd been led over here by a lunatic.

Mark and I stuck to the outside and watched Blues gathering down the street. Only a few were outside, but more joined them, putting their shoes on or going shirtless. Many were holding small black bags, but they knew we had them outnumbered, ten to one. Then another group of Blues gathered.

Five to one.

The Blues continued to pour out of the houses. It was only a matter of time before they had the numbers to feel brave enough to repel us.

"We've got to go," I yelled through the doorway, hoping Jackie heard me. She came running out with a large black sack, smiling. She held it up to me as a stone flew near her face. She lifted her arm and batted it away.

Putting her fingers in her mouth, she blew two loud whistles.

The tide turned. The blinded Reds staggered from the building even as Jackie stepped over one of them. Mark rushed to the side of a girl stumbling away from the door. I saw another girl frozen on the floor. I ran to her and gripped her under the arms. She weighed more than I'd thought, but I dragged her toward the opening in the fence.

"The Blues are coming," someone yelled.

I glanced down the length of the spoke and saw what must have been all one hundred of them. They had gathered their forces. The sight pushed me to find the strength to drag the heavy girl across the street. Ira moved next to me and grabbed the frozen girl's arm. After we'd dragged her to the fence, Ira turned and ran back toward the Blue house.

"Ira, no," I yelled, but she was already gone. I pulled the frozen girl to the other side of the fence. "There's a few more over there."

"No." Jackie slammed the fence closed. "They were slow and allowed themselves to be caught."

"Ira's out there," I said.

Jackie grimaced and looked over the fence.

A blinded Red stumbled out the door. Ira put her arm under his shoulder and guided him toward the fence. She wasn't going to make it. A stone landed near her feet and skittered across the street. It rolled toward the fence and into a hole.

The first Blue got to Ira and the blinded Red. He tackled them to the street. Ira got to her feet as the blinded Red punched at the air around himself.

"We've got to help," I said.

Leo grabbed Ira and turned to face us with his hand clutching her hair. His wicked smile made me want to throw up. He grasped the front of Ira's white shirt and ripped it down to her stomach.

"Help me," she screamed. Her bra and chest were exposed.

"Help me, help me," he mocked.

I moved to the fence, but Mark got there first.

"Don't." Carly grabbed my arm, but I yanked it away. "They'll do the same to you, or worse."

"She's right," Jackie said, but I had my hand on the fence with Mark. She looked over the fence and then at me. Taking a deep breath, she stared at the bag in her hand. "Dammit," she whispered under her breath. "Trade!"

The Reds and Blues both stopped at this scream.

The leader of the Blues marched Ira toward the fence. Tears fell from her eyes as she tried to put back together her torn shirt.

"I want everything you took from our house," Leo demanded.

"Fine…."

"And I want your stone. You know the one I'm talking about."

Jackie crouched behind the fence line. The Blues couldn't see her as she hunched over, cursing at the street below. She rose up, staring at me.

Closing the distance between us, she whispered into my ear. "I need you to make a stone." After the details had been revealed, she turned to the Blues. "Give me a few minutes. You touch her or the other guy and it will be a war."

I grabbed Mark and pulled him toward me. "I've got to make a stone. Can you help me?"

"Yeah." He looked back at Jackie.

I didn't wait for him to figure it out. I couldn't stand Ira being in their hands for one more minute.

The Reds moved aside for me as I ran to the door and to the back room Jackie had shown me the night before. Mark and Carly ran in behind me. I hadn't invited Carly, but I didn't have time to protest her presence.

"Get me sulfur, pencil shavings, and a solvent."

Mark's eyes went wide at the ingredient list, but he and Carly rushed around the room, gathering the materials.

"Do you know what you're making?"

"Yes." I didn't, really, but Jackie needed it to trade for Ira.

"Okay," Carly said in a dragged-out way as she pulled a jar of sulfur from the shelf.

With a bowl and spoon in hand, I waited as Mark and Carly placed the ingredients in front of me. Thinking of Ira being held by Leo sent enough anger through my core to mix the ingredients together the right way.

The stone clunked, and I used a black cloth to hold it as I rushed back out the door. The Reds turned to me as I walked past them with the stone in hand.

Jackie narrowed her eyes as I handed her the mustard-yellow stone. She took her time in the transfer, holding it away from her body. "I knew you could make it. Can you take this bag?" She handed me the bag of goodies she had taken from the Blue house.

Jackie closed her hand over the stone wrapped in black cloth and a wicked smile appeared on her face again. I sucked in a breath and hoped I had done the right thing.

"Are you ready for the trade?" Jackie said.

"I don't believe you," Leo said, and shook Ira. She whimpered and clutched her chest with both arms. "Place the stone in a bag and toss it over."

"Fine." Jackie's eye twitched. She dropped the stone in a bag and hunched over it before clutching it in her fist. "Put Ira and Dennis next to the fence and I'll throw it over. Allie will throw the bag of stones I took from you."

Leo pushed Ira toward the fence and kicked Dennis as he walked by.

"The stones, now, or I freeze them and let the house do whatever they want with their bodies."

The Blues grumbled in agreement. I saw the hunger on some of the boys' faces and I wanted to plow through the fence to get

Ira away from them.

Jackie leaned close to me and whispered, "Don't throw that bag, no matter what." She winked. "You're going to love what you just made."

I didn't have time to protest her schemes, but if she messed up the trade and something happened to Ira....

Jackie stood tall. "Okay, on a count of three."

Mark stood next to the fence, ready to snatch up Ira and Dennis.

"One. Two." She glanced at me and moved her hand back. "Three." She tossed the black bag. I couldn't help but stare at the high arc she threw it in. All eyes were on the bag sailing high above us. I barely noticed Mark grabbing Ira and Dennis from the fence opening. Other Reds took Ira and shuffled her off toward the house. All that mattered was they were safe.

Leo smiled and raised his hand to catch the bag.

The black bag spun in the air and as it neared Leo, I saw the pieces of bag break away, revealing the stone. Leo's eyes narrowed and when it got within a few feet of him another Blue jumped up and grabbed the stone.

It dissolved into his hand. The Blue grabbed at his arm, shaking and straining.

"What have you done, Jackie?" Leo demanded.

The Blue screamed as red marks streaked across his arms. He fell to his knees and tore off his shirt. The red streaks moved across his neck and down his chest. He screeched, and the Blues took steps back from him.

A girl pushed people aside and slid next to him. She hesitated at touching him at first and then grasped his hand.

"You are one sick bitch, Jackie," Leo said. He raised his hand and made a swirling motion. "I will personally make you pay for this, soon."

The Blues mumbled and groaned but started walking toward their houses.

"Wait." Jackie snatched the bag from my hands. "Don't you want your bag?"

Leo sneered at her and kept walking toward the houses.

"No, no, we need a teacher!" the girl next to the red-streaked boy pleaded. "Please." She glanced at the Reds.

Near the hub, I saw a person running down the spoke. Deegan, it looked like. His portly figured bounced as he advanced.

Jackie blew three sharp whistles and the Reds rushed to the nearest house door.

Mark moved to the fence.

"Mark, no," Carly said. "The teacher will help him."

The girl on the other side sobbed and screamed for help. The red-streaked boy collapsed to the ground.

"We need to get out of here," Carly said. "They'll pin this on Mark if he's out here."

We followed Carly. "Aren't we going back to the house?" I asked.

"No. I want to show you two something." She didn't go toward the house; she went back to the portal area at the end of the spoke. We entered the small hall and the screams diminished in its confines. I glanced back to see Deegan reach the boy and pull out a stone from his pocket.

"Is he going to be okay?"

"No," Carly said simply as she opened the door to the portal room.

My hands shook and I leaned against the door next to her.

"We've got to get out of here," Carly said. "Every day I'm here, it becomes more and more evident that we need to leave before it's too late."

Mark nodded.

"You okay, Mark?" Carly asked.

"Yeah, it's just that my stomach is in knots."

My stomach turned as well. With each passing hour, he touched his stomach more. The corners of his eyes creased, his breathing got more rapid, and he walked with a little less pep in his step. He tried to hide it, but I knew suffering when I saw it. The urgency of getting that life stone amped up each time I looked at him. "I don't know how much more of this Red versus Blue crap I can take."

"That's just surface stuff." Carly sighed. "It's not by mistake that people like Jackie and Leo are in charge. Sane people would try to work out a treaty of some sort, or at least find a civil medium to coexist in…." She glanced at the portal room. "After the jump, I did some exploring in the tunnels. I found this room, and if it's real, we need to find a way out of here. For everyone, if possible."

"Take us to this room," Mark said.

CH. 17

Carly held the door open for us as we ran across the portal room. Crossing the portal room freaked me out and I was happy to be in the dark hall beyond it. The hall illuminated as Carly held up a stone.

"Glow stone. Pretty cool, huh?" Carly said as she walked down the hall. "Ira figured it out in our stone room."

I ran my hand over the jagged divots and chiseled lines of the walls. The other parts of the Academy were smooth, stacked stones, but this hall looked as if it had been chopped out of a single block of rock.

Mark motioned for me to go first. The last time Carly had pulled me down this hall in total darkness, it had felt like the longest hall ever; with it all lit up, I could see it was only a hundred feet long. After a curve, light from the main hall bled into ours. Carly squeezed through the opening and into the main hall.

I rubbed my sweaty palms down the sides of my shirt and looked at the dark hall we'd come from.

"Don't worry, it isn't too far. But don't make a sound," she said. "I have a feeling the teachers might use this room."

I nodded and walked down the hall. Carly stowed her glow stone and kept another bag open, walking sideways with her hand near the bag.

"Expecting trouble?" I whispered.

"I don't like surprises."

"Why don't you let me go first?" Mark said.

"Please." Carly rolled her eyes.

He huffed, but kept to the back.

Carly kept a slow pace and glanced back as much as she glanced forward. I matched her and kept looking around. I had no idea what she expected to see, but it kept our mouths shut. She walked close to the wall and rubbed her hand along the stone as we moved.

She raised a hand and we stopped. "You hear that?" she whispered.

I squinted and turned my ear in the direction she pointed. I did hear it, a conversation not far away. Carly crept toward the sound, hunching low. Her hand moved along a wall and she stumbled forward. I grabbed her arm and saved her from falling over. She looked back and mouthed a "thank you" to me.

She pointed to the hall she'd found. The voices got louder as we tiptoed down the hall. I couldn't see the people behind the voices, but I understood the words and knew who was talking.

Verity's voice sounded weak, but her words were firm. "Who do you think you are, dropping in on us? I won't let any of you get a single one of them back."

Carly stopped near the end of the hall. I looked past her to the expansive room beyond. Small boxes filled most of the area, stacked high on pallets with shipping labels. She crouched low and ran behind a stack of boxes. Mark and I ran behind her and I did everything I could not to breathe loudly enough for Verity to hear it.

Carly slid a box over a few inches, which revealed Verity standing in a cleared area with the dad who had dropped from the ceiling sitting in a chair in front of her. He didn't move or even blink.

Suspended animation, courtesy of a stone I had made.

I covered my mouth and felt stuck in place myself.

Verity glanced our way, her gaze passing over our area without noticing us. "Bring the boy in. Let's make this quick. That damned booster stone our special gave me nearly sent me to the grave."

Carly looked at me and then back to the scene. If my heart beat any harder, they might hear it. Snooping and exploring were one thing, but this felt like we were about to witness something horrible.

Verity pulled over a chair. It scraped over the stone floor and she slammed it down five feet in front of the dad.

Priscilla and Professor Dill dragged a boy toward the seat. He tried to yell and fight but the tape covering his mouth muffled every protest. The boy's eyes went wide as they plopped him on the seat in front of his dad.

Verity moved behind the boy and ran her hands over his hair. She smiled and pulled on it. The boy struggled before Priscilla brought out a knife and cut his hand restraints and he yanked the tape off his mouth.

"Don't move," Priscilla said, pointing the knife at him.

"What did you do to him?" He bounced on the chair, moving it closer to his dad until Verity pulled him back a bit.

"He's fine. Think of it like he's frozen, but forever."

"Dad, can you hear me?"

Mark shook next to me and I knew he was thinking of rushing out there. I squeezed his arm hard and shook my head. I knew if we stepped out there or were found, we'd disappear like the students Carly had mentioned earlier.

"He can hear you, he can see you, and if you hugged him, he could feel you. Tricky stone, this is. One of the cruelest I can think of."

The boy wrenched at his chair and reached for his dad.

"Do you know why your dad came here? Why he attacked us?" Verity asked.

"I don't know. He's just an IT guy back home. He fixes phone service computers. I didn't know anything about his alchemy. I thought it came from my mom."

"I believe you," Verity said and motioned for him to go to

his dad.

He stood and rushed to hug his dad. His dad's body didn't move and he patted him, as if he was trying to feel whether his dad was real or not.

"We have to do something for him. He can explain, I know it. He's not a dark alchemist," he said.

"There's only one thing that can bring him out of this."

"What is it? I can make it for you."

"It's a life stone, actually. We'll have the ingredients for it tomorrow."

I almost fell against the boxes in front of me.

"A life stone? I'll do anything to save him."

"Don't worry about that. Think about your dad and what he needs right now. Can we trust you to stay in this room with him until tomorrow?" Verity asked.

"Yes. You couldn't drag me away."

"Good," Verity said, and smiled. She walked away with Priscilla and Dill. They left through a door at the back of the room. When I looked past the door, I saw another room, filled with boxes.

"Don't worry, Dad. I won't leave your side until we get you cured."

The idea of the life stone being created sent chills down my arms. If they had a life stone, I could get it from them and use it to cure Mark. It might be cruel to the boy sitting in front of his dad, but his dad had all time in the world to find his own life stone. Mark needed one now.

Carly touched my arm and pointed to the hall we'd come in through. We left the storage room and walked down the dark hall before entering the main hall.

"This is just as bad as I thought. They're making a life stone." She threw her arms out.

"Well, it's actually something I've been looking for," I said.

"Ugh. Didn't you hear Deegan in class today? It takes a life to create one. Maybe multiple lives. They're going to kill someone."

I had heard Deegan and vividly remembered the exchange. A life for a life, or as Carly had said, many lives for a life.

Mark rubbed his stomach and closed his eyes. Why did he have to keep reminding me of his impending doom? Dang Ms. Duval for not getting a life stone for Mark before I came into the picture.

"If they're going to take someone's life, who do you think they'll be taking?"

"If my suspicions are right, we'll be getting a new student tonight and a retirement tomorrow. God, I hope I'm wrong," Carly said.

The glow stone lit our way down the dark hall attached to the portal room. Carly pushed the door open and paused. She looked from me to Mark and then ran to the wooden door. She flung it open and we both ran through the room and into the next hall.

With the portal room door closed, we ambled toward the houses. My shoulders slumped and I dragged my feet with each step. The look on the boy's face as Verity told him the only way to save his dad stuck with me. If there was a chance to save one of my parents, I'd do anything too. The idea of the life stone being so close, yet still out of my reach, weighed on me. Getting it directly from Verity wouldn't be easy. I'd have to make the right stones, but even then, I'd have to be nearly on top of her to get a stone to touch her.

"What are you doing down here?"

I looked up to see Darius standing at the end of the hall.

"Uh ... nothing much." Carly went to Mark and played with his arms and chest and gave me a sexy smile.

"Just don't get pregnant," Darius said as he marched past us. He entered the portal room.

Carly kept rubbing against Mark until he cleared his throat.

"Do you know what this means?" Carly said, slowly letting go of him.

"Darius thinks we're into some triple sex action now?" I said.

"No. Well, maybe." She raised an eyebrow and looked at Mark again. "Darius only comes here when he brings in a new student."

"Wonder who the poor sucker is this time?" Mark said.

"A new student means someone's getting retired tomorrow. I'd bet the farm on it."

"Great," I sighed. "How do they choose who gets retired?"

"It's usually someone who's been here for a while and isn't performing."

Jackie seemed worried enough for me to create her a

memory-killing stone. She thought she'd be the next student retired. Even with Jackie's peculiar ways, I'd grown to really like her and the idea of her leaving sent me into a near panic.

"We have to stop it, then."

"Stop what?"

"I don't know. Stop the retirement."

"Don't get your panties in a wedge just yet. It should be a Blue."

I hated to admit it, but I felt relieved at it being a Blue. "I hope it's Leo." I tried to grab the words before they fell out.

Mark frowned.

"I didn't mean that," I said, but my slip showed on Mark's face and I saw him judging me. I was the worst person ever.

"Please. We all want Leo gone. That asshole's been here longer than anyone, but he keeps making rocks. His hate well must be infinite."

"What happened to make him so angry and filled with hate?" I wondered aloud.

"Well, he's with Jackie. So that shows he's insane. Maybe crazy people have a different level of emotions," Carly said.

He hadn't looked angry when Carly and I had seen them kissing.

The small hall ended and opened up to the long spoke. A group of Reds were staying near their houses while the Blues huddled around someone.

"There you guys are." Jackie ran up to us while glancing over at the Blues. "I've been looking everywhere. Why were you back in the portal area?"

"We—" I started to say.

"We just wanted to console Mark," Carly interrupted. "He's been crying a bunch over these stone wars. Kind of wanted to get him away from the Blues. They'd never let him hear the end of it if they saw him crying like a man-baby."

Mark pursed his lips. "Niagara Falls." He ran his fingers down his face. "Thanks for being there, ladies."

Jackie scrunched her mouth to one side and frowned as she stared at him. "Forget about the Blues. The Reds would tear him apart for being a little crybaby. Suck it up, Mark. You're not in grade school here. This is where the big boys play."

"Okay," Mark said. His fist was clenched at his side.

I covered it with my hand.

"And stop being a little bitch where Allie is concerned. She likes you, and if you don't start proving your worth, she's going to skip right down the road, leaving your Malki ass behind. A special like her could have any guy she wanted. Don't rest on your good looks. They don't amount to anything here."

Mark chuckled and shook his head. "Jackie…." I saw the witty retort building in his head, but he pressed his lips together and stopped.

"Good boy, Mark. Save it for the Blues. Speaking of the Blues…." She ran to the fence. "Your new member looks as pathetic as the rest of you. Nice heels. Did your pimp give those to you, or was there a sale at Whores 'R' Us?"

Jackie seemed to have a never-ending supply of insults

ready. I wondered if I should make her the memory stone. I was really interested in seeing what had made her this way, nature or nurture.

"Bitch, you'd better be stepping back. I can smell your wretched breath from here."

The Blues oohed and awed, exchanging high fives as the girl emerged from the Blues surrounding her.

I knew that voice. My heart stopped and I walked closer to the action. I had to be wrong.

"Is that...?" Mark began to ask.

I looked at him and shook my head in complete disbelief.

There, dressed in her tight Tetons shirt with her Friday F-me T-strap heels, stood my worst enemy. She faced Jackie with the same expression she'd given me for the last few years.

"Bridget?"

She did a double take and some of the bitchiness left her face.

"Allie? What are you doing here? Mark?"

"You two know each other?" Jackie said with her hands on her hips.

"Yeah, we go to high school together," I said with a transfixed gaze. Had she let go of her high school ways and adopted a new attitude toward me?

"Well, *I* go to school. *You* more or less loiter around with your stench," Bridget said and looked back at the Blues.

Nope.

"Hey, Mark. Good to see you, though. Is this where you two have been? The cops were at school today, asking about you.

They think you two ran away together."

"Why are you here?" I interrupted her conversation.

"Same reason you are, I'm sure. We're alchemists, right?"

"*You're* an alchemist?"

"What, did you think you have to be all emo to be special? Oh, you did, didn't you?" She leaned forward, putting her hands on her knees and pushing out her bottom lip.

I wanted to jump over the fence and punch her in the throat. I didn't want to hear any more words coming out of that face. My body shook, and I felt Mark putting his hands on me. I had felt wonderful coming here; it was a place where I could get away from my past and have a new fresh start, where I was special. A person like Bridget couldn't be the same as me.

"Oh, my, this is just sad," Jackie said. She reached into her pocket and threw a stone at Bridget, striking her in the neck. Choking, Bridget clutched her throat and struggled to get her next breath. After a minute of the Reds gathering to laugh at the spectacle, Bridget got to her feet and sneered at Jackie.

"Real mature, Jackie," Leo said, throwing a stone at me. I saw the black object flying at my face. Mark jumped in the way and it struck him on the chest. The rock broke and black goo spread over his shirt. Mark yelled and ripped off his shirt, flinging it to the ground.

"Oh my god," I heard Bridget say.

Turning to see what her codfish face was gawking at, I saw Mark picking his shirt up off the ground. I stared, much in the same way as Bridget. Those abs and chest. Ms. Duval had said,

"Stay strong," but this was Photoshop strong. Even the guys were lowering their brows, and probably questioning themselves.

"Put on your shirt, Malki. You're ruining every pair of panties in this place," Jackie blurted. "And probably some briefs as well."

Prying my eyes away from Mark, I looked at Bridget and we made eye contact. I thought I saw some of the hate leave her face and I hoped maybe my being the only person she knew here might smooth out the distance between us. Then she flipped me off and turned to the group of laughing Blues.

"What a skank," Jackie said with her hands on her hips and her head tilted. "She'll fit right in with the Blues."

I wished for a favor from the Almighty then. *Please retire Bridget tomorrow.*

CH. 18

Deegan was wearing his sash with the stones in class the next day. He jumped at each sound and kept looking at the ceiling while reaching for one of his stones. "As you know, the Academy was breached yesterday by a dark alchemist. Who knows how many would have gotten in here if not for Verity jumping us to a new location." He tugged on his sash. "In light of this, we're going to train room ten in some basic self-defense."

The class rumbled with enthusiasm. My stomach knotted up, thinking about that kid and his dad in the storage room. I was also worried about the impending retirement and Bridget being in the same building as me. The Blues seemed to know it as well. They didn't have the same spunk they usually did.

"Jackie, I hear you have a good throw. Can you come up

here?"

The Reds applauded her as she stood up from her chair. She took a deep bow and then walked over to the teacher.

"Here, put on a glove."

Jackie slid on a thin glove and held it up for the Reds to see. She turned back to Deegan. "Who do I get to peg?" She glanced at Leo sitting in the middle of the Blues.

"We're not hitting anyone. In fact, if we're attacked on a large scale, I expect all of you"—he gestured across the entire class—"to act as a unit."

"That's fine. I think most of the Blues are already a eunuch."

"No, I said...." Deegan shook his head and took a deep breath, then walked to the far side of the room. He pulled down a long sheet of paper with an outline of a human printed on it. "This represents a typical person. They will have their hands, face, arms and neck exposed. It's your task to hit them in the vulnerable areas."

Deegan walked back to Jackie and handed her a stone. "This is a practice stone. It doesn't do anything."

Jackie inspected the stone and then threw it at the paper target. The stone went through the paper and left a hole where its mouth would have been.

"Nicely done," Deegan said. Looking around the room, he said, "Let's get a Blue up here, Leo."

The Blues cheered and Leo took his time getting to the front of the class as Jackie took her seat. She leaned back in her chair and booed. He'd passed by her, touching her shoulder as he rounded the corner.

Leo threw and struck the neck. The Blues cheered at his accomplishment.

"Very good. Why don't we see what our special can do?" Deegan pointed at me.

I raised an eyebrow and he confirmed his point.

"Come on up, Allie."

The Reds applauded while the Blues jeered. I got up from my desk and knocked a spoon to the floor. After picking it up and placing it back on my desk, I made my way up to a toe-tapping Deegan.

"Okay, Allie. You can make stones, but can you use them? Sometimes it's more about the throw than the mix."

"Okay." I looked back with wide eyes at the Reds. Mark smiled and gave me a nod.

Deegan took my hand and put a stone in it. "Just do your best."

I gripped the golf-ball-sized stone and stared at the paper person on the wall, a mere outline of a person with two holes in it already. I glanced at the Blues. They were already snickering. I saw it in their stupid faces. I closed my eyes, as I really didn't want to see them watching me throw. The term "throwing like a girl" had been coined exclusively for me.

"Come on, you got this. Hit the thing in its paper balls," Jackie said.

I stared at the crotch area, reeled back and threw the stone. Maybe some divine intervention might happen and I'd strike the target … but no. It streaked across the room and struck a glass bowl five feet to the right of the paper man. The bowl shattered, and the pieces fell onto a stack of glass vials, breaking them and sending a million shards to the floor.

I winced and crunched up my shoulders at each of the horrific sounds. The Blues laughed and I couldn't bear to look at the Reds. Looking at the floor, I found my way back to my desk.

The rest of the class took a turn at the paper target and most made contact with it in some way. The target was a tattered mess by the time Deegan called Mark.

"I guess we should see what Mark can do," he said on a long exhale.

I alone started the clapping for him. The rest of the Reds joined in with a couple of soft claps before stopping.

Mark took the dummy stone in a gloved hand. "Name your part?" Mark asked.

Deegan rolled his eyes. "Fine. Right ear."

"His right, I assume?"

"Yes, his right."

Mark stood sideways. His eyes narrowed and I leaned forward. No one else had called out a target, and the ear was just a tiny bump on the outline of the paper man. Mark hurled the stone and it struck the paper with such force that it rippled. I couldn't see if he'd struck the ear or not.

The whole class leaned toward the shaking paper. Once it steadied, we could all see that what had been the right ear was now a hole.

"Very, very impressive."

No one in the room responded, but the Reds watched Mark walk back to his desk and for the first time, I saw something they had never given Mark before … respect.

"Nice throw," I whispered.

"I liked yours better," he replied, and I giggled.

The intercom warbled to life and I looked at the speaker on the wall. "All students, report to the hub for a retirement ceremony," Verity said in an upbeat tone.

Jackie clapped her hands and jumped up from her desk. The Blues slumped in their chairs at first, but Leo stood and soon the rest followed.

The Reds left the room first and I walked behind Mark. I didn't really think about the ceremony much now that I'd heard it was going to be a Blue. I didn't really know any Blues, besides the few horrible encounters I had had with them. I knew it would be wishful thinking to have Bridget be the one retired.

The hub filled up with students, divided by color. I rubbed the red scarf wrapped over my wrist. Some of the girls tied it in their hair or wore it as a kerchief, but the guys mostly wore it on their wrists.

Mark and Carly stood next to me. I wasn't sure where Jackie had gone, but I could hear her starting chants, taunting the Blues.

"It isn't normal to have two retirements so close together," Carly said. "They have to be doing this for the dad stuffed in the back room."

She had stated the obvious, and I definitely didn't want everyone around us hearing what we knew. If they needed to take a life, would the retirement be the life? If that was true, the person would be killed inside the globe, and not transported back home. If that was the case, everything in this place would be a sham. I took a deep breath and tried to convince myself otherwise.

I held my hand over my chest.

The crowd silenced and a few people mentioned Verity's name.

The crowd parted and gave her a clear path to the globe. She looked weary, but her quick steps didn't show it. Jumping up onto the edge of the stone wall surrounding the fountain, she waved.

"We have another joyous day as another student retires and goes back home."

The Reds clapped and I heard one screaming out, "It'd better be Leo."

I rubbed my hands together. I didn't want this happening to anyone, but the cheers drowned out my rational thoughts and I fought the urge to yell as well. I jammed my eyes shut and forced myself to think about what was right. This person, whoever it was, might be killed inside the globe.

Leo was standing near the front with his arms crossed. He seemed taller than all the others around him. Then I saw her. A few feet behind Leo stood Bridget. She hadn't noticed me, and it gave me a second to study her. She was wearing her blue in her hair, off to one side. Dammit, I hated that it looked cute. Would they pick Bridget after one day? Would they choose me after one day? The thought terrified me. Even if you truly went home through the globe, I didn't want to, not yet.

"Now, let's put our hands together for the lucky person." Verity leaned forward with her bright face.

I rolled my eyes and crossed my arms. How many of these ceremonies had Jackie seen? How many friends had she seen going into the globe?

"Ira Murray," Verity said with a big smile.

"Bullshit! It should have been a Blue!" Jackie yelled.

The Blues cheered as Leo stood with his arms in the air, turning to face them in triumph.

"Ira Murray, please come up here while I get the globe ready." Verity turned and threw a stone into the water. The water erupted around the globe and she threw another stone, freezing the water up onto the body of the woman holding the globe on her shoulder.

The globe opened up in slices again. Verity turned back around as Ira reached the fountain.

"Step right up, dear."

Ira took tiny steps, shuffling her feet. She kept looking back, blinking her eyes. I was standing in the back, but I thought they held tears. *Please, let me be wrong. Please, let Ira be going home.*

"Ira Murray has been an exemplary student and we all should strive to be more like her. Ira, we thank you for the time you spent here and we hope when you go back to the world, you can make it just a bit better than it was without you. Are you ready to go home?"

Ira looked back again. I took a few steps and she focused on me. I kept walking toward her and she kept watching.

"I ... I don't want to go in there." She turned and ran toward me.

I met her halfway and she looked up at me. Her sheet-white face greeted me and her hands were shaking. She glanced back at an advancing Verity. I didn't know what to do, so I hugged her tight.

Ira whispered in my ear, "Please, take care of Sir Joffrey." Tears filled her eyes.

"I will."

My heart leapt into my throat and I held her hand. Her eyes went from panic to a blank calmness. I looked behind her to Verity's hand on the back of her neck. Ira's limp hand slipped from mine.

"Ira?"

She didn't answer. Verity eyed me for a moment before turning Ira around and walking her to the fountain. She walked close to Ira and whispered in her ear as they reached the globe.

"She's ready," Verity called out.

Ira took the black bag and walked into the globe.

It closed around her and I gasped. I should have done something for Ira. I hadn't even gotten to say goodbye. I thought of her little pet hidden away in her room, her best friend, probably.

The globe vibrated, and streaks of light flew out from the small cracks. I rushed forward, close to Verity as she leaned near the silver boot of the woman holding the world. She reached to the boot and the stone fell into her bag.

Was that the final element they needed for the life stone? Thinking it could be Ira in that stone sent pains to my stomach. I looked around for a wastebasket as nausea washed over me. I pushed against my stomach and held it down.

"Thank you all for celebrating Ira's retirement. There will be no more classes today." Verity eyed me and hopped down from the wall. Her gaze didn't leave mine and I stepped back, hoping she wanted the person behind me.

"Allie, can I speak to you in my office?"

"I—"

"Now." Her big bright smile might have warmed most people, but to me it looked like a lion inviting a gazelle over for dinner.

CH. 19

I sat in the single chair facing her desk. The room felt smaller the second time around, and the mystique of the strange-looking bearded men on the walls had worn off. I took a deep breath and waited for Verity to speak.

"Yesterday, you made a very powerful stone."

I leaned forward and jumped on the statement. "I didn't know what I was doing. I just dumped all the ingredients in." Why was I being so defensive? I leaned back in my chair and tried to find a comfortable spot.

Verity took a small black bag and set it on the desk. The contents of the bag were most likely the remains of Ira. Or they could just be the common defensive stones all the professors carried around. Well, actually it seemed like everyone carried stones around. The way she looked at me, I thought I needed one on hand, just in case.

"I'm not disciplining you, I'm rewarding you." She brightened up enough to make her piercing eyes sting less. "If you could make that booster stone, I wonder what your limits are. I wonder if you could indeed make the stone I requested yesterday, but chose not to."

"I just get tired, is all. Making the stones is very draining."

"Perhaps." Verity smiled again. She seemed amused. "Is there something in the drinking water at Summerford?"

"I…. What do you mean?"

Someone knocked at her door.

"Can you get that?" Verity asked.

I walked to the door and opened it. Next to Priscilla stood Bridget. When she spotted me a wicked smile spread over her face.

"Look at this, two specials from one town, and at the same time." Verity stood behind me and I felt sandwiched between the two.

"Some are more special than others," Bridget said.

She was a special like me?

"That's all, Priscilla."

Verity motioned for Bridget to come in, but she was already strutting into the room. Pulling back her shoulders, she passed me. I wanted to shake her right then and there, and tell her all of this was so much bigger than our petty feud.

"I heard you broke the single-day record of stones made in

room twenty-eight?" Verity asked.

"Yeah, it wasn't hard once I figured it all out." Bridget sat on the chair.

I searched for another place to sit. *Guess I'll be standing.* Whatever. Let Bridget hang herself.

"Do you need me for anything else?" I asked.

"Yes. Please, be patient." Verity opened her cabinet.

Bridget got up from her seat and tried to see into the cabinet. She sat down once Verity had turned around with some materials. Turning in her seat, she looked up at me and winked. Could there be an evil wink? It looked like one. I frowned, not understanding.

"Now, Bridget, your friend here—"

"We're not friends," Bridget stated.

"Don't ever interrupt me again." Verity smacked the top of her desk.

Bridget slumped in the chair and crossed her arms.

"Allie couldn't make this stone. I was hoping you would give it a try."

"What does it do?" Bridget asked.

"It doesn't matter. It's a test to see if you can make it or not."

"I don't know. I can give it a try."

Verity winced. "It's not something you can simply *try* to do."

"I've only been here for a day, but one thing I know is, I can make these stones like no one else." Bridget looked over at me.

"Good. Then show me," Verity said.

Bridget pulled her chair closer to the desk.

"Just stand."

I hid my gaping mouth with a fake yawn, but I wanted to scream to Bridget not to make that stone. I didn't know what Verity planned on doing with a time stone, but I doubted it was to study it. I considered striking the bowl off the table. No, I had to wait for my moment. I had to get the life stone first; after that, all bets were off.

Bridget stood up from her chair and leaned over the desk, observing each item in turn. My heart began beating fast and I breathed hard through my nose. Maybe she wouldn't be able to make it. I hoped she wouldn't, but Verity had set out the challenge and I was sure Bridget would use her entire soul to make a stone I couldn't. She poured the liquid into a bowl and mixed the solids, the same as I had. There was no mist or clunk of a stone rolling around the bowl. Just a mixture of nothing.

"Did I pass?" Bridget asked, swirling the spoon around.

"No, you failed." Verity turned to me. "Allie, you're moving up to room five, and yes, before you throw a little hissy fit, you can bring your pet Malki along. As far as you go, Bridget, you'll be moving to room ten."

I shook my head. "Room five? I thought...."

"You thought no one made it past room ten? Well, when you can make a booster stone the way you did, we'd be wasting your talents teaching you anything less. I will see to your lessons personally."

My eye twitched and I wanted to scream at Verity about the things I knew she was doing and the people she kept in the storage room, but I only nodded. Telling her now would most definitely jeopardize Mark and keep me from getting that life stone. I leaned to my right, trying to get a better look at the cabinet holding all her goodies. The lock looked like a simple cabinet lock.

"You two can go now."

I didn't need to be told twice. I led the way to the teachers' hall with Bridget on my heels. She slammed the door behind me and even with my long strides, I heard her heels clicking along at a faster pace.

She brushed up against me and eyed me from the side. I glanced, not expecting to see her pleading look. It stopped me in my tracks, ten feet from the hub door.

"What?" I asked.

Bridget took a deep breath and glanced around the hall. "Listen, Allie, I know I gave you shit at Summerford." She closed her eyes for a second before scanning the hall and leaning closer. "This place is scaring the crap out of me. They *want* me to hate you, but I don't. They've asked me to do everything I can to make you hate me. They have ... things they're holding over me, so I'll continue to pretend I hate you, okay?"

Each word shocked me more than the last. They were holding something on Bridget, and she didn't hate me?

"Yeah, sure." Then I wondered if she was playing me, luring me in for some big prank. I tilted my head and tried to figure out her sincerity. "Are you crying?"

She wiped her face. "They keep making me relive my

trigger, or whatever they call it." Her crimson face shook as she spit out the words.

I knew what she was probably reliving. Mark had coaxed it out of her and had used a time stone to take it back. Bridget didn't remember it, but it still haunted me.

Bridget looked back at Verity's door. "I could have made that stone, but something told me not to help that woman."

I stared at the door. I had the same feeling, yet even with a crying Bridget in front of me, I didn't feel safe telling her that. "Look—"

She hugged me.

I tensed, expecting an attack, until her quivering jaw rested on my shoulder and her ragged breath landed on my neck. I hugged her back with my fingertips touching her back and my eyes open.

She backed away and wiped her face again, taking in a deep breath and sucking in her snot. "I'm sorry, but summoning the kind of hate I have for several hours today nearly broke me. How do you do it?"

"I don't know. I just feel it for a brief time and then let it go."

Bridget shook her head. "I can't let this go."

I opened my mouth to let her know that I knew what she was going through, but she wouldn't believe I had traveled back in time with Mark to right the wrong we'd done to her. I closed my mouth.

She laughed and wiped her face. "I guess I can consider myself lucky. Most of these saps can't seem to make anything."

Not comfortable with this new girl in front of me, I went back to the fundamentals. "Bridget, how is it you're an alchemist?"

"My mom is one. Oh, I'm so sorry, I forget about your mom."

At one point she and I had been friends. She knew a lot about me and used most of it to make fun of me, but she never mentioned my mom. It was a line she didn't cross, and I guessed that was one nice thing I could say about her.

"No biggie. Did your mom tell you about this place?"

Bridget looked at the high ceiling. "Not until a few days ago. Some guy named Darius was at our house a couple days after my mom showed me how to make a few stones. I thought she was going to have a heart attack, until he told her he was from the Academy and was taking me there." She laughed. "She seemed so happy to send me here. Why would she be happy to send me to a place like this?"

"Seems to be a theme."

She smirked and raised an eyebrow above her puffy eyes. "You and Mark have a thing still, right?"

I had an old knee-jerk reaction to avoid her eyes, but I continued to look at her as I answered. "Yes."

"Good for you. I about died when he took his shirt off today." She laughed and some of the friendly person I'd grown to like in my childhood reappeared.

"Yeah, well, they all treat him like a dog here because he can barely make stones."

"Your pet. I heard Verity."

I wanted to tell Bridget that Mark was ill, that he was dying and needed a life stone to save him. I could use a Blue on my side. I needed all the help I could get, but as much as I wanted to, I couldn't trust her.

After the urge left, I said, "We'd better get back to our houses."

"Blue *house*," she sang in her gangster voice, throwing a hand sign that looked like the letter "B." "Let me leave now, and you follow in a minute. I don't want them thinking I'm colluding with the enemy."

"Okay," I said.

Bridget walked the last ten feet and opened the door to the hub. I waited the allotted minute and went through the door. I picked up my pace as I thought about Verity going back to the back room with the life stone. That would be my best chance of stealing it from her. Maybe a few of those freeze stones would stop everyone while I did it. I would only need a second, and then I could use the life stone on Mark. I didn't care about the consequences afterwards.

I strode past the first Red house, searching the faces for Carly and Mark. I wanted to avoid them. I needed to get to the Reds' lab and make a few stones before we snuck to the back room holding that boy and his dad.

CH.20

"What's with the stones?" Mark pointed at my black sack.

I shrugged. "Protection." I glanced down at the bag and made sure it was closed tight. There was no reason to explain why I needed so many freeze stones. They'd find out soon enough.

We made our way down the endless hall and found the passageway into the storage room. Hiding behind a stack of boxes, we moved a few to give us a view of the dad. He was still sitting in the chair, with his son sitting in front of him. The dad hadn't moved an inch, still frozen in time. His son was sitting in a near-motionless state as well, slouched in his own chair, sleeping.

An hour passed and I knelt down next to the boxes, trying

to find a comfortable spot. My body was cramping, and I wanted to stand and stretch. Lifting my arms, I hit one of the cardboard boxes. Just my luck, it fell and hit the floor, and stones fell out of the box and bounced around.

The son stirred from his sleep and looked our way. "Is someone there?"

We ducked down and didn't move. His chair scratched across the floor and I held my breath as we huddled next to the stack of boxes. I closed my eyes and listened to the room. A few footsteps sounded, and were they getting louder?

A click and a thump echoed around the room, too many feet for a single person. I opened my eyes and dared a glance over the box.

"Is everything okay?" Verity asked, walking into the room. Deegan moved in behind her and stayed near the back wall. Verity ran a finger over the shoulder of the dad and moved closer to the boy.

The boy frowned and glanced at our boxes. "Yeah, I think I'm hallucinating. I haven't slept much."

"You're a fine son, Daniel. Are you ready to help your dad?"

"Did you get the stone to help my dad?"

"Almost. We just need one more thing, but it's going to be difficult for you."

"Anything. You just name it."

I knew the eagerness in his voice. I too would have done anything to help my mom, to bring her back. I also knew the danger of it and what Verity was about to have the boy do. I took a deep breath and waited for my moment.

Verity moved to the dad and ran her hand over the side of his face. She leaned in close and I saw her mouth moving next to his ear. Then she leaned back and said, "As you know, to break him free, we need a life stone. But what you probably didn't know is what it takes to make one."

"Just get me the ingredients. I feel as if I could make the philosopher's stone right now," Daniel said with his fists clenched at his sides.

"I'm sure you feel like you could, but this one only takes a couple of stones, held by a person who loves their father very much."

"I do. I love him."

"I know." Verity turned to him and with her gloved hands took out two stones from her pouch. Her gaze passed over our stack of boxes and I ducked down. I loosened the top string on my sack and picked my targets. I wasn't the best thrower, but how could fate let me fail when Mark's life depended on it?

Mark, wide-eyed, shook his head, glancing down at my hand.

Carly touched my arm and shook her head as well. They didn't understand that I had to get the life stone. And once they made one … I touched the bag of stones at my side and adjusted the glove on my hand. My fingers tightened over one of the stones.

"You just sit in that chair and with your bare hands, touch the stones together," Verity instructed.

At her words, I lifted up to watch her hold her hands in front of Daniel.

"These two stones."

"That's it?" he asked.

I controlled my breathing and timed my attack. Deegan would be looking my way, but I thought I could take Verity by surprise easily enough.

Verity cocked her head and shrugged. "Yes, but it's very powerful. You have to make sure you hold the stones together all the way to the end." She talked as if she was addressing a child.

"How will I know when it's the end?" He licked his lips and stepped toward her.

I knew something terrible would happen if he touched those stones together. I'd have to find another way for Mark. I wouldn't stay behind this stack of boxes and watch a kid die. Breathing deeply, I kept my hand deep in my stone sack. I wasn't sure which stone I was holding, but it didn't really matter. They would all work fine.

"Trust me, you'll know when it's over," Verity said. "Are you ready?"

Daniel sat in the metal chair facing his dad and nodded. "Give them to me."

Verity smiled, and her gaze passed over our boxes. I froze in fear, but her eyes didn't lock on me. I watched as she got close to the dad and leaned in with a wicked smile. Whispering into his ear again, she caressed the sides of his face and tilted his body forward a tad, giving him a perfect line of sight. She winked and turned back to the son, pulling the stones from her pouch.

This was it. I had only one chance to get it right.

Daniel wiped his hands on his jeans. Verity held the stones out.

My insides screamed to make it stop. I grabbed the stones with every intention of jumping out and hurling them at Verity. Mark touched me and I felt a cold sensation melting over the back of my hand. I opened my eyes wide and they stuck there. My mouth hung open in shock and rage filled me with so much heat I thought I could start a fire just by touching the boxes next to me. But I couldn't move.

He whispered, "I'm sorry."

I wanted to kick him and scratch his pretty face. How could he have put a freeze stone on me? I couldn't use my throat muscles to yell and warn Daniel. Even worse, I watched as Verity placed the two stones in his palms.

"Merge them, quickly." Verity moved out of the way so as to allow Daniel and his father a direct view.

No!

Daniel clapped his hands together and the stones cracked. A light grew from within his grasp, and Verity took a few more steps back. The light reached a blinding level in a few seconds.

I wanted to squint, but I couldn't even blink. The light grew so bright, I couldn't see him anymore. Then came the scream, a deep guttural noise, steadily rising in volume and tone, until it was an inhuman screech. I wanted to cover my ears. The whole room filled with the white light and the sounds of a person dying. I wanted to kill Mark for making me watch something so horrible.

Daniel's screams continued and I thought of his father, sitting directly across from him. I didn't even know his name. I felt a tear sliding down my frozen face. He and I were locked into seeing the horror, but I'd never hugged Daniel or tucked him into bed; I'd never told him a story or shared a life with him. I couldn't imagine the pain the dad was going through, watching his offspring being consumed directly in front of him and not being able to move a muscle or look away.

Feeling a warm sensation around my face, I blinked and shut my eyes and blocked out some of the blinding light. Even behind my eyelids, colors danced in my vision. Now, if I could only move my hands to cover my ears. The scream seemed to be never-ending. It wasn't humanly possible to have that much breath released from someone's body. The stones had to be draining him of everything from the inside.

Then it stopped. A second into the deafening silence, the light ended and the room fell dark. I opened my eyes at the sound of a stone hitting metal. The bright light had burned into my vision and I had trouble focusing on anything in the blur. I blinked hard, trying to clear my eyes, and found the chair Daniel had been sitting on. A stone lay on the steel chair, rolling around its concave surface before stopping. It was the last remnant of Daniel and the creation of a life stone.

I stared at the stone. It was something I'd been consumed with getting and there it was, a few seconds' dash from my grasp. But now, knowing how it had been created, I didn't want anything to do with it.

"He had some real gumption there at the end, don't you think, Dave?" Verity addressed the dad. She walked to the chair and picked up the stone, holding it above her, turning it in the light.

I desperately wanted my arms to function. I wanted to make Verity and the rest of them pay. *Damned Mark!*

I looked at him, wishing I could slap his face. He didn't look at me, choosing to keep his attention on Verity. His whole body shook and his face was crimson. Little bits of spittle flew from his mouth.

"I hope it was worth it ... you know, coming into my house, acting like you're somebody important. Don't worry, though. I'll find a way to send the others a message about what happened to you." She glanced back at the empty steel chair. "And your son."

She walked past Dave and left the room, with Deegan following close behind. My mouth moved, but my throat still wasn't functioning.

Mark hugged me awkwardly around my frozen limbs. "I'm so sorry. They would have killed you in a split second if you tried to interfere."

"There's nothing we could have done," Carly added from her position on the floor. Tears fell from her eyes and she sniffled.

I didn't believe her. They were both insane and wrong. We had just watched a boy destroy himself in a horrific way, directly in front of his father, and we'd done nothing. No, *they* had done nothing.

A warm feeling rushed around my neck and I swallowed.

"I hate you both," I tried to say, but the words came out garbled. Looking at Mark's face, I realized that he knew what I'd said anyway.

"I couldn't let you die, Allie." He shook his head and touched my shoulder.

I jerked, wanting to hit his hand off, but my arms still wouldn't work. "Don't touch me. I could have stopped it."

Carly shook her head and wiped her face. "No, you couldn't. She's fast, too fast for us. I've seen her demonstrations," she whispered. "Maybe if we all came prepared…."

The warm feeling spread over my body and I felt my fingers obeying my commands. Soon, all of my muscles began responding to my requests … not accurately, but at least they were responding.

I fell forward and Mark caught me. I tried my best to hit him and fell sideways instead. He ignored my outburst and lifted me to my feet before hoisting me up into his arms like a child.

"I think we'd better get out of here," Mark said.

"Wait," I interrupted. "I can walk."

Mark set me down on my feet. Pushing him back, I stared at Dave. His son had sacrificed himself under the assumption that his dad would be saved. In the end, they were both lost now. I took a step toward him and put my hand up to halt Mark from stopping me. I had a few nasty stones in my sack and would use them if I had to, but my sneer alone kept him back.

With each small, unsteady step across the floor, I glanced at the doorway the teachers left through. I wondered if it led back to Verity. I knew if I could manage a throw, I would have staggered down the hall after the bitch.

Dave was sitting propped up, looking at the empty metal chair. I stared at his eyes and thought they might follow me, or that his expression might alter. But nothing changed. He looked dead, and I cursed myself for making the stone that had put him there.

I touched his shoulder and pushed him back a little, so he wouldn't have to stare at the spot his son had just vacated. Leaning close to his ear, I whispered everything I wanted to tell him before I made my way toward the main corridor. I didn't look at Carly or Mark as I passed them, but I heard their footsteps behind me as I walked down the long hall.

After a prolonged silence, Carly spoke. "It's right here." She pointed to a hall I had just missed.

I adjusted my direction and walked down the dark passage. The light from Carly's glow stone lit the way from behind me. My legs loosened up and I managed a near-normal walk. I shook my whole body, trying to get rid of the last remnants of being frozen. I stopped at the portal room and turned to face them.

"I know I can't say anything past these doors, so I'll say this now to clear up any confusion. If you ever stop me from saving a life again...."

"We stopped you from killing yourself, you ditz, and probably both of us as well. The next time you want to put my life in danger, you'd better ask me first," Carly said. She wiped the sweat from her forehead with a trembling hand.

I opened my mouth and raised a finger but then stopped. I hadn't thought of them. I'd assumed I could freeze Verity, but what if I'd failed? What would she have done to the people who'd conspired with me? I pursed my lips together and didn't say a word.

"Don't you get it? This whole place is a lie. Verity just killed a student to prove a point. If she finds out we know anything, we'll be back in that room."

"Or the globe," Mark added.

"Yeah, we can't tell a single person what we saw." Carly paced in the tiny hallway. "I wish I could unsee this. I wish I'd never come to this blasted Academy in the first place."

I couldn't keep this inside. My soul had filled with sorrow, and if I had to bottle up another thing in my life, I felt as if I might explode. The words wanted to pour from my mouth, but I knew if I started I wouldn't stop. I turned and pushed open the stone wall, then darted across the small room. I didn't want to look at Mark and Carly. I didn't want to look at anyone.

The bright light and Daniel's screams wouldn't leave my head, so I ran. My legs felt free and I didn't look back. I ran all the way to my house door and up the stairs. When I reached my bedroom, I slammed the door behind me and jumped on my bed, burying my face in the pillow.

Another thought hit me and I wanted to scream. Tomorrow, room five, just me and Verity. Life stone or not, I had to find a way out of the Academy.

CH.21

The next morning, I crossed the hub with Mark a few paces behind. A couple of harsh looks were all it took to get some distance. I slowed down near the statue of Clymene. It'd once inspired the woman inside of me, thinking of her holding the world up, protecting it. But now I knew she wasn't holding the world up ... she was being crushed. This statue was just a snapshot of her futile struggle against the overwhelming pressure above her. Another second and the world would smash her into nothingness.

Many of the Blues and Reds walked by, but I didn't pay attention to them. I kept my focus on room five. Verity was sitting in that room, probably waiting for me with her vapid smile and endless pit of lies, hoping I'd make a stone for her. A stone she might use to harm others, or maybe even kill someone else. I wouldn't make a single stone again for the Academy.

"Whatever you want to do in there, raise holy hell, burn the place to the ground, I'm right there with you," Mark said.

I glanced back at him and kept walking. It was the right thing to say, and he knew it. I wanted him by my side and I wanted to burn this whole freaking place down, but I also wanted to be smart about it. They were right last night in stopping me. At best, I'd have saved the boy and we'd still be stuck in the Academy, eventually being killed. At worst, we'd all have ended up dead on the spot.

Room five.

A group of Reds and Blues loitered near me. I heard their whispered comments and questions. I hadn't told anyone but Mark and Carly about my upgraded status; and as far as Carly knew, no one had ever gotten above room ten. They watched as I stopped in front of the door and knocked.

I crossed my arms and tapped my foot. The Blues snickered and probably thought I had been pranked, but eventually the door opened. Verity stood there, studying me from top to bottom. I wanted to punch her in the throat and rip her fingernails off one at a time.

"Hello, Verity."

"President Verity," she corrected me. "Come in, and bring your toy with you, if you must."

I entered the classroom and stood at the doorway. I wasn't sure what I'd been expecting, but it wasn't a small library. Books lined the walls and only a few desks filled the middle of the room. I gasped at the sight. I hadn't seen a single book since arriving at the Academy. I couldn't help but smile. If I could have one alchemist wish, it would have been to have a library at my disposal.

A girl sitting at one of the desks turned and looked back at me.

"What's she doing here?" I asked.

"We needed a special stone made last night and when I looked for you, you couldn't be found." She raised an eyebrow. "Bridget filled in for you and did a marvelous job. Where were you?"

"I was —"

"It was my fault," Mark interrupted. "I took her to a hidden section of the Red house ... to be alone."

Verity gave the slightest roll of her eyes while she sighed. "Keep it in your pants. But if you must, please use the Academy-provided protection." She glared at him. "We can't have little ones running around here, now, can we?"

She turned and walked to her desk at the end of the room. The glow of the books surrounding me faded, and I felt empty again. Verity appeared as casual as always. Maybe murdering people didn't affect her.

Bridget turned and gave me a blank look. I stared at her and she turned back around as I sat behind her. I wondered which version of her I'd be getting.

"I can smell your foulness from here. Can you move farther back?" she said.

Well, that was cleared up.

I ignored the comment, but felt my anger building. This was the same thing I had done at Summerford, staring at the back of Bridget's head. Now we were who knew where. The hug and laughter we'd shared in the teachers' hall hung around me like a ghost and I started to question if it had really happened.

Mark took the seat next to me as Verity pulled a few dusty books from the shelves and placed them on the desk. The soft lighting illuminated the dust stirring up. The room smelled old and dusty, not like the sanitary feel of the other rooms.

"Pardon me. It's been a while since I've had a special to teach, let alone two." She thumbed open a book and skipped past a few pages. "Here we are. Have any of you heard of the alchemist wars of 1747?"

I shook my head.

"I suppose it isn't something taught in public school." She turned another page. "It was thought that one side had obtained the knowledge to create a philosopher's stone." Verity looked up from her book. "Come on, now. Tell me you've heard of the philosopher's stone?"

Bridget glanced back at me and shrugged. It sounded familiar for some reason, but I shook my head, failing to grasp it.

Verity sighed and closed the book. "There is an end game for alchemists, a stone whose powers are beyond comprehension. Some say it can give alchemists the power of eternal life; others feel it's the stone that will turn any metal into gold." She smirked. "A long time ago, a great and terrible war started over this stone and in the end, both sides took great losses, both personal and historical. In fact, almost all of the documentation on this stone was destroyed by one side or the other in this war. We've pieced together many of the stone diagrams, but most remain a mystery. I'm sad to say that the dark alchemists have been trying to destroy us good alchemists for a great many centuries." Verity walked to the front of her desk.

"I've never heard of such things. Why doesn't the world know about us?" Bridget asked.

"In the past, alchemists were more open about their studies, but most historians passed them off as pre-chemists at best. If anyone got close to knowing what we could make, a simple memory stone would be used."

I took a deep breath and squeezed my hands under the desk. I wanted to throw questions at her, like, why she would kill that man's son directly in front of him? How could she not be considered dark for the deeds she'd done? I kept my mouth shut for fear of spilling the wrong words and exposing Mark.

"It just doesn't seem possible to hide all of this." Bridget waved her hand around the room.

"You'd be amazed by what people choose to believe and what they choose to ignore." Verity turned back to her desk and grabbed the dusty book. "This whole room is filled with knowledge about alchemy. It's a collection some would kill for, just to look at for a few hours, and you have me as a personal guide. I know all of these books. I've pored over them and tried to make many of the stones. Some I can, and some I can't. That's why you're here, in this room with me. Room ten is too remedial. This room will challenge you. I will be directing you each day to make a particular stone. Whoever makes the stone first will have a significant victory for their house."

I wanted to throw up. She still wanted to play the houses against each other, even when I knew she'd killed one of us. I'd made a promise to Daniel's father, and I intended to find a way to keep it.

"Like what?" Bridget asked.

"I won't say specifically, but I will tell you this: you'll want to win for the good of everyone around you." Verity stared at Mark and then at the book in her hands. "Today's stone is one we've been trying to make for a long time. Aluminum dust, universal solvent, and two more ingredients. It's best you don't know what they are."

Probably baby seal oil or something equally awful. I could just picture Verity going out onto the surface of Antarctica to steal penguin eggs and club baby whales popping up for a breath.

"Is there something amusing, Allie?" she asked.

"No."

"Good, because these ingredients are of the highest level and one drop can be the accumulation of years of work. Come on up here and get them."

I hesitated at first, but walked to her desk to find a selection of vials and bowls divided into two pairs. I took the left-hand group of materials and carried them back to my desk.

Mark made like he was going to get up, and Verity spoke.

"Please, Mark. Don't kid yourself. The only reason you're here is because Allie thinks you help her make stones."

He didn't say anything, but mouthed a few words as he sat back down.

"Now, these aren't simple stones that you'd see in room twenty-eight. These are going to take everything you've got."

"What does it do?" Bridget asked.

"Let's not worry about what the stone does, as much as how you're going to make it."

Bridget clattered around the vials and the bowl of silver powder. She turned back to me so Verity couldn't see her. Her eyes went wide and she mouthed the word "no" to me. She widened her eyes even farther to punch home her meaning.

Of course it could be a trick, something to throw me off my game, to allow her a chance to make the stone first and shove whatever horrible thing the loser got in my face.

The aluminum powder sat in front of me in a bowl. I thought about aluminum being toxic and wondered if I should ask for a mask. Oh, well, I'd just hold my breath. I poured in a small amount of powder. Dust particles didn't float around like I'd feared. All of it clumped together at the bottom of the bowl.

I cleared my head as I took the vial of opaque yellow fluid and poured it in. The next one looked like plain water and had a pungent, vinegary smell. I shook as I poured in the solvent, while keeping my thoughts clear of any emotion.

With wooden spoon in hand, I stirred for what seemed like a long time, until I finally dropped it into the bowl. I took a deep breath and felt dizzy from the pressure I'd put on my head.

Verity watched from the front of the classroom. She frowned as I gave up and took a long breath when Bridget did the same. We had both failed to make the stone, and for another moment, I felt a bit of the poison Bridget had put in my blood drain out.

"You both failed. Very interesting." Verity rubbed her chin and moved away from her desk. "I thought you two bitches might be up to something." Hate filled her face.

I leaned back in the chair, unable to avoid her piercing stare.

"I tried my hardest—" Bridget began to say, but Verity stuck a hand in her face.

"Don't even think for one second that you two have me fooled. You think I would waste good ingredients on this testing stone? Yes, that's right, this was a test. I put out the simplest of stones that even your pet could have made." Verity closed her eyes and crossed her arms. "I blame myself." She smiled, and I recoiled from it. It was the same smile she'd given Dave before she murdered his son. "I haven't properly motivated you. I haven't given you a sufficient reason to make a stone, now, have I?"

"I'm sure we can make a stone. Just give us another chance," Bridget whined.

"I know you will. Bridget, if you can't make this next stone, I'm going to use a freeze stone on you and turn you over to some of the eager boys in the Red house. I'll make sure they have enough freeze stones to do whatever it is they want to do to you for a long and horrible time. And don't worry, you'll be awake enough to hear and feel everything."

Bridget whimpered and lowered her head. Verity turned to me and in an instant, threw a stone.

I recoiled, protecting my face, and I heard Mark moan. He held his hand and shook it. The tips of his fingers turned blue, and then it traveled down his fingers into his hand. His whole hand turned blue in under a minute. He kept shaking his hand and wincing from the pain.

"You're tough, Mark. Most people would be screaming by now." She stared at me with her hateful glare. "If the blue reaches his heart, he'll die. Not even a life stone would bring him back." She walked to the front of the room and continued. "Now, this is the real stone I need you to make." She pulled a beige cloth off a stand in the corner of the room. "You'd better hurry, Allie. He doesn't have much time."

Mark shook his head.

"If he dies, I will never make another stone for you again." I glanced at Mark and put my shaking hands under the desk.

Verity took a few steps closer. "Each second you wait, it works farther into his muscles, tearing down tissue and weakening his bones. How's the arm, Mark?"

I twitched at each side effect. Mark shook his head again, but he looked paler and gripped his arm tight. His face was filled with pain.

"Don't do it. I'll be fine," Mark croaked out. I saw the panic building in his face as he stretched his arm out from his body as far as he could.

Verity hovered near me with a smile. She knew she had me, and the rage filled me enough that I was sure I could have made any stone she wanted me to. "Fine, I'll make it. But heal him first."

"No. Is it getting close to the shoulder yet?"

Mark gripped his shoulder. The blue had already passed his elbow and was creeping toward his bicep.

"It won't be long now."

"Fine, but if you don't cure him, I'm going to use the stone I make on you."

Verity laughed. "You can try."

I would make a stupid stone, if it meant saving him. Just like the first stone, she'd laid out two sets of ingredients. I didn't pay attention to what they were and collected them. I set each vial on my desk and set my old mixing bowl on the floor next to me.

"Don't do this," Mark begged, holding his shoulder.

"Mark, shut up." I might have been too sharp with him, but I was already summoning my anger. Thinking of what Verity had done last night and what she'd threatened to do to Bridget was enough cause for anger. Toss in Mark dying next to me, and it sent me to an edge I hadn't known existed.

I didn't keep track of the ingredients as I poured them in. I didn't care if I was making a freaking atom bomb for Verity; I couldn't let Mark just die next to me. The wooden spoon dug into my hand as I gripped it hard. I spun the spoon around the bowl and waited for the sound of the stone dropping.

It plunked and clanked around the glass bowl. I grabbed it

with a black cloth and cocked back my hand, ready to throw.

"Done. Now stop it. Whatever you did to him, stop it now."

She glanced at Mark and threw a stone at him, hitting him in the chest. He caught it with his blue arm and the stone melted into his skin. He yelled in pain, jumped from the desk and stumbled past me, hitting the wall of books. He fell to the floor, grabbing at his arm.

A moment later, relief swept over his face and he wiggled his fingers. The blue was receding and the tan color of his skin returning. He stood and stretched out his hand, smiling.

I dumped the stone into the bowl and ran to Mark.

Verity tiptoed closer, staring at the contents of the bowl. Her brow crunched around her eyes as she approached and then her eyes went wide when she spotted the stone in the bowl. Her mouth hung open and she licked her lips. Lifting the bowl off my table, she cradled it like a mother holding her newborn child.

Another stone clunked around Bridget's bowl. "Done." She slumped in her chair and folded her arms.

I thought I heard her sniffling.

Verity turned to her with her mouth still open and gave her bowl a questioning look. She placed my bowl next to Bridget's.

"You both can leave. You too, Mark." Verity leaned over the desk, staring at the two bowls.

Bridget got up and rushed out of the room.

I touched Mark's arm. It felt ice cold, but at least the color had returned and it looked completely normal again. He made a tight fist and sneered at Verity's back.

"Leave," she snapped.

I pulled on him and we left room five.

Bridget was standing near the door, bent over with her hands on her knees, looking red in the eyes. Mark closed the door to room five and I took a deep breath. I had saved Mark, but at what cost? What had we made?

"You okay?" he asked Bridget.

"I feel like we just made something very terrible for her," Bridget said.

"I have the same feeling. Do you know what we made, Mark?" I said.

"I'm not sure. I've never seen those ingredients in my mom's collection."

"I can't come back here tomorrow and make another stone for her. It's going to kill me. Maybe not tomorrow or the next day, but if I have to keep doing this, I'm going to want to die." Tears filled Bridget's eyes.

I eyed the elevator door next to room five. "We won't have to stay here for another day."

"What are you up to?" Mark asked.

I clenched my jaw. The last piece of the puzzle had fallen into place and I hadn't even realized it. "I have a few things to get, and then, yeah, we're getting out of here." I just needed enough time to make a few stones.

CH.22

"What's going on in there?" Jackie called from the street below my window.

"Don't answer her," I begged. She would never take silence as an answer. "Take off your shirt and pants."

"Excuse me?" Mark had surprised eyes and a big, stupid grin on his face, but his hands had already moved to the buttons on his pants.

"We need to have a reason to be alone. If we don't, she'll force us down to another one of her block parties." I reached to the bottom of my shirt and pulled it over my head.

Mark stared at me in my bra. "This is a plan I can get behind." He tore off his shirt and pants in two seconds flat.

Staring at his body, I stopped at the red boxers. My breath

clenched in my throat, and I totally forgot what we were getting undressed for. Mark slid onto the bed and crawled under the sheet.

"You look good without a shirt," he said.

I looked down at my heaving chest, stuffed in a red bra. *Huh, we match.* Rolling my eyes, I jumped into bed next to him. "Don't get any ideas," I warned.

The door shot open and Jackie stood on the other side. Her mouth hung low as she took in the scene. "You little sluts," she said in a half-playful, half-jealous tone. "No wonder you've been hiding in here."

I pulled up the sheet to cover my chest. Mark rolled over onto his stomach.

"Can we have some privacy?" I asked.

Jackie ignored my request and skipped across the room. Sitting on the bed by Mark's feet, she continued, "I wouldn't be a very good house leader if I didn't make sure my peeps were being safe, now, would I?" She reached into her pocket and pulled out a condom. She placed it on Mark's bare back and then patted him on the butt. "Very nice ass, Mark." Ogling him, she looked at every inch of his body with hunger. "Damn."

"Jackie, get the hell out of here," I warned.

She laughed, but got off the bed. "Don't worry, I'll make sure no one comes up here to interrupt." She tapped her teeth with one of her fingers. "Do you need any pointers, Mark? I can tell you right now what kind of attention a girl like Allie deserves."

"No," I replied for him.

"The first thing you should know about a woman, down there, is —"

"Get out!" I yelled, and threw a pillow at her.

She laughed again, as if it was the funniest thing in the world. "Fine, fine, I'm gone." She rushed past the open door and reached back to grab it closed.

I let out the longest breath of my life. My body felt sweaty and I fanned my chest.

"She's an interesting one," Mark said, sitting up.

"More like crazy."

"I don't know. I would have loved to hear her advice about a woman's *down there* region." He smirked and held the condom in his hands.

I hit him with a pillow. "If you can help me figure out how to make a portal-the-hell-out-of-here stone, I'll consider giving you a personal lesson." As if I had a clue, but Mark perked up at the offer.

Looking at my stomach and chest, he nodded. "I'm going to hold you to that."

I pulled my shirt back over my head. Mark took much longer to put his clothes back on.

"So, what's this plan of yours? I've seen it on your face since we left room five," Mark said.

"The elevator."

"The one where Deegan had to dig through a large key ring that he keeps on his person, just to get it open? And how do we even know where we are right now? We wouldn't last one hour in Antarctica."

I took a deep breath and tried to come up with an answer. "I just know we have to get out of here. After seeing what happened to Daniel, I can't make another stone for her." Mark opened his mouth, but I talked over him. "She'll find another way to 'motivate' me tomorrow and the day after that."

"I agree with you. You can't make another thing for her. I have a terrible feeling each time, like we're doing a great wrong."

"You don't think I know? I made a freaking stone that locked that Dave guy into a perpetual nightmare. Who knows what my other stones have done?" It was hard to keep a serious tone while Mark was sitting at the end of my bed, shirtless.

"Fine, but we have to get the key from Deegan."

"Oh, God, yes, *yes*. Mark!"

He stared at me with a shocked expression and a bit of color hit his cheeks.

"Jackie needs to hear that." I shrugged. "I bet I just bought us a little more time before her strange ass comes up here to interfere again."

Mark didn't say anything for a while and then swallowed.

"You okay?"

"Yeah. I'm just not used to you calling my name out like that."

I smiled and covered my face. "Leave Deegan to me, but I need to make a few more stones to prepare."

We snuck down the stairs. A few Reds glanced at us but kept talking. We walked to the door behind the stairs.

"What if Jackie is in there?" I asked.

"So what if I am?"

I winced and turned to see her standing there with a cocked brow. "Oh, hey, Jackie," I offered lamely. "We were just...." I glanced to Mark for help.

"We were just looking for more protection. It kind of went quick."

I lit up at the thought and nodded.

Jackie frowned. "What's going on? And don't think for a second I believed your cat-like screeching up there, Allie."

I covered my face with my hand and tried to wipe the embarrassment away. "Come with us." I pushed the door open and found a few people sitting at various tables around the room. Some had materials set in front of them, while others were mingling in small groups.

"Everyone out," Jackie said. "Now," she added, and waved her hand at the door over and over again.

She got a few grunts and complaints, but they all left.

Jackie turned to us. "Now, why don't you tell me what selling your good name was worth?"

I didn't listen as I rushed around the room, grabbing the ingredients I needed. Jackie huffed as I remained silent, but I was going to make these stones before I worried about placating her. In a few minutes I had the stones I needed stuffed in my sack. I turned to Jackie.

"We found a way out of here."

The building shook.

"Not again, not this soon." Jackie stared at the ceiling.

"Wait, what do you mean, you found a way out of here?"

Verity's voice sounded muffled in the stone room, but we heard it well enough. "All students, report to your rooms to make booster stones. Room five, report to room ten."

Mark winced, grabbed at his stomach and fell to one knee.

I reached down to him. "Are you okay?"

"I'm fine." He grunted in pain and balled up.

"Diarrhea? I told you to stay away from the mystery meat in the cafeteria." Jackie shook her head.

I scowled at her. "It's not from bad meat. He's ill."

The building shook again.

"We'd better get to our classroom. You'll disappear if they find out you didn't help with the booster stones."

"Everyone will be gone…" I said to myself.

"What?" Jackie asked.

I pointed to the ceiling. "This is going to be our best chance of getting out of here."

I remembered the chaos it had created last time. Best of all, Verity would be locked in, trying to portal the whole academy.

Mark groaned again and rolled to the floor in a fetal position.

"Is he going to be all right?" Jackie asked, and knelt down next to him.

"Go. I'll help Mark," I said.

Jackie frowned and stood with her arms crossed. "If you two found a way out, I'm not leaving your side."

"Just go," I yelled. "I'll explain it all to you later."

"Fine." She stomped from the room just as the building shook again.

I wondered if another outsiders would be dropping in this time. Did the teachers have more suspended animation stones? I don't think I could consciously hurt another person again. Then I thought of the stone I'd made today. I didn't remember much, but it was a creamy, opaque color. I'd never seen another stone like it.

Mark winced again but got to his knees. I'd never seen him this bad, and I didn't know how to comfort him, but I knew what he needed. It was time.

I touched his head. "I'm going to leave you here, but I'll be back soon with something that will help you."

"I can make it." He got to his feet and winced in pain. "It comes and goes. This one is a bit worse." He looked at the floor and held his stomach. "I'm sorry you had to see this."

The lie his mom had told him for his whole life couldn't be contained. "Mark, you're not well. Your mom told me about your condition and how she's kept it at bay your whole life, but now nothing works. She sent me here specifically to get what's in Verity's office right now. A life stone."

Mark, bewildered, took a step back. "That kid *died* to make that stone. I wouldn't use it even if you did have it. It's all kinds of darkness. I'd rather die naturally with my soul intact, versus live and be damned."

"This isn't about wrong or right, Mark," I said between my teeth. "Stay here and I'll be back in ten minutes. Don't come for me. Promise?"

He pursed his lips and didn't say a word. I didn't like the way he was looking at me, like he didn't know me. I couldn't take that look and left the room. I'd felt the same way when I first saw the life stone, sitting on the chair … the remains of Daniel. The stone felt like a poison pill and if I had touched it, I would never have been the same. Maybe it still held the same fate for me, but sometimes your soul is a small price to pay to save the ones you care for.

With the sack of stones at my side, I walked down the spoke. Reds filled one side, and Blues the other. I searched across the street for Bridget. I couldn't leave her behind.

Someone bumped up against me. "You want to tell me what's going on there, Sporty Spice?" Jackie asked as she looked forward.

Another person bumped the other side of me. "Yeah, what's this I hear about you finding a way out?" Carly added.

I motioned for them to come close as we walked toward the hub. "I'm taking the elevator up and out of here. I don't care where we are."

"I thought you might have made some rope, or dug a tunnel," Jackie said.

I shushed her and looked at the Reds near us. "I need something first. Can you two cover for me in room ten?"

"Yeah," Carly agreed.

"Good. Meet me back in the stone room in ten minutes and we can come up with a proper way to secure the keys."

They broke off toward room ten as we entered the hub. I walked behind them a ways, getting blocked by the people rushing by. I spotted Verity talking with Deegan and Priscilla. I walked closer to them, careful to keep out of view.

The din made it hard to hear what they were saying, but Verity seemed furious and pointed to the teachers' hall. I heard one distinct word: "Dave."

Priscilla nodded and ran toward the teachers' hall. Deegan stepped closer to Verity and she placed an opaque, creamy stone in his gloved hand. The very stone I had made for Verity not long ago. His mouth hung open as he stared at it.

"Are you sure?" he asked.

"Do it."

Deegan turned and ran to the outer wall. I was sure he was going to the stone hole to launch it to the dark alchemists above. I didn't want to think of what horrible thing I had created this time, so I ran. Deegan would be next, but first I had to concentrate on getting the one thing I needed before leaving this place.

Next to my exit, I glanced around and darted to the teachers' hall door. The crowd in the hub had thinned greatly, as many students had already made their way into the classrooms. Verity walked toward the fountain with her back to me. Not sure what was waiting on the other side of the teachers' hall door, I pulled out a stone.

Opening the door, I slid into the corridor. Alone, I dropped the stone back into my pocket. I ran down the hall, glancing at the painted door cracked open to the endless hall I'd gotten lost in. Priscilla was probably running to Dave this very moment.

I stopped at Verity's large double door and when I twisted the handle, it opened. I breathed in relief. I only had enough stones to deal with the locks on the cabinet.

I closed the door behind me and passed by the paintings and ornate wood carvings all around the room. I darted to the cabinet behind her desk and pulled out an ice stone, almost pure white with blue specks on it.

I pressed it against the lock and watched it freeze into a block of ice. Then I took out a fire stone, half red and half black. Leaning far back, I pushed the stone onto the icy lock. When the stone touched it, it exploded. Bits and pieces of wood flew all around me, and the cabinet door swung open.

Stones were stacked nicely in egg cartons, filling much of the cabinet. I didn't think the life stone would be in anything like the other stones. I pulled a few bags from the cabinet and then spotted a wooden box with an alchemist's circle engraved on it. I carefully pulled the box from the cabinet and cracked the lid.

A green stone with two red lines lay nestled in the velvet lining ... a stone I remembered from the metal chair in the warehouse. The building shook again from another explosion. The green stone wiggled in the velvet pouch. Daniel's screams pierced my thoughts and I hesitated, my hand hovering over the stone. I couldn't go back once I took this stone.

I plucked the stone from its nest and dropped it in the small black sack.

I let out the breath I'd been holding and stood. The building shook and a few stones rolled out of the cabinet. I thought about grabbing a few more, because everything in the cabinet probably had some value, but I didn't want to risk taking something when I had no idea what it did. Or even worse, who the stones had been made from.

With the stone safely in my bag, I darted to Verity's door and slipped through.

I stopped at the double doors leading into the hub and twisted the handle. I spent a minute creeping the doors open enough for a slit of vision between them.

As I'd feared, the hub didn't have a single student in it. A few teachers were walking around the perimeter, watching the ceiling. I'd have to wait for an escape, or I could try the endless hall. The last time I had gone into it, I had to be rescued by Carly and now it had changed and might be changing again soon. No, I would have to wait.

"What are you doing in here?"

I turned to face a perturbed Priscilla. "Verity sent me to grab something from her office."

She glanced at Verity's door. It was the opening I needed. I hurled a freeze stone, which struck the door next to her and ricocheted back, striking her in the neck. She froze with a shocked look on her face and fell to the floor.

Without thinking, I ran to her and pulled her stiff body into the hall. With her stuffed away, I collapsed against the plain door, closing it. How had my life turned so quickly? Priscilla should be frozen long enough for me to make it out of here.

Five minutes passed and I stayed where I was, just in case. The rumblings had stopped and I wondered if the stone I'd created had anything to do with it.

"All students with booster stones, report to the fountain," Verity announced over the intercom.

I inched the door open until I saw the hub filling with students. Once enough people were standing near the door, I slid out and mingled into the crowd. I spotted Deegan near the hole in the wall, staring up. Then a massive explosion shook the building.

Pieces of the ceiling fell, nearly hitting a few Blues. People screamed and dust settled around us. Streaks of outside light shot into the room, illuminating the dust in their paths. I stared at the ceiling and saw three more stones falling. I knew what they were. We had been breached. Whatever my stone had done above, it hadn't worked.

"Get the booster stones to me, *now*!" Verity demanded.

I watched stones descending from the roof of the hub. Three stones landed near room five, striking the floor. As they bounced, they turned into humans, a woman and two men.

Utter shock stilled my movements. I blinked three times, making sure I wasn't hallucinating, staring at the women in the middle.

"Mom?" I whispered.

She couldn't have heard me, but she turned and we locked eyes.

"Mom!" I screamed, and ran toward her.

"Allie?" She took two steps toward me. Her just voicing my

name sent my heart sailing. She knew me, she'd come for me and she was alive. "Allie, you need to—" she started to say, but her last word came out garbled. She reached for her neck and fell to her knees.

"No!" I was too far away to stop it.

Students ran by in a blur, clearing out of the hub. Deegan threw another stone, but the man next to my mom slapped it to the floor and dropped another stone next to them. I ran, caught up to Deegan and passed him. I thought I had a chance of reaching her until the stone hit the floor and exploded in a dust cloud. My last image of my mom before she was engulfed in the cloud was the two men grabbing her and disappearing as quickly as they had come in. I kept running.

I reached the spot where she'd fallen and dropped to my knees, clawing at the dusty floor, breathing in the smoky air around the space she'd occupied. My heart pounded, but my mind hadn't caught up with my body. I'd seen her disappear, but I searched through the dust surrounding me. She had to be there. I clawed at the dirty stone floor, screaming.

She's alive!

Dirt filled my nails. I looked to the ceiling at the crack she'd dropped through. She could be right above, staring down at me. I raised my hand, reaching for the light shining through, and someone grabbed my arm.

"We've got to get out of here," Carly urged.

"My mom..."

She pulled on me again, but I shook loose.

Deegan and a few other teachers surrounded us. They looked to the ceiling and to the walls and into the dust cloud, searching for the same person I was. The dust settled onto the floor and kept a low haze. My body was too heavy; I couldn't move, even as Carly pulled and yelled my name. I felt as if I was in the middle of a jump, floating in the abyss. Everything around me went silent. I saw Carly's mouth moving and the teachers spreading out as they realized they were gone. All the while I was falling into my personal abyss. Had everything in my entire life been a lie?

"Stones, you fools!" Verity screamed.

I heard her powerful voice and looked to the line where Bridget was holding a stone near Verity's.

"No!" I screamed to Bridget, but it was too late. She placed her stone on Verity's.

We were going to jump.

Verity stiffened and the stone in her hand dissolved. She closed her eyes and fell backward, plunging into the fountain. Water splashed out onto the floor. I leapt to my feet, stretching toward the streak of light above.

The floor fell out from under my feet and the whole building shimmered ... and the bright light disappeared. I floated, feeling the distance between me and my mom expand. My footing finally firmed up on solid ground. I had no idea where we were, but my mom felt light years away. We could be on the moon or at the bottom of the ocean, but something told me that my mom wasn't going to find me again anytime soon.

The reality of my situation came at me as Carly yelled. She sounded so distant, her face contorted with fear. I stared at the space where my mother had been.

"Come on." Carly pulled me away from the dust cloud.

I allowed her to pull me along until I saw Deegan. He was the one who'd thrown the stone at my mom. She had collapsed under whatever horrible stone he'd used on her. I rushed in his direction, but he moved just as fast toward the fountain.

"Verity!" he yelled, not seeing my pursuit.

The water in the fountain splashed around and she lay underneath it all. I skidded twenty feet short of the fountain as the teachers grouped around Verity and pulled her out of the water. Her head rolled around as they lifted her out. Deegan knelt down, guiding her limp body to the floor.

I spotted the skin on the back of his neck, but my hand shook too much and I couldn't get a stone out of my pocket. He had hurt my mom, and if he'd killed … no, I wouldn't even think of it. Rage filled me as I stared at the teachers setting Verity's body on the floor. She hit the floor with a thud and water spread out around her as her clothes drained out on the stone floor.

I forced my gloved hand to steady enough to pull out a stone. Carly stopped pulling on my arm as I moved in a straight line toward the teachers.

"No, don't do this, they'll kill you," she whispered, but she might as well have been speaking to herself.

Carly stopped walking by my side once I got within ten feet of the teachers. Good, I thought. She didn't need to get involved in this. I had to do it on my own. I couldn't spend another minute in the Academy knowing my mom was out there.

I slowed down my approach and tried to show actual concern for the fallen Verity. Just a bit closer and I'd have Deegan.

The bald professor was the first to notice my approach, but it was too late for him. I struck the back of his neck with a freeze stone. He winced and slapped the spot like a bee had stung him and he was stuck in that pose, falling to the floor. The teachers froze in shock as great as any stone would have created. I used this second of disbelief to rifle through Deegan's jacket and grab his large key ring. I was getting out of there no matter where we were in the world.

"Did you just...?" Professor Dill dropped Verity's head. With surprising quickness, he pulled a stone off his sash. I saw the opaque color of the stone and the bright red streaks. Transfixed by it, I knew something of that color would probably kill or badly injure me. I took a deep breath and stepped back, but being within feet of him, I was an easy target. I mouthed an apology to my mom. I had only just learned of her existence and I had already failed her.

He wound up his arm and I continued to scramble back, keeping my gloved hand up. Just as his hand moved forward, a stone hit Dill's face. He dropped to his knees, the stone from his hand bounced across the floor, and he reached for his face in a scream. The other teachers reacted, grabbing for their own stones, staring at me with confusion and growing hatred. They didn't even notice the person who'd thrown the stone until she yelled.

"Suck on *that!*" Jackie roared, and she threw another stone, striking Priscilla.

Priscilla convulsed on the floor.

The bald professor pulled a stone from his sash just as a fist struck him on the jaw. He fell like a stack of cards to the floor, revealing Mark standing behind him. The muscles in his arms flexed and he glared at the pile of professors on the floor.

A woman in a black suit staggered back on her heels. "No, don't hurt me."

Bridget stepped over the frozen Deegan and gripped a stone in her hand. "Bitch, how about a nightmare?" She chucked a stone and hit the woman's face.

The woman screamed and flailed in the air like she was falling from an enormous height.

I gawked at my friends around me. They had just risked everything to come to my rescue. I blinked and glanced down at the keys. They gave me a chance I'd never really thought I had.

Jackie tilted her head in admiration for Bridget. Then she danced around the fallen teachers, splashing bits of water around Verity. She laughed and kicked Deegan the rest of the way to the floor before skipping over to me. "So, what's the big plan now, buttercup?" She could have been asking me about tea, or what movie we were going to.

"We're getting the hell out of here." I held up Deegan's large key ring.

Jackie clapped and laughed, looking at the elevator door.

"We don't know where we are. We could be anywhere," Carly argued.

Bridget let out a long sigh. "Anywhere is better than this place."

Mark shook his right hand. "I would normally agree with a cautious approach here, but I think we've outstayed our welcome." He looked at the array of teachers lying on the floor around us.

Just then, Verity groaned and Deegan moved a finger.

"What are we waiting for?" Bridget asked.

I didn't need to hear any further discussion. Running to the elevator door, I fumbled with the key ring, trying to remember what the key had looked like. If I was even a smidgeon smarter, I would have paid attention to Deegan when he used these keys.

I jammed a key into the lock and pulled it back out in frustration and tried another. Failure.

"Come on," Jackie said.

"I'm trying. There's like a hundred keys here." The keys clattered like laughter, as if their single goal was to see me fail.

I glanced back at the fountain. Verity sat up and looked our way.

"The dead just rose. We gotta go," Jackie warned, fumbling around with her empty sack.

I stuffed in another key, and then another, but none of them fit. I frantically worked down the key ring.

"She's standing up," Carly said with fear cracking her voice.

"Deegan's moving," Bridget added.

I took a split second to glance back in between keys. Deegan rolled on the ground and Verity had gotten to one knee. She stared at me and stole the breath from my lungs. Her normal look was scary, but her scary look was terrifying. I doubled my speed but fumbled the key and dropped the whole key ring on the floor, losing my place.

"Allie, we need to get out of here," Carly said.

"I'm trying!" The keys jostled into a metal meatball. I pulled them apart and found what I thought was the last key I had just tried. I stuffed the next one in and it didn't move. I sped through the next ten keys, but each didn't work. I had the terrifying thought that Deegan had taken the correct key off the loop and had stuffed it somewhere else. Maybe none of the keys would work.

I glanced back again and saw Verity pulling Deegan to his feet. She stumbled and fell back to one knee.

Mark pulled the sack from my side. There were a couple of stones left in there and they would both be effective. Let him throw them, I thought. I didn't slow down and tried another key.

"Here they come," Carly said.

I didn't look back. I didn't want to waste another second. "Help me, Mom, *please*." I had spoken to my mom sometimes as a child, looking at the sky, wondering if she was hearing me from above. I wasn't looking to the heavens anymore; she was in my world. I closed my eyes, looking for divine intervention, and selected another key.

I pushed it into the slot and turned.

The elevator door slid open.

"Yes!" I yelled and ran in. The rest rushed in with me and I looked at the panel inside the elevator and winced at the second keyhole waiting for a metal intruder. I grunted and moved a key toward the hole. The big key didn't fit the small slot. I shot around the ring, searching for small keys.

A stone struck the inside of the elevator and bounced to the floor next to Carly's foot. Mark threw one to match it.

I leaned to my left and looked out. I shook in shock at seeing Verity and Deegan only twenty feet away, close enough for me to see the wrinkle of anger spread over Verity's wet face and the stone she had in her hand.

"We aren't going to make it," Carly claimed, looking at my wad of keys.

I tried another small key, but it didn't work.

She took a deep breath and shook her hands. Grunting, Carly stared out of the elevator. "You guys had better come back for me," she screamed, then ran out of the elevator.

I reached for her, but she was gone. I watched her throw a stone and then I couldn't see her anymore. She'd given me another second or two and I sped through the keys, selecting another. I heard Carly screaming her battle cry and then silence. I slammed my eyes shut and hoped she hadn't gotten hurt. Maybe they'd just frozen her.

I picked another key. This had to be it.

A stone skipped across the elevator floor and hit the back wall. It burst open and yellow smoke poured out of it.

"Hold your breath!" Jackie called out.

Another small key failed as I ignored the smoke until it hit my eyes and burned them to tears. I held my breath for a few seconds, but I didn't have it in me to hold it for any longer. It sent fire into my lungs and forced a fit of coughs. Tears flowed and the world became a blur as smoke filled the elevator. My hands were my eyes. I felt the small key and ran my finger over the ridges with one hand while guiding it into the slot with the other, then I turned my wrist.

It worked.

The door slid closed until a small black shoe stopped it on its track. I leaned against the back wall and saw Verity's sneering face through the smoke. My friends coughed. I didn't think they had a single stone left to stop her. I saw Deegan's silhouette staggering behind her. I touched the life stone and planned on tossing it to Mark. If anything, I would find success in that.

"Screw it," Bridget said between coughs. She lunged off the wall and tackled Verity away from the door, forcing Deegan to backpedal as well. Some of the yellow smoke flowed out with her before the door slid all the way closed and clicked with a lock engaging.

I wanted to scream at Bridget and Carly, but the smoke filled my lungs and made me blind. The elevator moved upward and everything was complete darkness. I staggered around the elevator as we rushed to the top. My feet kicked something soft and I knelt down. At least I tried to kneel, but my legs buckled and I fell face-first to the metal floor. A body lay next to me and my hands ran over his stiff muscles.

"Mark" was what I wanted to say. Unfortunately, it came out in a gargle before I went into another coughing fit.

I heard him cough, and then another cough sounded from behind him. It had to be Jackie, but my eyes poured out tears and blurred my sight.

The elevator stopped at the top and the door slid open, smoke escaping into the darkness beyond. I tried to follow it and pulled my weak body from the elevator. I breathed in my first breath of fresh air and coughed it out. I sucked in another breath and held it. Lunging back into the elevator, I pulled at Mark's hand, but I could only move him an inch. I screamed and used all my strength before returning to a coughing attack.

The elevator door tried to close and I jumped, slamming my hand against it, halting its progress. I pulled my shoe off and stuffed it into the gap.

Blinking away tears, I went back to Mark. "Help me, Jackie."

She moved next to me and took Mark's other hand. She coughed louder and harder than me. Her red eyes bulged from her head and tears streaked down her face. We pulled, and once we had momentum, we slid Mark onto the roof of the Academy. A single light from the elevator lit the dark roof.

The door tried to close again, but my shoe held it open.

I shot to the ground and realized Mark had stopped coughing.

"Mark!"

He didn't move.

"Mark, wake up." I pushed him once, and then started

shaking his body. "No, no, Mark!"

I brushed the hair from his face and wiped the tears away. I leaned over him, my ear hovering over his mouth. I waited, holding in a terrible cough … and then heard it. A soft breath blew into my ear, sending chills through my body. I still had a chance to save him.

Sitting up, I stuffed my hand into my pocket. I'd only kept one stone and when I produced it, Jackie gasped. I knew she had words about it, but coughs filled in the blanks. I took my time and made sure to have good contact. I placed the stone on his forehead and watched it dissolve into his skin.

I scooted back and waited for something to happen. I wasn't sure how this would go down, but having seen the creation of this particular stone, I wouldn't be shocked to see angels drop down from Heaven.

Seconds passed and a weight built in my chest. Maybe I'd gotten to him too late, or the stone didn't work on him for some reason. I leaned forward to check his breath.

Mark lunged into a sitting position and inhaled a deep breath, like a scream.

I gasped and reeled back.

He looked around, confused. "Where are we?"

I didn't answer and barely cared. I rushed to his side and hugged him. He smiled and I coughed into his sleeve. He was going to be okay. The life stone had worked.

"What happened down there? I think Verity hit me with a stone," Mark said. "How long was I out?"

"It doesn't matter. You're okay." He was more than okay; he was cured. I didn't want to tell him how I'd done it.

"Those alchemists dropped in again, from the ceiling. I thought I heard you yelling at them," he said. "I watched you run right at them."

I wanted to shake him and make him realize what had just happened down there. "I saw my mom. She's one of those alchemists who dropped into the Academy."

Mark pushed me back and stared at me. "How is that possible?" he asked.

"You said she was dead," Jackie added.

"I thought she was, but she's alive ... and I think she was coming for me." The idea lifted me up and I drew in a fresh breath of air. Even as I said the words to convince them, I didn't totally believe them. How could she be alive?

Mark moved closer to me with a wide grin. He had lost his father, and I knew he would understand exactly the way I felt. "I'm so happy for you, Allie, and I want to hear every detail." He glanced at the elevator door moving back and forth, stuck on my shoe. "But right now, there's a very pissed-off president a hundred feet below us and we need to put some more space between us and her."

"Wait! We can't just leave them," Jackie said, and took a few steps toward the elevator. "Carly...."

I had the same thought, and stared at the vacant elevator. The door slid against my shoe and then retracted again. They were just a short ride down that shaft, but we had barely made it out of there and none of us had a single stone left. Bridget of all the people in the world had been the one to save us, to give us that extra second. It broke me to leave her down there, but that was exactly what we had to do.

"We can't leave the elevator working," I said, and walked inside the elevator. Only a few wisps of smoke remained but even those stung my eyes. I ignored it and put my hands on the electrical panel. If I could break an iPad, I could break an elevator panel. I found my rage easily and pushed the hate out of my fingertips. After a few seconds, I felt a vibration from the panel and smoke began to escape from the corners of the metal cover and the buttons. I yanked my shoe out and put it back on. The door stayed open.

"How the—?" Jackie looked at me sideways as I turned from the smoking panel.

"Let's go." I coughed. The stinging in my eyes had lessened, but I would kill for a bottle of water to flush them out.

Jackie paced near the elevator. "I can't ... I'm the leader of the Reds and they're still stuck down there. They might get punished for what we did." She took rapid breaths.

"We're coming back for them, but for now, we need to get away and find help." I pulled her away from the elevator. She kept glancing back but didn't put up any real resistance.

"Did you guys see where we are?" Mark gazed past our small platform.

I hadn't even looked past the roof. We rushed to the edge and joined him, looking over the city beyond the towering warehouse windows of the building enclosing our location. The platform we were standing on was about five feet off a dirty floor below. Mark hopped over the wall and landed on the floor.

He reached up for me and I slid down the side. He helped Jackie next.

Through the windows, I saw towering buildings and heard nearby traffic; even a few horns blared out. A helicopter flew by and I looked to the ceiling. Parts of the rusted metal roof had fallen in, letting a band of stars shine through in the clear night sky. Jackie stammered next to me, gawking at the sky.

"It's been a long time since I've seen stars," she whispered.

"I found a door," Mark called from far ahead in the warehouse. He kicked the door and on the fourth kick it broke open. He took a step back and then felt around his midsection with a confused look on his face. He raised an eyebrow at me and from the look in his eyes, he knew what had happened — but I'd have to apologize for saving his life later.

I glanced back at the open elevator. I felt so foolish now for not listening to Mark and realizing what the place actually was from the start. He had known. Now many more people were trapped down there. How many more would arrive there, thinking it was the Academy they'd been promised? I tried to make myself believe that I wasn't just turning my back on my friends. I knew it wouldn't be long before the Academy jumped again, but if my mom had found the Academy once, she could help us find it again. I just needed to find my mom.

I ran to the broken door with Jackie. We were free for the

moment, but leaving so many behind, stuck down there in the lie, waiting to see who'd get retired next, felt as if I'd built a prison of guilt for myself.

I made a promise then and there: we would get them all out of that hellhole.

For the latest information about releases, or if you have questions for me, visit me at: www.authormattryan.com or www.facebook.com/authormattryan.

Never miss a new release from Matt Ryan by joining the mailing list: http://eepurl.com/btCx_P

Made in the USA
Middletown, DE
27 December 2016